OMINOUS: BORDERS: COFFEE

PETER STANDISH EVANS

STEEL IMPRINT PUBLISHING

Published in 2012 by Steel Imprint Publishing.
In association with Acorn Independent Press.

ISBN 978-0-9571992-3-1

Steel Imprint
Publishing
— LONDON —

ACKNOWLEDGEMENT

Special thanks to Editor Leila Dewji whose keen eye, sharp instinct and solid advice have been of huge value in writing this novel.

My wholehearted appreciation for the talents of Angela Voges. Her wisdom and experience as the Master Editor helped tighten and toughen the novel into a form that Inspector Vasseur would surely acknowledge.

My gratitude to Cover Artist Tanja Prokop who caught the feel of *Ominous: Borders: Coffee* so perfectly and turned the book's cover into art.

ABOUT THE AUTHOR

Peter Standish Evans was born in Malvern, United Kingdom. He has two children and lives with his partner, artist Brigitte Maingard. He is a full-time writer, and has a published collection of poetry titled Red Winds Howl.

for Katya and Mark; always

*for my partner Brigitte Maingard whose
unwavering and erudite support never ends*

1

The Stalker was ten metres behind the target and catching up rapidly, too rapidly. She knew from experience the first connection needed to be perfect: the opening conversation, the eye contact, the make. There was too much at stake as usual. At this stage her controlling force was a heart-stopping infatuation, which would soon morph into desperate desire.

There was symmetry in the way the feet of the Stalker and those of her target moved. Only by taking the faster strides had the Stalker made up ground. She needed to slow down, to freeze time to control her heartbeat.

Obsession for her was not a finite science, and victories came only through sacrifice.

The gap was now eight metres and closing. *Failure,* she thought, *will mean months of depression.* At that moment Edith, the target, turned on her heels. She held her ground and surveyed the surrounding crowds, ignoring all the women. She did not detect a Stalker.

To any who might have watched her, Edith exuded strength, and a grace.

The man who sat at the table was immersed in his coffee ritual. The Proprietor of the café stood nearby on the pavement and watched as he always did, raising and lowering his heels, knees bent. None of the other customers noticed the Proprietor's routine, but with the concertina doors wide open, that man noticed everything. The Proprietor had ground the coffee beans and tamped the grinds in the small silver basket, applying perfect pressure from centre to outer rim. Once satisfied with his preparations, he had pulled the coffee on his piston machine.

The man raised the white cup. A golden tinted crema covered the surface and the cup was full to the brim. He brought his lips down to meet the coffee and tasted it, his senses on alert.

"A hint of wild blackberry and chocolate?" asked the Proprietor.

"More like the essence of a fine Frenchwoman," said the Inspector. "Fantastic." He took another long sip, and replaced the cup in the saucer next to the precise row of roasted almonds he'd laid out in the sun.

"Thank you," said the Proprietor, knowing Inspector J.L. Vasseur liked to remain incognito. "May I prepare a second cup?"

"What day is it?"

"Sunday."

"Then a cognac," said the Inspector.

As soon as the Proprietor moved away, the Inspector picked up the first almond, and flipped it into his mouth. He paused a moment to savour the salt of the Camargue and the delicate smoked flavour, and bit into the flesh. It cracked, and though to the Inspector this sounded like a gunshot, the other café patrons remained unmoved.

Inspector Vasseur remained uneasy in his chair at the café. The feeling that the air around him was developing a light blue haze would not leave him. He knew this instinctive warning too well. He lifted his small camera from the table before taking three wide-angle snaps of the scene. *The people, a street; a sidewalk;* Paris thriving on a bustling summer morning. He had a sixth sense that skated free over the most cobbled of Parisian streets. The camera logged the time and date, and the Inspector's notebook and pencil stayed where they were, resting on the metal table. His SP 2022 pistol remained hidden in its paddle holster the way he preferred. It sat beneath a light deconstructed jacket which he wore both summer and winter.

When Edith had turned around, the Stalker had drifted seamlessly into the crowd, slowing her stride to be natural; she was good, very good. From where he sat, the Inspector held his breath for the split second that he watched Edith's face – exquisite, almost sublime, framed by the sun. He reached for his camera again, but then she, too, was gone.

Vasseur blamed the blue air sensation that engulfed him on 'dark notions' – the thoughts and plans of people whose primary intentions were toxic. Most often his instincts proved correct, which was a shame. His Paris had been quiet these last days and the coffee had been rather special. Holding the cup to his lips with his left hand, the camera with his right, he snapped five more photos. Such was the nature of the café that no one took the slightest notice and the Inspector got on with the business of inspecting. Later he would look long and hard at super-enlarged copies of these photos, detecting a passer-by's sleight of hand that would intrigue him.

Notions of a feral nature drifted through the maze of these local alleys and cafés, seeking out new victims. In retrospect he would discover they'd even drifted into Camille Laroche's large two-floor apartment, despite the windows being sealed. It was to become home to meetings of the Fourth Coffee Society…

"Everything look usual to you?" said the Inspector with a broad sweep of the hand.

"Much as yesterday, fine and sunny, can't ask for more," said the Proprietor.

"And you don't feel anything strange?"

"Always, the world is too connected," said the Proprietor. "It's hard to see how these people all integrate, and that's the key, their integration."

On the other side of the river Seine, whose powerful flowing waters split the gracious city in two, a momentary impulse would shift normal perspective.

High in a building that housed academics and creatives, the artist son of a Spaniard from the Basque region propped a photo of a well-known politician on the family sofa. He then fired one shot at a range of three metres, which went straight through her left cheek. He had not expected the brash pop of the shot from the Glock 19, or the limited recoil. The consequences would also take him by surprise.

He put the gun back where he'd found it, albeit with only fourteen bullets in the magazine, placed a cushion over the hole in the sofa and headed for the streets. He'd blame the hole on a cigarette burn if necessary.

2

It was in Camille Laroche's apartment, with its sturdy shuttered windows, that the inaugural meeting of the Fourth Coffee Society took place. It was blessed by the attendance of its first and currently only two members. They were almost opposites, living on different sides of the River Seine.

For the fisherman's daughter, Edith Prideaux, a search for bigger society and artistic indulgence were the reasons she moved to Paris. She left Marseillan on the Mediterranean coast and moved to the city of intrigue. Edith changed her life of filleting her father's fish, and shucking oysters for her mother's eatery, at the time many Parisians were fleeing to the slower pace at the coast.

Edith was driven by an innate curiosity to explore the diverse districts of Paris. She had become an informal tour guide, soon at home in attractions as diverse as le Musée de l'érotisme and the Louvre. She was so ingrained with a zest for life that she became the essential travel accessory for many an enlightened and rich foreign tourist. Despite the economic downturn, Edith soon earned a substantial bank balance to match her skills. Her bookings stretched for years in advance, rather like the finest of Parisian restaurants.

Edith had no other plans at present although she did have a dream or two, and a persistent female stalker.

Camille Laroche was an accomplished composer and second violinist. For her, the words 'orchestra', 'society' and 'wine' all flowed as naturally as a nineteenth century Baudelaire poem might flow. They lapped along the banks of the River Seine, their sounds reaching the ears of all who swept on by. She lived alone in the spotless family apartment. Its décor and pride were handed down through generations, crowded with furniture and bric-a-brac, from Baroque to Bohemia.

Camille had an overwhelming lack of social acquaintances, a secret phobia that kept her busy after midnight, and a dubious male admirer.

With the long-term future of the Society in mind, it was as well that Edith, with her wondrous and tousled blonde hair, stood a fine head taller than petite Camille. Camille's short black hair, beautifully sculpted face and warm dark eyes wove their way through her myriad of furniture at great speed. They imitated her violin bow arm as it played, unleashing unrestrained energy. Camille exuded a sensual and magnetic attraction. It was a mystery she neither paraded, cultivated, nor understood.

Camille had realised that despite all her reservations, something had to be done to make close friends. The society idea had leapt into her mind while she sat in a bistro down near the bank of the Seine. Seated at adjacent tables, both drinking coffee, Camille had found herself responding in a friendly tone to a stranger's jibe about lone women. She'd surprised herself by suggesting they form a coffee society together. Edith, in need of new Parisian friends with whom she could enjoy loyalty, had encouraged the idea. They had diarised a first meeting, where they intended to discuss ways to attract many new and selected members. Such was the ease of their bistro conversation that almost immediately Camille had sensed that help with her many personal issues might be at hand. Though she knew little of this girl, she felt that Edith had radiated an aura of warm confidence.

On the coast, in Marseillan, Edith was seen as someone who embodied the deep strengths of Mother Nature. She had the confidence to lay herself bare in support of friends. She had a rare gift, unusual for one so young; Edith had steel.

"She's too damn fearless, and too damn loyal for her own good," said her father to her mother as Edith had left the coast for Paris. "She's the first to respond to storm warnings, rescue calls and possible drowning. It could lead to consequences one day."

"Take comfort," said her mother, "our sea doesn't reach Paris."

Edith's Stalker was furious to discover that Edith was visiting the apartment of another woman, carrying bags of what seemed like food for the evening. This was not how the Stalker envisioned life. Life should be Edith and herself, alone, together exploring the fascinating facets of existence.

The brass-framed name card next to the apartment bell had given the clue. The words 'Mlle Camille Laroche' said it all. The Stalker chose a position up the street where reflections in windows opposite gave clear views of the balcony of the fifth- and sixth-floor apartment. The building's street-level exit was in sight, and she'd decided the first contact with Edith could be made when she left to go home. The first interaction, she'd concluded, needed to be at night. The Stalker felt better at night and people were more approachable. Patience was needed. Then the upper floor lights went off. She switched to full alert, and all her predatory instincts came alive.

The Inspector did not walk past the loitering Stalker that evening. Had he done so he may well have afforded her a perfunctory nod. It was a trick he used to garnish a response from people, and to delve into the body language of those visiting or inhabiting his patch. Instead, Vasseur had stayed over on the Left Bank of the River Seine for the night. He walked the streets close to his home, trying in vain to damp down the sinister portent he'd experienced twice that week. One thought kept nagging at him: *was there a new opportunity for evil to weave itself amongst his people?*

Once home, he'd drink a glass or two of red wine with his food, and take it easy while he prepared his Pot au Feu, a slow-cooked beef stew, with the extra marrowbones he'd purchased. He needed a solid meal, there was something in the air, and dark ominous notions were stirring.

At the inaugural Coffee Society meeting in Camille's apartment, the two members agreed that the hostess would provide both the venue and the music. Edith would do more or less everything else. She'd write up the records of the meetings, provide coffee beans, the grinder, the French press, and clean up afterwards. This list would soon expand to opening the wine, finding the glasses and pouring generously.

In celebration, Edith served the first ceremonious cup of coffee with pride: Colombian beans from the Medellín region that she had subjected to a medium grind then and there. She brewed them for a full four and a half minutes in the French press. She raised her cup and proposed a toast.

"To us Founder members, and these dark and rich delights."

"I only wish we had champagne," Camille responded.

They agreed the Society would be the Fourth Society, Camille's apartment being in the fourth arrondissement of Paris. It was a district that lured more eclectic characters to its streets than most cities in the world. Characters who improved the daily life, and the Inspector gloried in the company such of free thinkers.

Taking a moment or two to enjoy the coffee that had travelled all the way from the southern hummingbird region of Rio Blanco in South America, Edith relaxed her shoulders. She let out an inaudible sigh. The very heart of the coffee's flavours warmed her. She felt that the coffee's subtler tones might be too intricate for her new friend's taste buds, and perhaps a touch over-roasted.

While Edith reflected, Camille went upstairs to her bedroom to escape for a moment. Escape was the same routine her orchestra conductors followed when rehearsals weren't going well. Or, more often than not, when Camille insisted that she needed to understand the intimate details behind their every decision.

Camille had confided in Edith of her life-long social isolation, blaming the influence of her father, who died along with her mother when she was sixteen. Camille endured years of nebulous life-coaching from the reluctant administrators of the family funds. She'd finally used a small portion of her inheritance to convert the apartment's historic *chambres de bonne*, the maids' rooms, on the upper sixth floor. These were expanded into a bedroom en suite, which included a small recording room and a large walk-in cupboard that held her classical music collection. It was her private space.

Left downstairs, Edith decided the second brew of the evening was needed and ground the beans more finely this time. They would be able to discuss and note the subtle taste differences between these and the medium-ground beans, and perhaps even develop ways to attract new members as planned.

Upstairs, Camille had sat on the edge of her bed with her hands over her eyes. She'd controlled her breathing; slow in, slow out. Socialising was her worst nightmare, even alone with Edith, and only generous quantities of wine could help soothe the experience.

Being one of the world's most gifted composers was easy by comparison. The music seemed to flow into her mind from channels of its own. From these channels emerged the most complex of passages, blends of precision and eternity, which she loved with a passion. That she'd locked her music away all of its life was as difficult to live with as being unable to play it in public. She had her own reasons, which were as solid as the history of Paris itself. Instinctively she knew that setting her music free in the world would also be the death of the cloistered life she clung to.

Thirty minutes or so before their own deaths, Camille's mother had said to her husband, "She's a sensitive child. It worries me that you isolate her."

"Talents deserve hard work. She's young and isolation is good. In any case I'll be there to guide her into the world my way, it's not your place to worry."

Camille knew only a soul such as Edith might help introduce her music to others. She needed help; life seemed one long struggle. For the last few months Camille had felt death creeping up on her, and she had no idea where it was coming from. How could you prevent what you couldn't see? Death had her in its sights, and Death could stalk Paris unseen.

She shook her head. *What was all this death stuff?* she thought. *Wine will wash it away.*

3

The meeting took on a life of its own choosing. Spirits rose for fine reason. Camille had been fortunate to discover herself heiress to a fine collection of wine, chosen and stored with utmost care by her late father. She was also the recipient of a substantial inheritance.

She wandered off and chose another bottle using the next-on-the shelf method. The wine, a 2004 Domaine de Marcoux – Châteauneuf-du-Pape was superb. Edith noticed the now cold French press of Colombian coffee, and decided to drink a second cup. She was surprised at how it had mellowed and had developed a whole new character: less chocolate, more malt. She decided to note down the results of this tasting.

Camille observed Edith scribbling, and looked at her watch; 23:58, perfect timing.

"I'm tired," she said smiling. "Make yourself at home Edith, Goodnight."

Watched by a bemused Edith, Camille went to the main door of apartment, took the keys off a hook nearby and double-locked it. With the keys clasped in her fist, she went up the stairway to her bedroom suite, shutting and also locking the staircase door between floors.

Despite not hearing Camille lock the stairway, Edith soon heard strains of violin music wafting around, rather like the Inspector's 'dark notions'. How, in hindsight, she wrote up this part in the meeting's records would be for Inspector J.L. Vasseur to reveal during his future investigations, should he wish.

Some hours after his satisfying meal on the other side of the river, Inspector Vasseur had gone to bed early. It had been a quiet day by Parisian criminal standards. He carried the ominous warnings to bed with him, and consequently tossed and turned so much that it was just as well he slept alone. At night, during that time Paris found itself sheltering under the shawl of darkness, he was able to do much of his thinking undisturbed. He was comfortable in the knowledge that, at night, the wiliest of city life were convinced they were hidden from his informed and prying eyes.

By day his visual instincts peaked, and Paris once again became exposed, became his city. He loved the uniformity of the gunmetal stone buildings with their historic height restrictions. They existed in stark and solid contrast to the continuous movement in the streets and walkways they sheltered. By day, those buildings spilled their occupants out, ready to ferret amongst the many shops and restaurants where Parisian life loitered. He loved walking those streets, especially the street-side food markets. Here the vibrant colours sprang to life, displaying the reds and greens, blues and burnished browns of the day. He listened to the voices of the people on the streets, all proud, loud and clear. There were few secrets in the markets of Paris; working people had little time for such subterfuge.

Shopkeepers' voices competed for time and custom, adding to the chaos of what daily became a living street-art, a foil to the grand setting and the planned order of the city. In that daylight glare, the presence of the deviants usually stood out clearly to the Inspector. Their existence was neither as bold as the buildings, nor as sensual as the markets. This was his Paris, chopped in half by the river Seine, whose waters caressed both sides of its own islets. These small islands were the river's defiant acts of possession, its solid safe havens. On either bank of the Seine were what the Inspector regarded as the old moneyed guard of the Right Bank, and the students, artists and intellectuals of the Left.

Locked in Camille's apartment, alone on the fifth floor after midnight, Edith had scooped up the bottle of wine and gone out onto the tiny balcony to taste the Marais vibe. Shivering despite the warmth outside, she drank the wine fisherman-style straight from the bottle. It hit the spot.

The Marais, though dark like dark coffee, was wide awake and she took a deep slow breath as her eyes shifted up and across each building opposite. She froze her gaze for a second at each window, staring with the intensity of a hunter, before scouring the nooks and crannies of the street below. Edith searched for that someone, a predator, perhaps even some stalker she'd sensed might be watching her lately. Someone who remained as still as the sky that night.

Her sixth sense had bristled, and she realised she was tired of taking evasive actions. Once again she lifted the bottle to her lips, the motion slow and deliberate. She did not scare easily. Edith had learnt to be prepared the hard way, having lived her childhood outdoors on the coast. She well understood the perils of the sea, and the hidden threat of the riptides that could whisk you away at nine or more feet per second. The fishermen Edith grew up amongst were hardened by a world of no second chances. They knew the random coincidences of nature were all-powerful and unexpected. A watchful eye was imperative.

Extreme loyalty was embedded in Edith's psyche, and she used her fierce inner strength to help protect her family and friends. Looking out over the Marais from the balcony she consciously recognised that tides of a different and dangerous nature might exist in Paris. Scanning the street below one final time, she decided it would be wise to raise her guard, which might have slipped. She did not detect the Stalker, who had left a few minutes earlier with other commitments to meet. Edith re-entered from the balcony and, having searched around for another key to the main apartment door, decided it was a wiser option not to disturb Camille.

Instead of walking back over the bridge to her home in the Latin Quarter, she retired to the guest en suite bedroom, where she fell asleep, naked, at 03:17.

Less than an hour later, at 04:09, the body of a young female, later identified as Arianne Morel, was discovered on the bridge over the river Seine, known as the Pont Neuf. She was found sitting propped up against the wall in a small alcove on the bridge. Her long black hair draped over her left shoulder, covering the arm that was tucked into her coat between buttons. In her cold hidden fingers she was clasping a €100 note. On the top of her right hand, which lay on her lap, was a symbol drawn in permanent black ink, and underneath was scrawled the word 'Venus'.

4

In the apartment where he'd fired the bullet through his mother's favourite sofa, a confrontation took place. Marko Segura's builder father, Gorka, asked him what the hell he'd thought he was doing. This was no bullshit cigarette burn. The mother and sister, still in a state of shock, stared at the two of them, their faces vacant.

"I was looking for my money... I found the gun."

"There is no money, we need to eat."

"I discovered that, and I need a new sketch pad. Why do you keep a gun?"

"The same reason you install a virus killer on your computer. How many bullets are in my gun?"

"I don't know."

"Well that's why you don't have a gun."

"So how many gigs are in my computer?" said Marko.

"Idiot," said his father. "None, I sold the damn thing."

"What the fuck?"

"You shot your sister's cat behind the sofa. Now get out. Don't come back until you put food on our table, and take the cat with you, bury the poor bastard."

"No," said the sister with determination. "I'll do that."

It would be another two hours before the young Marko, accompanied by a local boy and a Greek girl, would walk past the Inspector. The Inspector saw the pain in the youth's face and sighed. He knew the look was of a troubled soul, one of many facing the new dawn of financial uncertainty. Marko had taken the gun with him. There were fourteen bullets left in the magazine; he'd counted them.

The week before the girls conceived their coffee society, a pseudo-psychoanalyst sat behind his impressive desk in Paris. Since his arrival in the city, Zuppin had not seen the Paris the Inspector so loved. He'd seen the hordes, the black funds changing hands, and another opportunity to explore the dark side.

He was not a registered therapy practitioner, having fled the law in Germany a year or so before. He ditched his previous pseudonym, renamed himself Zuppin, and set up a phony therapy practice in Paris. The one constant was his faithful receptionist whom he'd kept in tow.

He had prepared his consulting room for a meeting with Edith's female stalker and a strange male psychotic patient. He'd set up a PowerPoint presentation, run through the slides and was satisfied. With two hours to kill before the event, he put on a sombre classical CD to fill the room with sound. He plugged in the modified electro-convulsive machine he kept under his desk, strapped the electrodes below his calves and turned it on to a low setting. As the first surge of power smacked into his body, he took a hard hit from the whisky bottle and called for his receptionist. She had heard the dull throb of the machine's pulsing bass under the music; in fewer than thirty seconds her heart rate had accelerated and she waited for instructions. She braced in anticipation and shuddered as soon as the bite of the electric pulse moved from his body to hers. Within an hour she had changed roles, tying his hands behind the chair, moving the electrodes up to his inner thighs, and boosting the jolts.

The pseudo-analyst welcomed his patients, without introductions, to the dimly lit consulting room. He advised them they'd been hand-selected to participate in live clinical experiments. He had blended various psychotropic drugs, and tailored them for cutting-edge mind control. He'd a proposal to put to them, one with considerable financial reward.

The male patient had an emotional disorder that fused with his delusional traits. The Stalker, the female patient, struggled with her compulsion to meet, befriend and control her targets. Analyst Zuppin beckoned the Stalker to stand beside his chair, and instructed the male to sit at the other side of the desk for the presentation. She was soon aware of the analyst's fingers crawling behind her knees. She wondered whether this was a necessary part of the research, or extra reward on top of the thousands of euros that Zuppin was offering for each research session. She inched away.

The Stalker accepted the position of camera operator. She was to be discreet in filming the male in public as he experienced the emotional and physiological impacts of the drugs. Once she'd departed, Zuppin continued the discussions for an hour or more with the male, persuading him to undergo a hypnosis session to prepare for the trials. The patient left the clinic with a firm promise of twenty thousand euros, to be paid to him in cash the following day.

The man walked two blocks away from the clinic. He dragged his hand along the stone buildings as he passed, feeling the time-worn textures, trying to infuse a sense of calm into his thoughts. He turned right, stepping off the pavement, and made his way down a narrower street, looking for a quiet bar. He'd sit and read his pocket-poet book; its well-worn pages gave him comfort and the words offered another view of perspective. He needed to feel calm again. He was no fool; he knew his psychosis was drifting into dangerous territory. He thought of death daily, his own death. He looked down at his outstretched hands; they were still, and as solid as a rock.

The analyst walked around the night streets with the Stalker, discussing shots in variable lighting conditions. He had not been happy with the first practice session, the grainy outcome and camera shake. Once satisfied that she'd got the hang of things, he left her the new camera, digital cards, batteries and a charger. He told her to remain available, and advised her to collect her cash in future from the male patient. She was to hand him the card from the previous filming session each time he delivered a new brief.

"So he'll be the Paymaster," she said.

"Yes, the Paymaster."

The body of Arianne Morel had not been moved. Three hours and fifty minutes' sleep had been more than sufficient given the circumstances. The Inspector wondered if there was any correlation between the strong sense of unease he'd felt at the café and this murder on the bridge.

Stage-managed, thought Inspector Vasseur. Arianne had spent most of the night with her boyfriend after sharing a few drinks with friends. She'd left his apartment at 02:15. Having walked back to hers little more than a thousand metres away in the Latin Quarter, she'd showered and changed into work clothes. She was on her way to work at the bakery when the killer struck. There was no sign of blood, and when her body was moved those present saw the vivid bruising on her neck. Inside the coat, in Arianne's left hand, was the green euro note.

"A ligature killing," said a young assistant whom the Inspector ignored, resolving rather to bide his time and wait for the lab reports. He'd learnt a long time ago that the concepts 'obvious' and 'reality' were often poles apart. After extensive questioning, her boyfriend was allowed to grieve. The Inspector, convinced of his innocence, wandered deeper into the Latin Quarter to drink his first café express of the day. He needed to think about the handwritten inscription on the €100 note, 'Limited Edition 1/7'. The team needed a clear plan of action; that alone would take a miracle.

The Inspector laid ten almonds on the table, turning the first and seventh at right angles to the others. He held his right hand palm down next to them, and contemplated the black symbol on the victim's hand; a scratching that resembled the number 7. It was the Russian or European version, with a line drawn across the middle of the upright.

The previous evening, before falling asleep, Camille had listened to two classical works by lesser-known composers, performed by an orchestra based in Moscow. She had carried the same secret to bed most evenings as she had since she was eight or nine years old. She felt the weight of this secret might sink her, and had long since resigned herself to that fact. However, she felt a growing sense of confidence from the natural strength of her newfound friend. Edith was unlike most of the orchestra players she mingled with. She was so secure in herself, that Camille believed she was the person meant to guide her out of this nightmare.

Camille had hidden her extraordinary talent from the world. She was hounded by her father's threat to confiscate her violins if she insisted on composing music before she'd mastered the classics.

By day she practised the 'great works' as her father called them, including Berlioz, Debussy and Saint-Saëns. By night, while drifting near the edge of consciousness, she composed the most alluring and compelling music in her head. She felt the music wove itself, using her as the conduit.

These works became her secret collection. Unlike subconscious dreams, Camille was able to recollect the pieces the next morning note for note. Her compositions were of differing attitudes, all so wrought with a melancholy as deep as the mother lode, or as vibrant as France itself. She struggled to classify them. Over time she learnt to hide them from her father by tagging them all under the composer pseudonym *Kovchenko*. She recorded each one, and added them to her ever-growing collection.

Kovchenko became one of her father's favourite composers. He was unaware of her subterfuge, and many evenings requested her to play the music of "the great man himself".

"Now there's an example of a remarkable composer," he declared.

Camille vowed to discuss her music collection and obsessive behaviour with Edith; Edith seemed selfless, in harmony with life, and grounded. The first person of that type she'd ever met. She would confide in her how she dreamt up new characters in her head as friends. It was a comforting form of escapism, and she might tell her about the supportive therapy sessions she had with Lacey. Sessions with Lacey managed to calm her. She yearned for normality, whatever that would turn out to be.

<h1 style="text-align:center">5</h1>

Officer No.1 sat with the one man in the police force he admired the most. While others may have been reticent about being frank with the Inspector, officer No.1 knew the Inspector preferred him to speak out, if only to nudge thoughts or fill in background details.

"The ligature was leather, perhaps a belt, they tell me. It had coarse edges. Forensics is running more tests."

"It takes only one hand to hold the victim with a belt. It would look more natural to observers, one hand behind her neck. Two hands would look like an attack. The belt might suggest it wasn't premeditated, but I think it may have been – perhaps our killer doesn't like to touch."

"A male?" said the officer.

"Yes, that would be my assumption. I've been mulling over the crime scene. What's your take?"

"All looked natural, no sign of blood, too simple."

"Exactly, killings don't normally look this natural, especially strangulations. Where was the venom, the anger? I've also been thinking about the messages left by the killer."

"The euro note, the number on her hand, Venus?"

"What do they tell you?"

"Mixed signals?"

"Completely. I think I've seen this before. This says to me that we might have two minds at work here: a killer and a murderer."

"At the scene?"

"No, this may be a first-time killer, following instructions from the real murderer, someone in the background with motive. Alternatively we are facing a single individual, perhaps with multiple personalities. The murderer would have the motive, the premeditation; the other personality would act on commands."

"So what do we do?"

"Unscramble all the signatures, see which are from the killer, and which may be from someone else. We decipher them and tear them apart. Remember, in this case, the consciousness of the killer might not be the consciousness of the planner."

An hour or two after the discovery of Arianne's body, Camille woke and decided to action an idea that had crept into her head at the Society meeting. She would invite the man she'd noticed attending recent concerts to be their next society member. He'd been brave enough to approach her at the Claude Debussy concert, having talked his way into the musicians' after-concert drinks. To Camille's surprise he'd showered her with attention. She was impressed by how he'd countered her strident verbal attack with banter. Perhaps he could be her second new friend. He seemed interesting, though rather insistent, and as far as she could gather he was a traditionalist baker with a serious axe to grind.

The slight morning wind she loved tempted Camille to go out walking. She always walked to rehearsals and concerts, but today the new lure of random left and right turns was calling. She layered her black look as usual, wearing an ultra-fine deerskin leather jacket over a sleeveless shirt. She'd throw the jacket over her shoulder if it got too hot; her arms could do with some sun. She'd threaded a faded calfskin belt into the metallic loops in her black skinny jeans, and had used extra thick laces in her trainers. She was ready, and she never went anywhere without a violin to hand, her talisman. The dark, creased-leather violin case, which had belonged to her maternal grandfather, held the violin that had been his only, and her first. The thought of the walk cheered her spirits. She would emulate Edith, and walk with a newfound strength on her foray into the outside world. It was a world far removed from the politics of the orchestra.

The Pompidou Centre was its normal hive of activity. The fusion between those sitting idling away the time and those on the move created a fervour that reminded Camille of a strident cadenza. She paused to listen to the sounds around her, enjoying their random structures.

It's the tone of life here at this moment, she thought, deciding to share the experience with Edith. She wondered which of the senses Edith would have focused on: the smell was stale, the colours were vibrant, and the sound discordant. She'd suggest they go there together and visit the exhibitions, which she'd never been to see.

It was less than two seconds from the hard bump on her back to the disappearance of her violin case into the crowd. Although lots of people would have seen it happen, they vanished as fast as the case. Only two witnesses remained, sitting on the pavement staring at the victim. They could sense the cold blankness that overwhelmed Camille as she turned and turned, looking at the crowds. No one else took interest, and all Camille heard was a silence.

"Bastards," said one of them, a Greek girl. "They've just stolen that busker's life."

"I know them," said Marko's sister. "They live over the river in our district, let's help her."

"Marko wants us to find those street kids."

"He can settle his own scores," said the sister. "The violinist is confused, we can call someone to help, or take her home. I was looking at her case, it was interesting, beautiful."

In the week following the reasonable success of the first Fourth Society meeting, Edith spent a long evening selecting the coffee for the next gathering. She crafted the inaugural minutes, capturing what she felt was the essence of the two Founder members' discussions. Feeling that Camille as an arty musician might relish the touch, she'd sketched pencil drawings of a 1900s Risler and Carré silver coffee pot in the margins. Coffee, unlike a society, she'd realised, seemed to have no borders. Well after the clock moved past midnight the thought struck Edith; coffee was the ideal new passion to live alongside her fierce sense of loyalty. It gave her time to reflect, a time to glory in life and memories, and to savour the long moments outside the hustle and bustle of city life.

While Edith was writing up the minutes, the Stalker had prowled around outside her apartment. She hoped Edith would emerge to take her tourist party on a fine-dining experience. Those dinners were always easy photo opportunities for the Stalker, while Edith's attention was focused on clients.

The Stalker gripped her camera in her right hand as one of the two men who'd propositioned her that night refused to take no for an answer. She decided to give him one final chance to move on before she'd smash the camera in his face. She had her own victim to set up, and men were never a part of her final plan.

The Inspector met with officer No.1 again to discuss developments in the Morel murder investigation. He chose a quiet café where they could talk in private.

"And your opinion?" asked the Inspector.

"I doubt this was a one-off killing, too many signatures with the body. The '1/7' marking suggests that we can expect seven killings. There seems no specific reason why this particular victim was chosen. We can't find immediate cause, no arguments, nothing to single her out. She was wearing simple work clothes, and not loitering."

"We should keep an open mind. The big question is, if we can't catch him first, where will the killer strike next? The bridge may be a random place – I hope not. If he sticks to bridges we can focus our attention. What about the baking angle?"

"We're whittling that down from a hundred associates to the low tens. She was universally liked, a hard worker, a happy soul. We're looking now at her previous workplace."

"Time's not on our side. It was a half-moon on the night she was killed, which may be nothing, but a full moon is around the corner. I want you to step up feet on the street over that period. I know you'll have the support of the team."

"They're working around the clock."

—∘∘∘❖∘∘∘—

In the days after the first meeting of Society, analyst Zuppin had asked the Receptionist to call the student. He'd earmarked her as the backup plan, in case the Stalker didn't cut it when the filming got heavy. The student Lacey had approached the clinic some time earlier wanting to study therapy. After discussions, she was considering joining his weekly anxiety-trauma study group. She seemed keen and not connected to the other students, which suited his needs.

The analyst was testing and retesting his new camera equipment while he waited. An hour later, Lacey bounced in, the broad smile dominating the space between the blood red beanie, the sunglasses, and the light cotton scarf around her neck. Her denim jacket collar was pulled up, and the analyst's eyes were attracted to her T-shirt slogan: 'Think on the edge'. It stuck in his mind.

"I've got a proposition to help you pay your fees," he said.

"Why? I can pay if I join."

"Dim the lights and stand here by me to watch the slides," he said, annoyed she was wearing jeans. "You'll understand, we'll discuss it."

Three minutes later, the student walked out of the consulting room. Lacey advised the Receptionist to tell the analyst to stuff his offer and his fucking tutorship, she had books on therapy practice at home that never abused her.

A pity, thought the Receptionist. *Imagine that body joining our games.*

30

6

As the day crept amongst the city life, the Inspector saw the same young team of potential revolutionaries. This time there was a second girl with them who could have been the twin of the leader. She was carrying a black plastic bin-bag and looked distraught, so distraught that after a brief moment of deliberation he decided to approach them. He paused them in their tracks with a flash of credentials.

"Everything all right?" said the Inspector, "Interesting bag?"

"My dead cat, going to bury it," said the sister.

"That's our own business," Marko told her, feeling the weight of the gun in his back belt getting heavier and heavier.

"And it's my cat," said the girl, "I'll tell him what I want to."

"Then my condolences, go well." said the Inspector.

"And how do you propose we do that?" said the boy as they left, the words echoing in the Inspector's mind long after they'd gone.

"I should have shot the interfering bastard," said the boy.

"You already shot my cat," said the girl.

They hunted for a piece of loose stone, which the second youth found down one level near the water. They placed it with care in the bag with the dead cat. The sister purchased a medium sized padlock. She borrowed the shopkeeper's black marker pen, and wrote 'Xavier RIP' on one side of the lock, before walking up onto the bridge with its view of Notre Dame.

"Amazing!" said the Greek girl.

"It's the right place," said the sister, "the river keeps flowing, it's a border between here and there, and my cat still has other lives to live."

"You think it's Schrödinger's cat?" asked her brother.

"Similar, mine's floating free in a different space."

Marko's sister dropped the bag into the waters of the Seine. They watched it plummet all the way down and into the water, not hearing the splash as it hit the surface. Then she clamped the lock onto the steel mesh of the bridge alongside the hundreds of others. It sparkled in the sun and the glint warmed her heart. Turning away from the railing, she threw the keys over her shoulder into the river to join the cat.

"Swim well," said the sister. "You'll get your revenge."

"On who?" said her brother.

"Some evil shit. Let's go put the gun back."

"Until next time I need it," said Marko.

"I'm saying goodbye, then," said the Greek girl. "Your dad's as hard-assed as mine. See you later."

"Wait, I need to talk, I feel funny." said the sister.

"What?"

"Like I've got other voices in me."

"Where from?"

"I don't know. They'll go. I need wait here awhile."

"Okay, then I'll leave."

The Inspector watched the bag's journey down to the water, as did two of his team who were on undercover bridge duty following Arianne's death. They let it be; they were after bigger fish. The Inspector currently had ten of the thirty-seven Paris bridges over the Seine being watched by his men. They needed to be on full alert during the dark hours of the early morning. It was a tough time and his team were up to their necks in it. He hoped the dawn killing would be a one-off, but somehow doubted it; 'signatures' were calling cards, which often meant more to come. He crossed over to the Left Bank and sat at an arbitrary café with a good coffee, and struggled to get the youngsters out of his mind. Perhaps he'd have his own some day, but what kind of world would he bring them into?

As they walked away, a quartet amongst a tide of many, he surmised these young adults might well have parents who were fighting the poverty trap, as were many. They had a determination in their stride and, like thousands of others, could end up in Che Guevara T-shirts somewhere, throwing stones. He knew the boy's accent; he'd pick up their scent downwind sometime. He wished he could counsel them now, focus their anger on the side of the good guys – but then, who were the good guys?

The second meeting of the Fourth Society started at 20:11. Edith was surprised to be greeted by a subdued Camille, who remained mortified by her first conscious attempt at enjoying the outside world. The violin incident was something she wouldn't share with Edith. Her father had been right: evil was everywhere. Worse still, Edith would have somehow dealt with those people then and there. She was grateful the girls had helped her home and embarrassed that she hadn't thanked them.

Edith decided to ignore her own sixth sense. Within moments of the start of the meeting a solid knocking on the apartment door interrupted the two Founders. *A man's knock,* Edith thought, and though the meeting had been underway for fewer than five minutes, Camille had been itching for a break. The knocking was fortuitous. Before the interruption Edith had relished a sip or two of her first coffee of the evening, which she'd brewed using newfound skills. Camille, on the other hand, having gulped down her cup with a foresight rather than intuition, rushed to the door. She made no comment on the quality or subtlety of the flavours.

Michel Lumière arrived at the second meeting at 20:18 carrying a large paper packet.

Solid, tall, curly-haired and unusual, thought Edith. It was a while before he finished his detailed inspection of the fifth floor. When Camille refused him access to her private sixth-floor suite, he turned away from her. He marched to meet Edith with open arms and a purposeful stride. The whole episode amused her. The brooding aroma of her coffee received his same single-minded attention. He handed her a packet of traditional baked Baba Au Rhum.

"They have an aroma to complement your coffee," he added. Each was in its own box, their batter was a glorious brown, infused with rum and topped with a whipped vanilla cream. Her mouth watered, more so when Edith noted there were three, not two, Babas.

He was forewarned, she thought, and added them to the macaroons on the table.

"Oh," said Camille, "he's the new member."

With a new confidence, Michel blurted out his news far sooner than intended. He revealed that he was horrified by the murder of a dear friend in the early hours of dawn. The girl was a boulangerie apprentice he had trained the previous year. She had great potential to be a traditionalist like himself. She'd been enticed away to a modern rival bakery, one concerned only with cash. It was one without principles. Under the circumstances of his revelation, no one claimed to be enjoying the coffee. The death was a tragedy that would bring them all closer to the intrusive wiles of Inspector Jean-Luc Vasseur.

The Inspector, the Founders would discover, was a charming, forthright and handsome man.

With the touch of rum on her lips, Camille hurried to the next-on-the shelf wine supply. She returned waving a bottle of 1989 Clos du Marquis, much to the consternation of Michel, who feared for the safety of wine from the St-Julien estate north of Margaux.

"Mon dieu," was all he said.

The wine poured, Edith tabled a further issue that would change things forever. She said it had occurred to her that responsible Founder members should be au fait with coffee, to guide future members in a fitting manner.

"We need expertise, like your father's knowledge of wine," she said to Camille, who laughed.

She suggested the Founders go on a field trip to Ethiopia, the origin country of coffee. There, they offered a certified three-day course on how to conduct a Traditional Ethiopian Coffee Ceremony. Ethiopia, she added, produced some of the finest Arabica coffees in the world.

The words "conducting" and "finest" had resonated with Camille, and the idea of a break away from orchestra's rehearsals sold her on the idea. Michel imagined an exotic hotel, the girls, sultry Ethiopian sundowners on the sun deck, and he too was on board. He would never have believed he was not central to their dreams; such was his naivety.

Edith had only once crossed national borders, far out to sea, when her father told her they were no longer in French territorial waters. It felt bizarre; in every direction of the compass, French waters had looked identical to international waters. The borders were invisible.

In a repeat of the first meeting, a minute or two before midnight Camille followed the door-locking procedure, as if in a trance. This time Edith heard the click of the lock in the staircase door. She smiled and, with a new bottle in hand, invited Michel onto the balcony. She proceeded to drink the wine fisherman-style, straight from the bottle. This was fast becoming her tradition. She handed him the wine, and he took a tentative connoisseur's sip, finding the sharing of the bottle with Edith sensual, erotic even. Such notions had never entered Edith's head. She perceived the drinking to be between comrades, platonic. When Michel mentioned his reaction to her, she suggested he go to le Musée de l'érotisme to get a clearer understanding of eroticism.

"I've learnt that erotic exists alongside love. Go sometime with an open mind," she said.

"I will. You should come with me."

"No, some things you do alone," she said, and changed the subject. Love was the last thing on her mind with this man. During the evening Michel failed to get the concept out of his thoughts; it stayed festering with him for many hours.

When the moment suited her, Edith went to bed, leaving him on the balcony. It was 03:11 and the meeting had ended.

Left to his own devices, Michel poured himself a generous whisky, a Balvenie twelve-year DoubleWood, to which he added a similar volume of water straight from the tap. That way he could taste Scotland and Paris in one great glass. Confused at being locked inside the apartment, he realised he'd missed a come-on signal from Camille. He searched for the spare key to the main apartment door, and then sat in one of the many chairs to enjoy his drink and reflect. He soon allowed fantasy and reality to blur. These were dangerous thoughts.

He knew he loved Camille's beautiful face more than any face and, set against her black angular hair, it was very Parisian. He wondered why he felt lost trying to communicate with her; it was easy with Edith. He imagined Camille on stage, looking over the concert audience and longing to be alone with him. It made perfect sense, mad lovers, the traditionalist and the violinist. He was desperate to walk, to supress his crazier thoughts, to find somewhere else to drink.

At 05:48 the body of a second young girl was found on a bridge in Paris, this time on the Pont Saint-Michel, rather close to the Left Bank. The Inspector ruled out coincidence. He felt an unusual chill, one with a source deep in his psyche. The body of the second victim Natalie Fillion was also found in a seated position, blonde hair covering her face and left arm tucked into her jacket. People who had walked past in the early hours would be of crucial interest to Inspector

Vasseur who was smartly on the scene. The area had been cordoned off and the pedestrian who'd found Natalie had given an initial statement to the team. The Inspector would visit the pedestrian later that day to ask what made her stop before discovering Natalie's demise. He preferred eye contact and first-hand information.

Police photographers captured the scene in better light than the Arianne crime scene. When Natalie's body was moved, the bruising on the neck was visible and similar to that sustained by Arianne. He would wait for confirmation from the forensic team. Perhaps they could shed more light on the tool of strangulation. Natalie was another apprentice on her way to work at a bakery. She clutched a €100 note in her hidden left hand inscribed 'Limited Edition 2/7'. The symbol drawn on the top of her right hand looked at first glance to be the same black ink, and this time 'Mars' was written beneath it. The lab would run their tests.

<h1 style="text-align:center">7</h1>

Rising, for once well after the sun, Camille seemed surprised to find Michel in the apartment and let him out without much ado. He was distracted and not interested in lingering and she had work to do, a new recording to make. Eyeing the empty Balvenie bottle she glanced towards the guest bedroom, the door open. She then went upstairs again to record.

Emerging from deep sleep, Edith listened to the music from Camille's violin as it drifted down to the fifth floor. Later she cleared the table, made herself a coffee, and was amazed that Camille could practise whilst the apartment remained a mess.

Each to their own, she thought.

Camille descended from the sixth floor wearing black, total black. It was a simple cami dress with ultra thin shoulder straps and fine pleats, which carried over to the midi leggings under. She wore stub leather boots with the toes cut away, her toenails painted black. Edith realised she had never seen her wear anything but black. She lingered over that thought.

"That was delightful," she said, "it reminded me of a free wind, a soft spirit."

"It is a piece called *Motherlands* that I'm dedicating to Arianne."

"You wrote it?"

"No, *Kovchenko did.*"

"Great choice, I've never heard of him."

"I'm hungry," said Camille "and I need a coffee, let's eat out."

At a café in Rue Mahler, Camille fiddled with her tarte chocolat crumble, grappling with ways to confide in Edith without scaring her away. Thirty-five minutes later, news filtered through the café of the second bridge murder, rumoured to be yet another baker's apprentice. She wondered if Michel had also taught this girl. Camille liked absolute certainty around death, and was not comfortable with these bizarre deaths so near. These deaths were associated with someone who'd been in the same apartment as they had the night before. It made her shiver.

She would close her curtains for a while, that helped her cope, and she would play louder no matter how much the neighbours complained – she would feel safer. Edith gave it some thought and dropped the subject. She could sense that more than the incidents alone troubled Camille. She reached across the table to clasp her hands, which made Camille uncomfortable.

"There's something else haunting you, tell me about it?"

"There is, and it's ridiculous", Camille said, "I'm so composed playing violin. I'm so relaxed among musicians; I'm useless with real people. Now I've even lied to you."

"Musicians are real people," said Edith, "we only have slight differences. I swim well and I love showing Paris to people. You are an expert violinist. Apart from that we only look different. We all eat, and sleep and laugh, and you're never useless with me."

"There, that all flows so easily from you, that's why I need your help. Before I could play my violin with confidence, this music started appearing in my head at night. It happened once or twice a month at first. In the morning I remembered it all. I could play it in my mind. Later, I played the music on my violin and noted every piece to paper."

"That's so amazing, your family must have been so proud."

"My father stopped me, he said I needed to learn to play all the masters first, but I had this master composer in my head, so I lied and invented a composer named Kovchenko. I said he wrote the music and they believed me. They loved Kovchenko, they didn't know any better."

"Was there ever a real Kovchenko composer?"

"Not that I know of, I made people up all the time. I only developed an obsession as I got older. I was scared that my music might include passages I'd heard and copied from other composers, that my subconscious was stealing their work. I started checking and checking the works of composers from all over the world. To this day I've found nothing."

"So, you did compose *Motherlands*. What's the issue now?"

"I can't stop the checking process, one last time, another final time, and again, over and over. I've composed so many of my own works that it drives me crazy, and still I've found no music that I've copied to this day; it's all my original work."

"Hey, just get out there and play your music."

"I can't, understand me, I'm obsessive. It's the repeated 'checking' that is the phobia; it eats me. I've bought massive amounts of vinyl and CDs, thousands, every composer I can find; it takes up so much time. I know it sounds crazy, and it is. I'm desperate to beat it."

"Some professional counselling would be wise."

"I tried that once too, he seemed in a worse state than me, sitting there wrapped up in silence. Now I only have my Lacey therapy sessions left," said Camille, deciding to keep the details of the Lacey sessions to herself, therapy being private. "I need your help to end this obsession, to start sharing my work."

"I'll try. The trip in the meantime will do you good, help break some habits, and we'll get to know each other better."

"I hope so, thanks."

Edith sipped her second coffee. It was still hot and she wrapped both hands around the cup, not for the warmth but for the comfort. She was pragmatic: in her own life she would follow her instincts and act, but then she'd never met many creative types before, especially in such an intimate way. She'd need to think about her friend; about any advice she might give her. She'd heard complex discussions in the art galleries over many of the great works. These discussions often seemed disjointed, devoid of normal meaning. They had led her to believe there was a world out there she had yet to comprehend; a world where language and words took on surreal interpretations. The last thing she wanted to do was to interfere in Camille's creative process. This was not a matter of life and death, or so it seemed to her.

8

The Inspector's team had compiled and hard-filed a list of one hundred and thirty-seven contacts in connection with the girls' deaths. Many of these had tenuous connections, some with bad records. He pinned those allocated to himself down one by one, and sought their take on the tragedy. He meandered through the issues and surrounding events, honing in on the essence, the killings. He always took a few notes as guidelines.

"A reminder of your helpful points," he usually said.

The pedestrian said she'd thought the second victim Natalie was ill, her hand was inside her coat, "I thought stomach pains", and said she'd gone to offer help.

With the Arianne post-mortem report completed, the Inspector and his team reconsidered all the available information. The list included people living on or near the Pont Neuf, people in the baking industry, friends and acquaintances of Arianne and Natalie. Known local criminals did not escape the net. The Inspector had visited family, and revisited the boyfriend a number of times, even though he still suspected his innocence. He was working non-stop, but this was nothing new to him; there was a killer out there and the team were drawing up an expanded list. Stones were being turned over.

Michel had been forty-second on the original contact list for the first bridge death. Now, like all baking acquaintances, he moved up the queue. Time had become a precious resource and a key in the battle to prevent a third bridge death.

At 14:42 the Inspector found Michel doing rounds of the Lumière family baking business. It was a solid and established boulangerie-pâtisserie, passed on to Michel and his brother from generations before. Michel believed they owned about six retail outlets too many for a traditional specialist. A single outlet would have worked far better. His brother thought along different lines, but his brother made every effort to avoid getting involved in the business in any case.

There was no avoiding the hard and direct stare of the man who entered the pâtisserie as if he owned Paris itself. When the Inspector introduced himself and suggested a coffee at the café for a quick chat, Michel felt relieved. He was proud to be consulted on his views, and insisted on bringing along a box of amandine. He immediately felt the physical presence of the Inspector. Vasseur was imposing; tall, lean and tough, and despite his own build, Michel began to feel intimidated.

"Something to wash down our coffee," he joked and, noticing no reaction from the Inspector, thought *perhaps there'd been the faintest of nods, a camaraderie.*

They ordered two coffees and sat at a table an arm's length from the traffic, sporadic as it was.

"It is a tragic matter," said the Inspector, pausing as he cleaned his sunglasses, waiting for a response. He had seen the faint expression of relief from Michel outside the patisserie, and then the dull joke. *Mixed signals*, thought the Inspector, who noted the strength in the man's forearms and shoulders, and wondered if he still kneaded the dough.

The report on Arianne suggested she had been escorted alive to her resting place. A leather ligature had been tightened around her neck, and she may have been on tiptoes, choking even as she was moved to her last moment. The perpetrator must have been tall, strong, and callous. The investigation team dubbed the killer the 'Wolf'. He came out of nowhere, avoided the cameras, and was most likely a male who sat with his victim while she died, before arranging the body into position. To passers-by they would have looked like a couple going about their business. It was a brutal business. The team continued to consider whether or not either Arianne or Natalie knew their killer, they followed that thought.

The Inspector was in no mood for lightness, and neither was this baker who was keen to offer his traditionalist conspiracy theory. Such was his gripe at the baking industry's plight that the Inspector's concern increased. *Were boulangerie workers mere pawns in the business?* he thought, as Michel Lumière cited the inhumanity of people he termed cash-bakers, who stole the best staff from the real boulangeries. He bemoaned that Arianne had been tempted by cash, and crossed sides. The Inspector, having requested his interviewee's blessing, scribbled a few notes to "capture the essence of your experience". Michel was eager to be heard.

Eager for what? thought Vasseur. *This man has an industrial obsession that borders on the absurd.* He noted a few more details on the bakery conflict, thanked Michel for his time and requested he stay available for further discussions. Michel nodded and the Inspector took his leave, having a long list of people to see and little or no time before bureaucratic pressure would mount. Criminal minds came in many baffling guises; he would keep an eye on this man. He had to admit the amandine had been delicious; he would revisit them another day, by himself.

Craving a drink to help piece the puzzle together, Michel ordered another coffee and water. Having had visions of Arianne the previous night, he decided a clear perspective of this mess was needed, and wondered why he'd not mentioned the pending trip to Ethiopia. He surmised Inspector Vasseur had only requested inside information on the industry. For that purpose the Inspector had found the best source for the underlying truths. He would be pleased with their discussion and must have gone away satisfied.

"Michel," said the Inspector returning out of the blue, "where did you say you were last night?"

"The Fourth Society meeting, in an apartment in the Marais."

"Ah, the Marais, and you were there all night?"

"Yes, from eight o'clock to around six-thirty this morning."

"And you went home to change? You look freshly dressed."

"Yes."

"Puzzling," said the Inspector "that's a long society meeting." He made another note in his book, took down the contact details of the other members, looked up at the sky, and walked away.

Michel finished his coffee. He had no idea if the coffee was Colombian, Ethiopian or Guatemalan. Somehow he wished he held a whisky in his hand, and he wished the Founders were already winging their way to Africa. Had the Inspector pencilled him in as a suspect?

No one did such things in their right mind? thought Michel.

There were phone calls during the day bouncing between the female Founders, more to than fro. Camille was forever calling Edith with her 'latest thoughts', as she called them. This was usually the same thought swung round and round, which was rather perplexing. Edith consoled Camille whose musings such as "… did we rush to invite him?" and "is baking run by the Mafia?" all interwove into a cord of thought that convinced Camille she was on their death list.

"Whose death list?" asked Edith. Camille failed to reply, saying rather that as she was packing for Addis Ababa it would be more convenient if they held tomorrow night's meeting at a bistro. Edith agreed, though she thought it absurd that Camille was packing before the flights and hotel were even confirmed.

The officer No.1 wanted the Inspector's input and was glad to get a gap in the busy interview schedule. The Inspector would be thorough, they could rely on that, and he'd smell rats where others would fail. He had a gift, one the force needed, and intuition was almost impossible to learn.

"It's all rather unusual," said the Inspector, before tasting his coffee a second time. He longed for one of the Proprietor's specials, but was loath to hold meetings there; it was his private refuge. He sat instead at a café some five hundred metres away at a table with a grand view on all sides. Here he could watch people pause at the crossroads, and he was amazed at the body language of people when paused. It spoke volumes, and warning signs were easy to read.

"Well, one thing's clear," he said. "It's the same killer."

"Yes."

"Sum it up for me," said the Inspector.

"He left three similar signatures, with the victims. This second victim also worked at a boulangerie, and was also killed on a bridge."

"Of more significance," said the Inspector, "is that the bridge is upstream, and Venus and Mars are a natural sequence. We have the start of a pattern, we can begin to tighten the net, and focus the A team."

"Where?"

"Upstream bridges."

"Do we pull the downstream teams off?"

"Never, it may be a ploy. We can't take risks with lives. We need find another angle to help pinpoint the killer. This was his second killing. It gets easier to kill, that's the danger. His 'alter-ego' might not relish physical involvement. If we get the killer we'll stop the deaths for a while."

"Someone in baking?"

"Possible, not yet probable. The second killing still shows no sign of anger, no pent-up rage."

"Why?"

"Good question. Do you remember my first law of complex crime? How do we decipher two random coincidences where they intertwine?"

"Separate them as soon as possible."

"Right. We need separate those messages left with the victims, and decipher them."

Camille decided it was time for another Lacey therapy session. The situation had progressed since her last one, and there were new developments to consider. She left the bags mid-pack, and exited the building's back door to the street. She pulled a black hoodie over her head, tucked another violin case under her arm, and stuffed her free hand in her pocket. When Rue Saint-Paul met the Quai des Célestines, she turned in the direction of Pont Neuf and walked along the Seine, pausing briefly to take in the music of the river water. Today it plunged its way into the distance, the sounds compelling her to cross the street to listen to the magic, to hear its own symphony with ever-changing forms. She looked back at the buildings she'd walked past. They stood tough and rigorous, *like the sound of a double bass.* They were strong enough to last forever, built from huge blocks of stone, all uniform, all classic by nature.

At that moment she knew the river was crucial to Paris and her own life. It added the melody and the spark to the city, as did the Parisians themselves. From her apartment in the Marais, she could only see across the street, or further if she gazed up into the sky. *It's better for my privacy,* she thought, and then wondered for the first time why she needed so much privacy. She loved this city. She knew the subtle mixtures of tension and passion allowed her the space to compose the music.

She turned right into the Rue des Lavandières to arrive at the bistro, the same bistro where she held all her Lacey sessions. She did not need a reservation at that time of day and her friend welcomed her again.

"All the usual?" he said, and she nodded, hungry and thirsty. She opened the violin case and took out her notebooks. This would be a long session and therapy needed fuel.

"Are you expecting someone?"

"Of course, Lacey," she said, and her friend looked at her.

"Of course," he repeated. "We look forward to meeting her one day." Camille stared at him blankly; *they all failed to understand therapy.*

The Inspector, having mounted the creaking staircase, was allowed through Edith's apartment's tight security. It had been fitted at the absolute insistence of her father. Having had his own credentials scrutinised, the Inspector was confident that unannounced visitors would never disturb Edith. He smelled the coffee, but no offer was forthcoming, so he got to the point. Edith confirmed her first meeting with Michel was on the night of the second Society meeting. She showed him the notes she'd taken which included precise times and, when asked, allowed him to read the first meeting's minutes. These were the minutes that were never ratified and included a brief addendum of the locking-up incident, an issue that might later raise its head. She told him that to the best of her knowledge, Michel must have been locked in at 03:30, about the time she'd fallen asleep. When she woke up, he was gone. Camille had said she'd let him out. Edith maintained she felt comfortable in his company and told the Inspector that they were all going on a foreign trip together, to learn more about the origins of coffee.

"Ah yes, coffee," said the Inspector, still hopeful. "My experience tells me people are not always whom they seem. Please err on the side of caution. You've only recently met this man."

"I'll trust my own instincts before being too cautious," said Edith. "They allow me the freedom to enjoy my life. Thanks anyway."

She thought about his advice for a while after he left and decided she was right in her belief. Instinct was a part of her family make-up. That was how they predicted the sideways tides of life, how they avoided danger and how her father kept his fishing boat safe at sea. She kept her promise to the Inspector not to tell Camille of his pending visit. She understood his explanation; he would prefer Camille to give her own viewpoint on matters. Edith had no idea what that viewpoint would be, the unexpected being a large part of the charm of her new friend. The Inspector thought about Edith's instincts all the way to Camille's apartment. They were worth thinking about.

9

The Paymaster arrived unannounced at the Stalker's home with a briefing for the next assignment, and details of the venue where she'd be filming. She could go and test the camera and lighting settings in advance. It was still some way off and the date hadn't been set. He gave her the cash. He stared at the pictures of the Founder women still posted on the wall.

"What the fuck are these? Are you moonlighting? Taking photos for someone else?"

"No, they're mine. I'm practising."

"Don't lie to me, we both need the money."

She insisted the photos were for her own use, to keep her skills sharp. He did not believe her, yanked the belt from his trousers and whipped her two or three times across the chest, buckle first. She never flinched, and as quickly as he started, he stopped. She'd survived an upbringing of violence, and knew when taken by surprise, the best reaction was no reaction, especially when unarmed. She wished she'd just kicked him in the balls, but there hadn't been a chance. Though she enjoyed a bit of pain, it needed to be on her own terms. He stared at her, punched her in the stomach, and belted his trousers. While she lay on the wooden floor, he crossed the room to the wall, and stopped in front of the photos. He ignored the many photos of Edith and focused only on three, which included Camille. Pointing at the dark-haired girl in the photo, he asked, "Who is she?"

"A fucking violin player," she said. He pulled one of the three photos down, folded it twice and tucked it into his pocket-poet book.

"Bitch," he said as he went down the stairs, leaving the door ajar. The Paymaster stood for a second or two outside in the sun, trying to ground himself, lines from a page in the book still playing on his mind:

we trigger our thoughts like mirrors
propped at strange angles in strange doors
disfiguring the dark waters upon which our
lights will shine

He took a step, paused, and took another step, feeling the need to go to a bar and study his photo; take a hard look at this girl. *Unusual girl in the picture*, he thought. *What triggered my attack switch? I'm the Paymaster, the controller.* He accepted the name the analyst had labelled him with; it gave him both authority and anonymity. The psychotropic drugs sometimes gave him emotions. He was ready for a woman. He'd go home and look hard in the mirror to see if he could find any emotion. He needed to kill his violence switch. It was unreliable, a hazard, it needed to be turned off.

Camille never thought to check the man's credentials; she opened her front door like a lamb. Inspector Vasseur felt he could have kicked it open with ease in any case. She offered him wine, and when he adjusted the music volume he detected concern. He accepted tea.

Chalk and cheese, these girls, thought the Inspector after fifteen minutes. He scribbled down *she talks in riddles*. From the level in the bottle she was only on her first glass and, with no empties lying around, he deduced this would not affect her answers.

Fine taste in wine.

She had much to say, though little that answered his queries, and in the end he decided it was wiser to let her ramble on. She claimed she'd met Michel once or twice. She hadn't given any thought to letting him stay the night. Was he involved in something? She wasn't sure if he'd left the apartment during the night, and could not remember exactly how they'd first met.

"After an orchestra concert I think," she said. "I think he mingled with the musicians, they must know him. I'm always wrapped up in the music after a concert; I don't remember that sort of detail. Perhaps I knew him before. How did he know about the Society?"

Delusional perhaps, thought the Inspector, *chops and changes, she's odd, might well be her way.* He decided not to read too much into it, but was intrigued when she showed him the key on the hook at the door.

"I always keep it there, and there's another spare somewhere." she said.

The Inspector recalled a different story from Edith, and left the building trying to reconcile the two interviews, his concern on the increase.

Smoke and mirrors, he thought, *unusual girls. Michel had better be the warm-hearted man he purports to be.* He made a note to instruct the team to watch the man's movements.

Despite the Inspector asking Camille to keep their conversation to herself, she called Edith before he'd left the building. She recounted her version of everything about the visit. The Inspector would have recognised little of the version Camille told Edith, and he had a natural gift for recalling the spoken word, at least for a week or two.

"I'm tired of all the questions, and choosing answers for people," she told Edith. "Sometimes I feel they want too much, and I don't know which answer to give, so I give the one I think they want."

"And who are these people questioning you?" said Edith

"The people I meet anywhere."

Camille was adamant she needed her free time to advise the orchestra committee of the trip, and to co-ordinate her wardrobe before the final pack. Edith changed the subject and agreed to call Michel to inform him of the venue change, wondering just how one could co-ordinate black, black and black. Edith mentioned to her that she'd locked Michel in with them all night. Camille retorted that those sorts of people have ways and means, and thank God she'd locked her staircase.

"Habit," she said. She did not elaborate on exactly who "those sort of people" were, or what particular "ways and means" she was referring to.

Enjoying a whisky, Michel was bemused at the level of guilt he'd felt in the company of Inspector Vasseur. On a whim he invited Edith to join him for sundowners at Au Rocher du Cancale, promising to order up food for her arrival.

It would be a few hours before sunset, which did not deter Edith. She did not change her outfit for the drinks and dressed with casual style. Though Edith was aware of her physical attraction, she seldom thought of it. She enjoyed her physicality; it was inherent in her being.

The variety of food spread on the table reminded Edith of times with her father when the platters of fresh seafood overflowed. She smiled at the memory and tackled this selection in the true hearty Marseillan spirit. The sounds, smells and memories of the beach came flooding back.

Alone in her apartment, Camille moved away from thoughts of deaths, leaving the memories of Arianne and Natalie to their own devices. She never thought to dedicate any of her compositions to Natalie. She'd dealt with her parents' deaths all alone, and that was enough death for a lifetime. Her current problem was of a different and more important nature. Which of her violins, none of which was a Stradivarius, was the most suitable to take on the trip? She phoned Edith to invite her to the apartment to give an opinion on the violin. Hearing Edith was alone with Michel having mojitos with double tots of rum, she felt disappointed that the friends were fragmented. Surely they all could have drinks together? She asked Edith to come over as soon as she could. Edith said she was having fun, and she later needed to check visas and confirm the travel arrangements.

"And I need time to draft the proposed charter for the Society."

"My decisions are also important," said Camille.

"I'm sure they are, and I'm convinced you'll make the right choices. You'll also need to respect that my time is as important to me as yours is to you. Do all the violins have cases?"

Dragging the call out as long as possible until she could almost taste the mojitos, Camille hung up. She opened a bottle of wine without once glancing at the label and sat, glass in hand, staring at the violins, feeling somewhat deflated.

Why should they be forced to drink alone? she thought. *I would have kept them company.*

Buoyed by the wine, Camille decided to call Michel, but failed to get the anticipated invite. He rushed her off the phone as his new acquaintances converged on Edith, too cheerful for his liking.

Later in the evening, when Edith made excuses and departed, Michel wondered why he'd neglected to share the details of the Inspector's visit with her. He dismissed the thought.

The Stalker was not as neglectful and, having followed Edith to the venue, she remained a shadow in the background at the café, before trailing her home. Edith's sixth sense was as sharp as a blade. She checked her CCTV footage as soon as she was indoors and could see nothing amiss. She relaxed and removed the Sabatier oyster knife from her bag. She stroked the polished wooden handle and spun it in her fingers before placing the knife under her pillow, as usual. It had been a gift from her mother. Checking her IT system, she noticed more amateur attempts to hack in, but the tightened defences had held. Her website was crucial to the tour business and generated many bookings, so she made a mental note to out-hack the hacker after their Ethiopian trip.

The wall in her tiny home was covered with photos of Edith, and the Stalker looked them over for a considerable length of time before selecting a red marker pen. On the whiteboard mounted onto the adjacent wall she created a new list headed 'Contacts' and wrote 'A-(female)' and 'B-(male)' underneath. Although she now knew both Michel and Camille's names, she could not bear to actualise them; the reference tags would do fine. She was not happy with the possessive streak she could see Michel developing. However, having followed Edith for well over a month, she knew he would not be taken seriously. She wrote that down.

To revisit her strategy, she selected a blue pen and drew five columns under the heading 'Photos'. In them she wrote 'date order, outfits, mood, location, rating'. She spent the next hour rearranging some photos on the wall, grouping them by the clothes Edith wore when photographed, before crossing out 'mood'. This girl seemed immune to mood, she was always happy. The Stalker sat on her bed with a drink in hand, staring at the collage on the wall, searching for other character clues. It occurred to her to correlate the number of times each outfit had been worn since Edith met Camille, and compare the results with her own personal like or dislike of these outfits. She could use this method to track Edith's thought patterns, her traits. She was determined to get into Edith's head, and also her bed. She usually did.

Hours passed, but she found no patterns. Everything remained random. In a fury she hurled her vodka bottle against the wall, which also had no effect. It bounced off still intact and the Stalker grabbed the pestle she used to crush garlic and ground it into her left hand; it broke the skin and drew blood, but she felt little pain. Sitting on the floor in frustration, with no clear direction, she realised there was no other way but patience. Given time, and clear thought she would work out Edith's dreams and get into her mind. She'd get help to instruct Edith's computer to forward mail and diary entries to her own. Realising more photos were needed to sustain the process, she cheered up. She loved the chase, despite all the obstacles.

There were a few days left until the Paymaster set the time for the next filming assignment. She would hide this private business well away by then. The cash for filming his antics was becoming crucial to this new lifestyle. It was expensive to monitor Edith in the restaurants she visited with tourist clients. The new earnings covered her needs. She could get used to this lifestyle. Having decided Edith was the girl she'd been searching for all these years, she was determined to succeed this time, at any cost. The analyst would not get the details of the Edith episodes out of her. This was her secret, and he'd suggested nothing to help her stalking addiction from previous case facts. He only seemed interested in the intimate details and the sexual conquests. She failed to understand why he needed the receptionist to listen in on some of these sessions. "Second opinion," he'd said. He could go and get his kicks another way in future. She picked up the vodka bottle and drank again, heard a light tap on her door and stood facing the Paymaster, again without forewarning. She stared at him without changing her bland expression. For now, she needed him. Later, she could change the rules.

"Good news," he said. "He accepts the films, there'll be more."

He thrust an envelope into her hand.

"You've paid me already."

"It's not yours, don't open it. Give it to the violin girl when you see her and make it soon. She needs to get it. She'll understand why."

The Stalker stood at her open door for a minute or two after he'd walked away. How did he know Camille well enough to write to her? She decided now was a good time to deliver the message; she went back into her room, had another shot of vodka and got ready to go out.

She stood outside Camille's apartment in the same spot as on the night of the first meeting and smoked. She always smoked cigarettes when waiting; it was the best cover. The windows were shut as they had been on that previous night. Seeing no movement for twenty minutes, she decided the smartest approach was to slip the envelope under the door and leave. It was easy, and she was gone five minutes later.

Inspector Vasseur sat, notebook in hand, scribbling the occasional word or two. He drew hieroglyphics amongst his words, adding arrows and exclamation marks. Then, frowning, he drew the symbol from the victims' right hands on a new page and looked at it. It resembled a modified seven, an ominous seven with the top section resembling a blade, a challenge, a warning. He then wrote the words 'Venus' and 'Mars'.

He usually enjoyed the pre-dawn in the Marais, but tonight he had a real bastard to sniff out. He was on a sidewalk down from street level that ran along the River Seine. The dampened sounds of the water moving past heightened his sense for other noises around. He registered an occasional engine, laughter, shouting from an apartment alongside the river.

The Inspector took out four roasted almonds from the stash in his left coat pocket. After rolling one around between his fingers, he placed it on his tongue before enjoying the crunch that released the dense flavour. Once again he dragged his eyes across the bridge, moving them in a grid pattern up and across. He noticed two new forms, one staring in his direction and the other walking, or rather hobbling, as the head bobbed up and down. The third form had been there for some time, a cigarette glowing as the person took another drag. The Inspector noticed the smoke curling up towards the light above; it made him thirsty, but not for water, there was sufficient in the river. He took the cap off his coffee thermos and, using it as his cup, poured a full measure. It was piping hot and wonderful. He replaced the cap with regret; the dawn was still some way off.

He took a random €100 note from his wallet and with an open mind studied both sides. Holding his breath, he rubbed the note between his thumb and forefinger, *two notes, both €100, he'd need help from these notes, something out of the box.* He breathed again. There might be a way; they were high-denomination. He wrote again:

Why leave money with dead girls; message (hand tucked in – private); to whom; 1/7, 2/7 limited edition; bridge; why repeat 7 on the right hand? – take with one, give with the other? Run a tracker on the euro notes.

Timing himself, he drew the seven symbol, filling in the spaces as the Wolf had done. Well under a minute. He then underlined the section of notes and put a 'z' through the line as he always did, and the time and date.

The air's still pre-dawn, he thought, before making a note to check the wind speed and direction at the time of both Arianne and Natalie's deaths. Sound carries on the wind. He slid the pencil out of his top pocket before selecting four more almonds. Eating the smallest first, he sketched the symbol from their hands on a new page, the same black symbol, noting to check the forensic reports. He looked up at the sky. Paris was almost still and the dawn had yet to arrive. The smoker had moved on.

10

The scheduled time for the informal Society meeting was 20:00. Camille was the second to arrive at 20:31 and ordered a drink, even though Edith had a coffee in front of her.

"A double gin and tonic," she requested, explaining she was following an orchestra friend's advice to gear up for malaria. "It's the quinine in the tonic, I'm told on good authority."

"Who mentioned they have malaria in Ethiopia? Anyway it's low risk in Addis, and the high altitude is more likely to make you sick."

Michel walked in at that moment: 20:39. He remained loyal to the spirit of the Society and ordered a coffee. Camille had decided after an about-face that she was quite impressed by the minutes concept after all. That morning she'd explained the finer details to a second violinist and a first violinist. She looked forward to hearing all the interesting things she must have said at the last meeting, of which she had no recollection. When she was advised that the minutes had been abandoned at her insistence, she had to be reminded once again that she was not chairman.

I need to be, she thought, instead saying, "What else can I do? I'm no good at making coffee or pastries."

"Well you did provide the venue and wine," said Michel, "so perhaps next time you can play your violin as well."

"I'd like that, I'll try."

The gin and tonic went down well – so well that she ordered her second before her fellow Founders had sipped the last of their coffee.

"Look at this," said Camille, "it came under my door. People are strange."

Edith took the envelope and opened it, read the contents and handed it to Michel before calling the Inspector.

"I'd prefer if you met us here, and please, straight away," she said.

"Eight minutes," he said, and looked forward to meeting her again so soon.

"Who was that?" said Michel.

"The Inspector."

"Is that necessary?"

"Yes," said Edith. Camille looked at them both.

"It's only some idiot," she said.

"An idiot who knows you play violin," said Edith.

The Inspector ordered a coffee and Michel gave him the envelope.

"So you've all touched it," said the Inspector. "That's a shame."

He opened the envelope, and hand-scrawled on the page was the message:

> *part one: if you play the violin once more in public I will kill you, slowly, in three movements like a concerto.*
> *part two: when we are together you will play for me every day.*
> *part three: we will be together forever.*

The Inspector took out his notebook and tore out three pages. He handed one to each of them. He excused himself to Edith as he lifted her pen, and gave it to Michel.

"I want you each to write your immediate thoughts about this message on the paper, name them, and hand them back to me. You first, Michel – and I hear you're going to Ethiopia as well."

As Michel wrote, the Inspector said he hoped for a happier occasion when they could join him to drink more of such fine coffee, but now there was work to be done. With all three papers and the message in hand, he said he was pleased they were flying the next day, which should take Camille out of harm's way. He would look into this letter, which appeared to be a serious matter, thanked them for the coffee and left.

He walked two blocks away, went into another café and sat down to read. He immediately compared the handwriting to Michel's, and then he read the scripts. Camille wrote a single word – 'nonsense'. Edith mentioned a possible link to the person she sensed was stalking her. Michel, who'd lingered over the task, went into a diatribe as to how people would be overwhelmed by Camille's looks and talent.

The air in airports the world over is distilled, sucked dry of any character, and vacuumed of all that makes it sweet. Personality changes are rife in airports, and mood swings run rampant. Logic goes out the window.

Edith, of course, was an exception and, try as she may, she found it hard to grasp the circus that played out before her. Camille had adopted the persona of a rock star. It was a persona that is not usually welcomed by flight attendants of airlines, or the repair and maintenance teams of hotels. She blazoned her family history and political connections before her and, astonishingly, some doors – including those of the VIP lounge – opened. Had her father owned the world's most famous bank and all associated airport lounges, perhaps not? When had Edith become the owner of the largest tour company in Paris? And Michel, said to be an esteemed critic of airline food, flying secretly to test Air France, would have been amused to hear they were flying Emirates. A concerned ground staff member felt it fair to warn the cabin crew.

Edith, in a moment of brilliance, had booked her own seat five rows behind Camille and Michel, whom she had advised were most lucky to be seated together. She took Camille to one side.

"What's all this bullshit you're spouting? Just be yourself?"

"It's hard. I'm scared and this is what happens, I start attacking everyone."

Edith took her hand and hugged her.

"There's little to be scared of. A bumpy ride is the worst that can happen."

"No, I'd like that, a Disney ride. It's these people asking me questions, not trusting me, intimidating me, while you and Michel are so calm."

"That's their job," said Edith, "and I can promise you we're only calm on the outside. Try slow breaths."

There had been a number of eyes from both sides of the law watching the members of the Fourth Society checking in. The Inspector's officer was unaware of the Stalker who in turn had the officer mapped on her radar. Officer No.4 was not used to being watched himself and did not possess the sixth sense that Edith so enjoyed. The cameras monitored them both.

The Officer managed to learn that their return tickets were for a week-long trip to Addis Ababa. He gleaned little else of importance, noting that Michel's luggage was twice the size of the women's, which seemed unusual. Also, Camille was carrying a violin case, which he presumed customs would put under deep scrutiny.

Listening to the officer's report some time later, the Inspector surmised the extra luggage might indicate a longer intended stay. He took a mental note of his officer No.4's limitations. Within sixty seconds Inspector Vasseur had sourced the name of their hotel in Addis. He contacted a security connection within the Addis French Embassy, and requested he keep a discreet eye on the tourists, especially the male.

The Stalker was aware that Edith had inspected the people in the terminal on more than one occasion. She used the utmost discretion taking photos, which were essential for her wall. She managed half a dozen or more photos of Edith, and two or three extra where Michel or Camille were also in the picture. Studying their body language in these photos might give her insights into the nature of their relationships. She snapped one of the officer as well. Was he also a stalker?

Had this assignment been for the Paymaster, she felt certain he would have been impressed by her skills. She was even tempted to tell him of her feelings for this girl. She was building more intimate plans for Edith, which vacillated between the usual quick sexual relationship and a full, long life together. They might even enjoy stalking as a team. That opened new fantasy worlds, and her female partner could punish her if she made mistakes. She decided it was better not to tell the Paymaster anything, especially of her planned break-in to their apartments during the trip. He might inform the analyst, who would be furious that she was keeping back information as a patient. The analyst had said that in his patient relationships he never passed information on to the authorities. He was his patients' law, first and foremost, and he insisted that they kept their sessions secret. She would keep a tight lid on her plans for Edith.

It was 00:36 in Dubai when they entered the airport concourse for an eight-hour stopover. The travel companions attempted to co-ordinate their rendezvous for the second flight. Camille refused to change the time on her watch, insisting that it was still 22:36. Their logic didn't cut it with her.

"I'm French," she said, "I'm staying that way."

"See you at boarding time," said Edith, smiling and squeezing Camille's hand. Michel was already striding off with great haste.

With team spirit temporarily splintered, Michel headed for Pint 19, Camille to the food gallery, and Edith decided to go for a swim in the complex pool. She would follow up with a drink in the concourse; something long and cold would do the trick. They had another flight, and there were more borders to cross.

11

It was business as usual in Addis Ababa, some four hours' flying time from Dubai. Kelile Benyam, son of the founder of an independent coffee company, was looking forward to receiving the French guests. Both the city of Addis Ababa and Kelile's Traditional Coffee Workshop team were well prepared for their Parisian visitors, or so they thought. The workshop team had all retired to bed for the night. Kelile's younger sister, Gabra, had handmade the name tags: Camille, Edith and Michelle for the three French women. She believed it might be difficult to tell them apart. She loved their names and looked forward to learning more about Paris. Gabra wondered who would win the coveted prize and lead the coffee preparation at the graduation blessing. On the first full day, Kelile would drive them through the city to acclimatise, as per Edith's request. She'd especially asked to visit the bustling Merkato street market, the largest in Africa and a pride of the city. On day two, work would start in earnest.

Michel strode into Pint 19 like he owned the place, getting increased satisfaction from his social drinking this past week.

There seemed to be more interested listeners for his stories in Paris lately. *Was it the increased confidence gained through close association with Edith and Camille that attracted people?* he pondered. He ordered a Heineken and, halfway through the beer, or some thirty seconds later, realised that this was a holiday. It should be a mojito with a double tot of rum, and he waved both arms for the barman's attention.

"You wave so much, are you drowning?" said the barman.

Do they serve alcohol in Ethiopia? Michel wondered and presumed they did. It was to be party time with his girls, and champagne and mojitos would soften them up; they would soon fall for the charms of his worldly self. He hadn't realised the airport bar would be so big and sat isolated, thinking about Edith's extraordinary power. She had a calm assertiveness that did not tolerate fools. A man could travel the world with a woman like that. They'd be invited to the best parties and dinners. Their hosts would admire them as a couple, admire their wisdom and her taste in men, which was discerning to say the least.

Amazed at his own ability to integrate with all types, he'd labelled Camille the introvert. She was secretive and talented; he'd heard that from the people seated near him at concerts. He knew she'd waited to share inner secrets with him on the trip. He had no doubt she was searching him out in the airport. He'd enjoy being found.

Camille hardly gave Michel a thought, and hadn't much since inviting him to the Society, apart from some concerns about his connection to the poor victims.

His drink was soon gone and the barman replaced it. Michel nodded in appreciation. There was a lot of thinking to do as the Society was influencing his life. The chairman slot might well suit his own purposes. Imagine being chairman of the Coffee Society when there were fifteen to twenty female members all seeking his attention for one reason or another. He almost patted his own back. All those thoughts, and the paths they led him down, took an hour or two of his imagining. He checked his watch and was glad he had a huge capacity for alcohol. He'd be the last man standing; the cognoscenti in Addis would appreciate him for that.

The mystique of coffee was becoming more and more challenging to Edith. The more she discovered, the more there seemed still to discover, and the more rewarding it became. She was determined to bring back as many varieties as possible to Paris. She would ask the others to make sure that there was space in their luggage, believing Michel would have lots of space in his two big cases. She had butterflies in apprehension of the ceremony course. She'd read that the genuine Ethiopian coffee ceremony was one of the great experiences of a true coffee lover, and a proud moment for all attending to share. She'd been surfing the Net for coffee information, and reading as much as possible before booking the course. Her numerous attempts to interest the others were unsuccessful, and she assumed they were way ahead of her already, studying in secret for the course. Why else did Camille disappear upstairs so often? Why did Michel hang around cafés all day?

She avoided the Pint 19 to allow Michel time to the play the crowds unfettered, and took her time over the swim in the airport pool. The feel of the water rushing over her body was mesmeric, and floods of happy memories rolled in and out of her thoughts as she swam. She stretched her arm far ahead and reached for that extra few centimetres before cupping the water, to stroke it back past her body. It felt amazing, she felt amazing, and she swam on.

In the concourse and alone, Camille smiled to herself. Did they think her so naive as to miss the next flight? She was a violinist and timing was a key essence that enriched her life. She was happy being on her own in such strange surroundings, though she checked and rechecked that the violin was secure in its case. Even though she couldn't pinpoint her whereabouts on a map, she knew she was completely safe. There was no time to pamper her phobia. She would relish freedom for the time being.

It was between borders in the airport concourse building that Camille's life underwent its first significant shift of the trip. She checked her violin for the umpteenth time, this time stroking it against her cheek. Out of the blue, a Chilean traveller with family en route to Singapore requested her to play for them, to bless his family on their trip. How could she refuse?

"I'll play *Motherlands* for your family," she added, "a short piece." While not her first public solo by any means, it was the first in such an unusual setting, and the first solo of her own composition.

A nearby lone Canadian tourist recorded the entire performance on his iPhone and went on his way, convinced he was in love. An American traveller clapped so much that the authorities thanked Camille for the entertainment. They asked her to please forgo the encore the growing throng were demanding. They also gave her a dinner voucher, which she thought unusual as it was long past midnight. The voucher went into her wallet as a memento, and another small portion of her fears was stowed in the violin case alongside the 1828 J.F. Pressenda violin. She wondered if she should have bought the Francesco Ruggieri violin instead. It might have been more suitable for airport acoustics. She contemplated a world airport tour, wondering which airline would fund it, *perhaps Virgin or Turkish*. She'd heard from a cellist they were exceptional airlines.

She was so taken with her various plans that she'd no time to react when the Canadian passed again on the way to his flight, hesitated to kiss her cheek, and was gone. Camille loved this airport. She wondered why some spectators had handed her high-denomination dollar bills. *The airport equivalent of presenting soloists with flowers,* she thought, looking around to confirm there was no florist in sight. *They'll need florists before my world airport tour.*

Under the new circumstances she contemplated flying on the next plane back to Paris, where she felt fate was awaiting her. *They'll think I've missed my flight,* she laughed, giving no thought whatsoever to the death threat that had recently come sliding under her apartment door.

The Paymaster stared at her photo, which shook in his hand. He rubbed it against his face, much as Camille had with her violin, and then stared hard at her eyes. They spoke to him, whispering words from his book only he could hear:

> *when the quartet spins in circles, the lights will glow*
> *on the moon*

And he thought, *yes, violin girl, I'll come for you, when the lights glow.* It was just as well he'd no knowledge that she'd already defied his instructions, and played in public. Camille hadn't given it a second thought.

<h1 style="text-align: center;">12</h1>

Twenty-seven minutes before the Founders' aircraft took off from Charles de Gaulle airport, the Stalker decided to follow the man she'd noticed keeping an eye on the team. *Who the hell was he, what was his business?* She drifted back into the airport's moving morass, watching and waiting for his movements.

First, he had gone to the washroom. He left there drying his hands on his trousers, had drunk a beer at the airport, and caught a shuttle bus back to the city. The Stalker sat one row behind him, and she decided whoever he was, he was not a professional. His mobile had never left his hand, and his first call was to a female colleague whom he called 'honey'. His tone had been frivolous, teasing, and soon sexual. From habit, the Stalker had taken out her own mobile, opened a voice memo app and pressed the record button. He made two more calls of a similar nature to other females before calling the wife at home. He'd be in late, meetings, he told her.

The Stalker had it all on record. She followed him off the bus and only when he entered a Police Authority building did she realise she'd hit gold dust. What was their interest in the three travellers? With Edith away she would have time on her hands and needed a new game to play, at least until the next filming session was scheduled. She wondered about these filming sessions. Her mandate was to film the Paymaster at night from some thirty metres' distance. She was to be discreet while he went about interacting socially with various people, at random, under the influence of the drugs. That was fine and dandy. There was so little light to work with at night that she felt the films must be grainy and dark. That was the analyst's problem, given the conditions he'd set. Perhaps he blew the films up to large scale and clarified them somehow. She'd seen the projector in the office. How else could he evaluate the subject's emotional reactions and responses? Those responses all looked rather meek and mild to her as she battled to use the viewfinder, never sure what she'd captured in the dark. It was the analyst's money and she wasn't about to complain. Perhaps the analyst was so cash-flush from all his patients' consulting fees that her payment meant little to him. She contemplated asking for her counselling sessions to be free as well, but decided against pushing her luck, which was currently strong.

The analyst sat facing the Paymaster and queried what exactly he'd felt during the drug-induced experiment.

"I felt thirsty."

The analyst covered his eyes with his hands, head shaking.

"And that's it? For twenty thousand euros, that's it. You must have had other reactions, exhilaration, sadness, inhibitions, anger? These drugs alter emotional states, make emotions vivid, powerful, bring out feelings locked away inside."

"Well, I have no recollection. Either your drugs or the hypnosis caused that. I felt thirsty. I wanted a drink, and I wanted to read my book. Perhaps I have nothing locked deep away. After a drink I felt better. You have the films. Look at them, don't ask me."

"What about emotions?"

"That's your job."

"So how do you feel now?"

"Still thirsty and I want to watch the films."

"Well you can't. You've been well paid and those films are a part of the experiment. They're for analysis only, confidential."

"I always bump into this 'confidential' crap," said the Paymaster, "and what if the drugs are causing permanent damage to me, what then? What about the hypnosis, what the hell is that for?"

"That's why I pay you so well, for the small risk. The experiment can't do a fraction of the damage the cocktail of alcohol and recreational drugs you swallow do. You can stop these experiments anytime you want."

"No, I'll carry on, I've got plans for after."

"What plans?"

"A new life."

"Right," said the analyst, "you all have new life plans. They never happen."

"That's the first intelligent thing you've ever told me, and it's crap."

Inspector Jean-Luc Vasseur knew things were difficult. His routine of four almonds every half hour had crept up to twelve or sixteen, and that was a sure sign of trouble.

He linked his fingers in front of him and turned his palms outwards, pushing his hands away from his body, stretching. He stood up from his desk – which was his least favourite place – and arched his back. He thought again of the Spanish girl's cat. How many times had it arched its back in its life? He hoped that when his time came he too could have such an unusual funeral. Satisfied with the stretch, he took two more almonds from his pocket without thinking. After a brief ritual juggle he'd placed them one by one into his mouth where he relished the roasted crunch.

The window offered the best light for viewing a €100 note from his wallet. After staring at it, he concluded the bridge metaphor was too obvious. Each euro denomination had a bridge image on one side and a window image on the other, modelled not from any reality, but from a design relevant to the chosen era. He knew which Parisian bridge the €50 design was intended to have on it – that is, before the decision was made not to use actual bridge images. He'd had a look over the Pont de Neuilly bridge and surrounds the previous day. He had found nothing to connect it to the bridges over the Seine or the two murders.

The team had hoped that hobby enthusiasts of the three main euro-tracking Internet sites might throw up a lead. The websites allowed registered currency trackers to load unique serial numbers of individual euro notes in their possession onto the site. Next, they'd spend the note back into general circulation. In time they hoped another tracker, in another city, might load the same note. The sites then flagged the movement of notes that received more than one loading, building the note's travel pattern. It was a long shot, but two euro notes had ended up in the hands of dead girls in Paris.

The report he received from an assistant showed a hit on the first €100 note. It was in Berlin, some fourteen months before Arianne's murder. They were about to run the second euro note through the system. Had the killer or his master carried the note from Berlin to Paris? Possible. Where and when did the euro tracker spend the note back into circulation? If in Berlin, where, exactly? The team would need to find out. The killer might well have picked up the note in that same shop or venue it was released back into, giving the team a near date and location of the puppet-master, or the Wolf. They could then start to search for unusual traits. This was a long shot; they needed a break, and soon. The lab advised the only prints on the notes were those of the murdered girls. *Fastidious*, thought the Inspector. These were careful and premeditated actions. They would catch this 'Wolf' bastard and give him a real name. A request went out to their European counterparts for crimes leaving victims holding euro notes, and for any violent crimes on bridges. Was there a grudge against the euro or the girls, or both? He decided to take another walk along the Seine to get feedback from his team working incognito. He would chat to traders he trusted, and to other dominant communities in the Marais and the Latin Quarters. This crime would break sooner or later; he needed it to break before a third killing.

Officer No.4 left the building at 18:06. The Stalker was some distance away and clear of the perimeter vision of the CCTV cameras. It took the officer a while to walk deeper into the Latin Quarter, and into a bar where he took up a seat facing the main entrance, his back to the wall. He fidgeted, and adjusted his crotch at least three or four times before the female joined him. They kissed on both cheeks, and once on the lips. The Stalker felt her bile rise; she took a long sip of her rum and soda, ordered another shot of the rum and mixed it in. This 'meeting' could take a while, but she had all the time in the world.

The sharp sound of a slap caught the Stalker by surprise and the female left, rubbing her hand. Officer No.4 was left sitting looking down into his drink holding one hand to his cheek. When the Stalker came and sat at his table, he frowned.

"I'm also having a drink after a fight... with my man," said the Stalker. "We may as well commiserate."

"Why are you fighting?" he said.

"He hates sex, I love it," she said. "A drink will douse the flames."

"Well well," he said, "at least we're on the same side."

"Was that your wife?"

"No, she's at home, she thinks I'm at a meeting."

"Look," she said, "I've got to go now, but why don't we meet soon, same place, have a few drinks, have some fun? Give me your number; I'll call you when I can make it. I might run a bit late because I work long hours. Have a drink or two and wait for me. Tell your wife to go out with friends that night." She took his number, had a final sip of her drink and was gone.

After their encounter officer No.4 arrived home early, and in good spirits.

"How was the meeting?" asked the wife.

"Interesting, and with possibilities to improve certain matters," he said. "It's going to be continued one of these nights."

"Well then, I'll arrange to go out that night myself."

"Yes, do that, I was going to suggest it," he said, much to her surprise.

Yeah, like hell, she thought.

The Stalker looked up at officer No.4's apartment. He'd left the bar some ten minutes after her and never once watched his back. She'd followed him; she noted down the address, smiled and turned to go back to the Latin Quarter, her heart beating a little faster. She loved a challenge, and Edith was away.

13

Ignoring the French attitude that citizens never needed to venture beyond their own borders, the Founders' travel fever ignited once more. It was a nervous group of Founders who disembarked in Addis Ababa. Michel, having had Camille sound asleep on his shoulder for over an hour on the second flight, was in love yet again.

Leaving the aircraft was akin to stepping into a radical new world for the Founders. Kelile, their host for the trip, emerged from the terminus to walk them through the system. He ignored their initial hesitation, elevating them to what Camille imagined was VIP status. Kelile stared at Michel. This was not the Michelle they'd been expecting, and he decided this wasn't the appropriate moment to upset any euphoria. He would tell them later that as was their tradition, the course was for females only.

The city of Addis Ababa combined tall new structures rising in an indiscriminate fashion from the squat concrete buildings of the past. There were people everywhere. The hum of activity grew as they watched. While Camille seemed comatose, Michel glowed. He saw an enhanced beauty as she blinked, turning her head as if panning on a new life. He saw little else. He did not see her fear as she stepped out of the security blanket she'd been wrapped in all these years. He did not sense her afterglow at having played her own composition in the Dubai airport a few hours earlier.

Only Edith was aware they had crossed a border, leaving France behind. Perhaps having sailed many times out of sight of land had helped her. While the other Founders might have read her body language as acquiescent, it was rather a respect of another culture and another nation. Camille, wide-eyed, could not refrain from commenting on the lack of French signs, and the absence of fresh baguettes when needed.

Michel took total charge of Camille's luggage. In the hotel lobby seventy-five minutes later, Camille requested her violin case, and Michel's heart froze. He'd taken it from the overhead locker, and then? She insisted that he go back to the aircraft and fetch it. She might need it soon.

Edith marvelled at her friend's newfound self-control. Lessons were being learnt. Up in Camille's hotel room, one glance out the window revealed the distant shantytown dwellings, which would have been heaven-sent to a photographer. She would've preferred an auditorium, with enhanced acoustics. After her airport concert Camille already regretted not having flown back home from Dubai, but to what? She knew deep down it would be wise to spend this time with Edith, who would help her build confidence. She would need large doses to tackle the outside world; the world her father had said was tangled up in danger.

Camille decided to take her first bath of many that day, succumbing to the temptation to test out the Dubai duty-free bath salts purchased from her stack of gifted dollars. Edith would wonder where Camille's endless supply of dollars had come from. From the comfort of the bath, Camille fretted over the J.F. Pressenda violin which, now that it was lost, had become her absolute favourite.

After a quick shower and shave, Michel decided the Piano Bar seemed the best spot to plan his strategy; *how to hunt down the violin and fresh baguettes.* These, he felt, were the keys to unlocking Camille's heart. He would soon return a hero with the trophies. Once he'd located them they could tan by the pool, sipping drinks, and rush to his room to make love before lunch. Yes, that would be the life, and they could then embark on many sexual adventures together. This temporary loss of the violin might turn out fortunate. He knew for a fact that Edith would want to join their wanton activities.

Unaware of Michel's plans, and taking the obvious course of action, Edith and Kelile drove back to Bole International Airport. There the Emirates ground staff had the violin and case intact and well cared-for. Prize in hand, they drove back to the hotel where they discovered Camille had gone incommunicado. Their knocking on her door went ignored, and they decided to save the good news for dinner.

The pre-booked Merkato tour took place and Edith was the lone tourist, fulfilling her pre-trip wish to experience the opposite role to tour guide. She was later dropped off at the hotel, elated and with a new take on hustle and bustle, having added a wave of new scents to her memory. She loved her first breath of the Ethiopian experience, the endless stalls of local food, and she knew she would visit this city again. *Michel should not miss this*, she thought, *he would taste everything.* Her guides were fascinated by her enthusiasm, and she picked up all the exotic fruits, holding them to her nose, relishing their subtle and differing aromas.

There was strength to this city that rivalled Paris in different ways. The power of Addis, Edith thought, was willing her to understand those differences. What struck her was the way the wind swirled free, rushing between, around, and over the buildings. In Paris, by contrast, the winds seemed forced to follow the same streets the people walked. As a relative newcomer to Paris she'd noted that so many of its buildings were uniform in height and form. Addis did not have the symmetry of Paris, but that was not a fault. She had no preference as she observed Addis in action, a free-for-all feeling, jumbled buildings, each with its unique character and surrounds. Paris was hewed out and stacked by man, block by block. Addis Ababa felt like it was built by nature itself – the product of many men and women. They perhaps worked for their own purpose, not pulling in the same direction with the same end in mind. *Why should they?* she thought. Both cities stood their own ground, stood with a unique sense of defiance. The gardens and trees in Addis had decided for themselves where they'd like to be, rather like the beaches near her hometown, Marseillan. Somehow the trees and fenced gardens in Paris acted as if the decisions had been taken out of their hands, as if they should grow where they were told to grow.

Edith promised herself she'd spend more time in the parks of Paris, her chosen home. She'd experience Paris from a new perspective; see what Haussmann had envisioned when he'd remodelled the glorious landscape in the nineteenth century. That was long after the French remodelled themselves in the revolution. She regretted that neither of her friends had joined her on this excursion. Her two hosts had an insight to life she found interesting. She listened when they talked, and they listened when she talked. The Coptic cross she'd purchased would remind her of the ethos of her new Ethiopian friends, and her Taytu handbag would grace Paris in suitable fashion.

After finding the king-size bed in her room rather comfortable, Camille discovered the minibar. She never gave a thought to the bill she would later be presented with. She started to see the positive side to the violin saga – *yes, the team were onto it* – and Edith had a way of succeeding with such matters. It would be tragic to lose yet another of her violins. She slept on and off with her pillow wrapped around her head and the sheets pulled up high. It seemed to do the trick. She had no qualms about not answering the knocks on the door, and rationalised that she was not yet used to her bedroom being a public domain. Once the violin was returned she knew she'd feel more relaxed. Travel, she decided, was not as bad as she'd imagined, and touring via the hotel windows seemed an adequate solution.

Kelile had a way about him that Camille found fascinating. He was calm, controlled and complete in a way foreign to her. He seemed to want for nothing and his smile rose up from the depths. She decided that she would sit next to him at the table, and selected elegant yet feisty earrings to complement her eyes, polished black stones set in gold.

At 19:25 Addis time, she strode forth on an adventure from her room, bold and glamorous, heading for the appointed dining room. Kelile, Gabra and Edith stood and welcomed her with the surprise of the rescued violin, and the staff clapped. She arranged for the violin to be dispatched forthwith to her room, adding a request to restock the minibar.

In his quasi safari outfit, Michel now seemed rather out of place in Addis and he was horrified to see the time was 19:50. He and his new friend Hank were somewhere 'special' as promised. They were having countless Ethiopian beers with the locals, who were being offered massive rewards to retrieve the violin. The locals were now negotiating upfront payments. Michel's excuse that he had not exchanged euros for birr did not seem to deter them, and the 'special' bar became rather dingy in retrospect.

Without a goodbye to his new and persistent acquaintances, Michel hurried to find a taxi. He commandeered a *blue-devil* taxi all to himself, paying to be the only passenger. He took time to adjust to the blaring sound of gospel music pumping through the speakers. He couldn't fathom the writings inside the vehicle, but his heart warmed at the sight of the Brigitte Bardot photo alongside one of a Coptic cross. He held on for dear life.

Despite giving the driver instructions to speed to the hotel, which he regretted almost at once, he managed a stop to purchase local *injera* bread for Camille on the ride back.

He had failed to appreciate that its round and flat appearance was different to that of a baguette. To boot, it flopped around without the slightest tendency towards crispness. He took one or two bites, modifying its appearance and testing if the quality was up to scratch. It was, in an unusual way. He kept on checking the quality from time to time to be certain, and felt damn good. Valour was returning to his soul and a violin hunter needed sustenance. Camille would be missing him.

I'll be fashionably late, he thought.

At the dinner table Michel assured them that he was well on his way to pinning down the location and recovering the violin. It had been sighted around; that's what his reliable and well-paid sources were telling him. Edith informed him of its safe retrieval with a thank you, and Camille nodded, acknowledging her graciousness. When Edith said the coffee course was for women only, Michel perked up. *He was destined for wild adventures, and Paris was already full of coffee.*

14

Skipping the Addis hotel breakfast coffee in favour of the real thing on the course had been a big mistake for the girls. The first workshop commenced at 09:00 and there would be no rushing to brew. Drinking coffee would be the final act of the morning. The Benyam business was already a hive of activity. Wooden desks were piled with files, and mountains of stacked sacks of green coffee beans were all being readied for packing. The trucks carrying the shipping containers queued and backed up in the yard, waiting to be stuffed.

On the flat concrete roof of the three-storey building, a rural home setting had been recreated. It represented a compound or *gebi*, using different examples of rustic dwellings from the south-west and the east of the country. Edith loved the open-air veranda feel, which had a welcome like a typical Parisian café. She could smell the embers of yesteryear, and coffees long drunk. Camille thought the builders had gone home early, leaving the place unfinished. She baulked, assailed by the cacophony of noise, the trucks, forklifts and shouting voices. She appreciated being a good three storeys above it all.

Kelile opened the workshop, welcoming the visitors from Paris. He amused the assistants by saying a famous *male* baker of Paris wanted to take their course. He told the gathering that the diversity of top-quality beans in Ethiopia produced a wide choice of coffees, with many subtle flavours.

"Our local coffee culture," he said, "has a ritual respect for nature, friends and family. Some of our beans are amongst the finest in the world. I hope today's coffee lives up to standard."

Before he departed, leaving them to the course, he said he looked forward to the final ceremony. The female guests from Paris would lead the preparation.

Camille felt he combined understanding with an air of calm authority. These were traits missing from most men of her life. Raising her hand for attention, she requested a cup of coffee, which everyone thought was hilarious, and they laughed and clapped at her joke.

"We love European humour," said Kelile as he left.

The coffee ceremony was ingrained in the daily life of Ethiopians. The commitment to communicate and spend time together in this ritual meant more to many of the locals than the drink itself. It reminded Edith so much of Sunday family dinners in Marseillan, and the wonderful seafood meals that were prepared by her grandmother. They were events never to be missed, where the family shared the unusual and interesting moments of their past week. It was strange to see such a glaze in Camille's eyes, but it was comforting to know that she too was enjoying the moment. Edith loved the indoor-outdoor feel of the rooftop. The sky seemed especially close to her.

As a young girl Edith had learnt to shuck oysters at home, and the deftness and speed with which she handled her oyster knife would stay with her for life. She was a quick learner, and applied herself to this new course. Edith's fervour was catching and soothed Camille somewhat, prompting her to hug her friend. It was the first time she'd hugged someone in years.

Camille was grateful that Edith would be on hand to do the coffee preparing, whatever that entailed. She could see Edith was full of confidence. Meanwhile, she'd grown rather partial to hiding in her hotel room and might soon pretend to feel a migraine coming on. It crossed Camille's mind to send Gabra a catalogue of Krupp burr grinders and the latest choice of home roasters, which would make things a whole lot easier here. It was a miracle she kept these ideas to herself. Especially the part about two cups being more than ample for one sitting, and the three cups that participants drank in this ceremony being excessive. She would later learn the cups were rather small.

Maybe I do have a little confidence in myself, Camille thought, *when I play violin on stage or in airports*, and she smiled to herself. When Camille presumed the first day's session was nearing its end, she had no idea that they would sit for yet another hour during which three rounds of coffee would be served. By the third round – the blessing round – she was more than ready to leave.

To an untrained eye, it would come as no surprise that when Gabra mentioned her early ratings of the participants to Kelile, Edith received ten out of ten. Camille managed a polite three. He decided that a tour of the workings of an independent coffee export house might lift Camille's spirits. It would boost her interest, acknowledging the violin incident must have been hard on her. He asked Camille to be his guest that afternoon at around 15:30. He would do his best to spark her interest in the euphoria of coffee. It was disappointing when visitors did not fully engage in the course, and he needed to support his sister as best he could.

In the fifth pawnshop in Paris visited by the Spanish sister and the Greek girl, they found an array of tattered musical instruments. Camille's violin case was shoved in amongst them.

"What do you want?" said the attendant

"Do you ever sell this shit?" said the sister. "I might need a cello."

"What for?"

"An ornament, what else?"

"I don't have any."

"I can see that. I'll come again."

"Come alone, it's cheaper that way."

"I might," she said, and they walked back out onto the street.

"Creep," said the Greek girl.

"Not the first and not the last. My brother owes me a big favour, and the violin's there for the taking."

Officer No.4 was sitting at his desk when the call from the stranger he'd met in the bar came through. He spoke to her in the low tones he used when talking to his sources, although he wasn't taking notes.

My lucky day, he thought, and they arranged to meet the following night in the same bar.

"I'll go there after work," he said, "about eight. I'll tell the wife to go out again, that way we can take our time."

"I'd like that," said the Stalker, "I'll get there when I can. It might be after ten. You can tell me all about your exciting work when I see you."

"No rush, I'll have a beer or two and eat."

It took Camille five minutes to decide on a layered look with a black, silk-blend vest over a fitted long-sleeved T-shirt. She'd wear black jeans and gladiator sandals, which she'd thought were just the thing for Africa. The cellists back home had recommended the sandals following their trip to Turkey, and she believed Istanbul must be hereabouts.

Kelile drove her to see the many aspects of the coffee cycle. The destination turned out to be a plain concrete two-storey building, which she would later describe as run down. It was not run down, it was functional and spotless. 'Box-shaped' might be the suitable architectural description. Disappointment was written all over her face, and from the moment the security guards searched her bag on entry Camille seemed unable to recover her equilibrium. She showed little interest in the tour and Kelile tried to keep the conversation moving in a charming way. Camille wished they could forget coffee for the time being and just sit down and discuss how to go about building sublime worldly confidence, similar to his. That would be the highlight of her trip.

When Kelile excused himself from the sampling room for a moment, Camille chose a few 250-gram packets with handwritten labels. She was not au fait with the sampling concept. These would impress the other Founders no end. It did not occur to her that she'd removed packets of beans roasted and prepared for a professional buyers' cupping later that day. She had no idea that certain top-end coffees were subjected to close security in these parts, where hijacking targeted the best. A container of the finest Arabica coffee was black gold, and at times could be hijacked to order by grey trade syndicates.

The private security guards upped their interest in Camille on exit. They discovered she had no receipt for the coffee packets and Kelile, caught off guard, had no immediate explanation. The moment Camille admitted she'd helped herself, security wanted to question her further. She offered to put them back at once. They said the packets were required as evidence. Camille asked if they realised she was a tourist.

Kelile defused the issue, suggesting they take details of the hotel she was staying at. They agreed, and called their superiors to report the incident. At the security company headquarters there was jubilation; perhaps they had their first solid lead to one of the syndicates behind coffee hijacking, a foreigner.

Headquarters called the French Embassy whose representative had arrived by the time Kelile returned. He did not appreciate this escalation of the incident. They did not accept his view that these were random packets taken in the mistaken belief they were free samples.

Dinner was held in the hotel again. Camille relived the sample incident with a nervous yet uncharacteristic gusto, and the other Founders found her story hilarious. The red wine flowed and for the second night in a row the hotel's French restaurant felt like home. Edith promised herself something authentic the next night, a taste of genuine Ethiopian cuisine, whether they accompanied her or not.

The French representative arrived with his shadows in tow as the third red wine was doing its round. Michel proffered the bottle. The representative turned him down, and requested details of all three members' travel documents. Camille was instructed to proceed to her room after dinner, and to remain there until notified otherwise. They advised that the incident had now been reported to the local authorities. The Embassy representative had negotiated for Camille to be confined to her hotel room, at this stage.

"In the name of the devil," she said, "I'm under arrest." Camille stood up and left the dining room, having no idea that someone would be hovering outside her door all night.

The Paymaster remained furious with the analyst. He'd become a pawn in his experiment, not a patient. If he couldn't watch his own films to gauge emotional responses, then why didn't the analyst give him real feedback? If it weren't for the money, he'd raid their dispensary and leave. A time would come for that. He'd leave only with his new woman and her violin. *Perhaps there is progress*, he thought. *I can feel the woman is waiting for me. I can feel her needing me. I'll touch her body, touch all over, gauge her responses for myself, and if she lets me down I'll punish her. I can think of ways to punish her.*

He removed his Böker Kalashnikov knife from his pocket, flipped it open with the thumb-tab. He ran his finger down

the side of the black blade. When they were together he'd buy
one for her. They could slice their dried meat together, wash
it down with vodka and listen to The Doors. He wondered if
she could play '*Strange Days*' on her violin. He'd make her do
it, and he would sing for her.

15

The Inspector knew he could expect another murder in the sequence some time soon. Alternatively the Wolf might go to ground. Both would be a disaster. The Inspector sought justice before another murder took place. He was disappointed that the €100 notes the victims had clutched were wiped clean of prints. He returned to his bench by the Seine to mull over unclear thoughts, which had accumulated the past few days. Coincidences happened – he had long since learnt that – so was the murder of two baking apprentices coincidence? Given that the time of morning when the baking industry went to work coincided with the time when the killer seemed to strike, it would raise the probability somewhat. Streetwalkers, insomniacs, late-night revellers could all become targets. Michel's diatribe about opposing passions running through the industry made the Inspector retain the baking angle.

The Inspector knew probability and possibility were different concepts, but he needed to consider both. The bridge location did not seem to be random. Why murder on a bridge? It was a boundary, a crossing, a midpoint… it all ran through his mind and some thoughts were written into the notebook. He had widened the search across Europe for similar bridge killings.

The €100 notes were a means of communication, perhaps more. 'Limited Edition 1/7' and '2/7' spoke for themselves. The symbol on the girls' hands seemed a vicious interpretation of a seven. It was not lucky for some. The obvious solution was seven planned murders, but these killings were not the obvious type. His team had decided the signature information was not for public consumption, and they had kept it that way so far. Let the killer go public on that if he wished. Some killers had been tempted out of their comfort zones on such issues in the past, desperate to explain their messages.

'Venus' and 'Mars'. The Inspector knew he could in all likeliness expect 'Mercury' next. It depended on how pernickety this killer was. The planets' distances from Earth changed as they moved in orbit, and Mars made it more complex by having an elliptical orbit. Was this was a signpost to the location of the next bridge murder, and would it be one bridge further away from the second crime scene? If yes, he'd predict murder three could be planned for anywhere from the Petit Pont to the Pont de la Tournelle. If the Left Bank represented a quick exit for the killer, it would be near the Left Bank. He had to prevent a third murder.

Knowing she was an overnight flight away from the safety of her own apartment in the Marais, Camille decided the best approach was to take photos through her hotel room window. Edith could email these back to France, and the Inspector could give them to the Special Forces. They would rescue her as they had with others in the past. With that comforting thought, she realised she'd been holding her breath and relaxed. She spent a comfortable first night under house arrest. She woke with the sunrise, refreshed after only three or four hours' sleep. She loved the complete lack of responsibility that came with confinement.

It had not dawned on her that seated on a chair in the corridor outside her room was a guard posted by the Embassy. The guard was instructed to sit there and not restrain Camille in any way. He had listened to her potter about on occasions during the night, and presumed she was planning an escape, which kept him vigilant some of the time. He'd balanced a matchbox on the door handle for added security and it stayed there, only removed for room service delivery and tray collections. He wished he had his own corridor service to order food and drink, and decided to request his employers implement it at the first opportunity. A man needed sustenance for such tough assignments.

At 07:00 Edith arrived to console her friend, only to find Camille in high spirits. Camille began handing over lists of the things needed for her incarceration. These included special strings for her violin to counter the high altitude. She'd added a request for the plans of the large open areas in major world airports, and a Corsican fig jam packed with fruit, made in the solid style she loved. Edith took the lists downstairs to breakfast to look over, and laughed well before the airport request.

Michel mentioned he'd received a disturbing message from his brother. The brother claimed there were major cash-flow problems in their business, and all were unforeseen. This was a mystery, and he needed to fly to Paris for an urgent meeting. He would fix matters and return. He was sure there had been some accounting glitch, and knew from experience not to let things fester.

In the Latin Quarter of Paris the Paymaster held a bottle to his lips at the bar, the dim lights annoying him as he tried to reconcile instinct and emotions. He was finding it hard to tear the two concepts apart, and blamed this foreign city for his dilemma, unsure why he'd ever crossed the border into France in the first place. What had he been trying to escape? It was lost to his memory, and every time his mind delved into the past his hand instinctively touched his Böker knife. It lay on the bar stool unopened, resting between his thighs, ready: ready for what? Camille's photo lay next to the knife and he picked it up again, and stared at her. All he felt was a desire. He needed to protect her, so he placed the photo between pages twenty-four and twenty-five of his pocket-poet book and felt comforted. He would kill for her or kill her, and he questioned why he thought such thoughts. This was love, perhaps he needed to take her across borders to understand love, to touch her. His instincts rose to the fore, his emotions subsided and, gratified, clarity filled his mind. There were no borders between his real home and this city, there never had been, just a mountain or two; and there were no borders between real love, she would know that.

The Stalker wore jeans and a long-sleeve red chequered shirt, the same outfit that had hidden the welts from the Paymaster's attack, as they healed. Once again, she did not want to attract attention – it was time to be the master thief.

The light pain of the cloth rubbing on the still sensitive skin sharpened her senses and reminded her to stay grounded. The Paymaster would get his just deserts soon enough, as soon as she'd found an alternative source of funding and built up her own slush fund. She would use his belt on him. She was certain of that. She was now documenting her filming and taking notes on movie-making to improve the quality of her work. She hoped to take videos of Edith on her return to Paris. That would be amazing, the films came with sound, and the voices might be the catalyst to succeed in this latest project. She loved the watching, waiting, and planning, but preferred the conquests. The cycle trapped her and she kept spinning onto new targets. One day she would settle down with one of them, perhaps even Edith, if only she could get to know her. In the meantime she looked forward to meeting up with officer No.4's wife.

It took the Stalker thirty-five minutes to penetrate Edith's apartment building, and another twenty minutes to reach the third floor. She manoeuvred herself into a position to render Edith's cameras ineffective. She then took out her own camera and started scanning the door, the frame and surrounding areas on 35 × max zoom. She took pictures where necessary and noted a camera at eye level less than a centimetre in diameter in the doorjamb. She took pictures of the lock. *An unusual beast,* she thought, but knew the tools she'd need to crack it. *Why so much security?*

The procedure was similar at Camille's apartment, which at first look seemed far less secure, and was. By the following morning her preparation was complete and she'd fashioned a modified lock pick, a tension wrench for Edith's door, and a standard key for Camille's. She felt her heartbeat lift, and knew this would be a buzz.

The Stalker was more cautious at Edith's apartment the second time around, not sure of what she was up against. Once inside the building, and up the staircase between floors two and three, she donned a balaclava. She wore it until she'd masked the camera in the doorframe. This done, she removed the balaclava, fearing interruption by other tenants. If interrupted, the 'concerned cousin' routine worked like a charm. She spent a further five minutes checking the door and jambs for alarms and inserted the first pick to rake the eight pins. With her heartbeat increasing, she heard the knock as the tumbler triggered the timer alarm. "Fuck," she said, and turned, but not before the second camera on the lift shaft took the pictures that Edith's system would download to its hard drive.

At Camille's apartment there was little resistance, just one neighbour on the third floor who watched her go past and a door lock that came from the Ark. Once inside, the antiques and wine collection amazed her. They were of no immediate concern. Her affinity with Edith was growing daily and she needed crucial background information. She continued the search for correspondence, which she now realised was a greater challenge than she'd believed. There might be a need to hack their phones. That was one way to know Edith better than she knew herself. She'd get to the position where she could anticipate her every turn and reaction, to take control and manipulate her heart. Each challenge increased the excitement. The Stalker felt she was the master at this game.

Working fast, she was soon through the staircase door and into the suite upstairs. Finding the violins in their cases laid out on the bed, she stared at them for a full minute before shaking off the trance and continuing her mission.

How could Edith like this woman? she thought. *She's a relic of the past.* She felt an urge to trash the place, but instead ran her hand over the case of each violin in a vague ritual, before entering the music room. The labelling and the setup impressed her, with walls of stored vinyl and branded CDs.

"Shit," she said to herself, "no files, no pictures, no trace of Edith anywhere."

The Stalker shuddered at the memory of standing in the shadows outside Camille's apartment the night when Edith first stayed over. She wondered where Edith had slept, and forced the thought from her mind for the time being. She'd seen her drinking on the balcony, and her eyes shut tight at the memory. The clothes racks produced black after black, almost all black except one or two red and denim accessories. *Perhaps she's a closet Goth violinist? Who was this other woman to Edith?* If only she'd succeeded in accessing Edith's apartment and getting the lowdown on her personality, but she hadn't. She now realised she needed a professional hacker's help to get into Edith's emails and mobile. Those might hold the clues to her real character.

The Stalker felt a wave of disappointment and was aware of how long she'd lingered. The swathe of black and the fastidious order of the sixth floor perturbed her. It was a complete contrast to the bohemian clutter of the fifth floor. She took the box of recordable CDs and DVDs she'd found; she could search through them at her leisure at home. They might well contain email backups. She could put them back later if she needed to cover her tracks. She believed there were still a few more days before they returned from their trip, and time was on her side. The Stalker retraced her steps and locked the apartment door.

16

Michel's thoughts during the flight home left him feeling confused and guilty. Camille had little of substance to say to him and Edith seemed disinterested. Both of these things left him feeling flat. Where was his Parisian panache? Where was his quiet bravado and charm? He shrugged. Was he suffering from some bizarre travel fever or did crossing borders play havoc on his psyche? Was he caught in a no-man's land? He decided to mull things over for the next day or two, and hoped the Founders would forget all the blunders before his return to Addis.

When he stepped back into Charles De Gaulle Airport he felt relief, yet had no idea why.

Passport Control, as requested, notified the Inspector's department of Michel's re-entry. Thanks to administrative bungling it took eighteen hours before the message reached the Inspector's desk. The Inspector was furious to get the news so late, and also perturbed that Michel had returned early to Paris. What had changed? He still had an open mind about Michel's possible involvement in the murders, and he'd keep it that way.

Someone, he surmised, *was the puppet-master of these killings.* He requested the Embassy in Addis to check on the girls' welfare. The report-back was positive, with the added details that sense was beginning to prevail in Camille's case. He resolved to hunt Michel down for further discussion.

The Proprietor knew that Inspector Jean-Luc Vasseur was mentally computing his options. He moved the surrounding tables further away to allow Vasseur more space to breathe. With officer No.1 being debriefed, breathing was needed, and it was unorthodox for the Inspector to meet any of his officers here. The report on the second €100 note had been received, and this note had also been uploaded onto the note-tracking system in the same batch as the first. The probability was now high that whoever carried the first note to Paris had also carried the second. If they could trace where and whom the notes got moved on to in Berlin, they could investigate the receiver. Officer No.1, the most tried, tested and astute of his team, had been to Berlin to flush the card from the pack. The result was both positive and negative.

Leon Voormann had loaded the serial numbers of the banknotes amongst a batch of ten onto the tracking system. Days later he had used all of them in a deposit payment to a financial advisor known as Kurt B. Huber. Huber had disappeared overnight from his rented office a year or so ago, one step ahead of the law and the planned litigation from enraged clients. His credentials proved to be false. All the tailored plans were identical, despite his clients' differing investment needs and instructions. The financial script of the market dealings had all disappeared as well – that is, had there ever been any. The officer was waiting to receive an ID sketch the Germans had collated and would get it to the Inspector as soon as available. They would circulate this in the financial world of Europe in the hope someone would recognise this man. Then perhaps they could get to the next link in the chain, and discover to whom the notes were moved.

"Go back to Berlin on the first flight and ferret. Get me a sample of the man's writing, and anything else you can glean," said the Inspector, "and remind me again why you brought officer No.4 onto our team. He seems incompetent."
"He has a unique gift we need," said officer No.1.
"Which is?"
"He speaks Mandarin."
"Pity," said the Inspector.

The Stalker waited outside the apartment block of officer No.4 an hour before she was due to meet him at the bar. As predicted, the wife emerged arm in arm with two friends some twenty minutes later. She followed them to a bistro two or three blocks away and their mood was already festive. Inside they ordered a double round of drinks, which further lifted their spirits. It took the Stalker forty minutes to infiltrate the party.
"You're having much more fun than my colleagues," she said, and gestured over her shoulder. "Another round for my new friends," she ordered. She was welcomed into the circle. Within the hour they were swapping mobile numbers for a future night out. Giving them all a farewell hug, she excused herself saying it was time to go, and that she had to work the next day.

She moved fast to get back to officer No.4, and was confident he'd hung around waiting for her. She would need information on why he'd watched Edith and friends checking into their flight. She'd soften him up tonight; lead him on for a night or two before getting the information she needed. After which he could go on chasing his other girlfriends. She'd have some fun with his wife, much more to her taste and good-looking too.

When Kelile arrived at her hotel suite, Camille felt at ease. They settled on sandwiches and biscuits and she confessed she enjoyed being locked up. It gave her freedom, the strange kind of freedom she was used to having.

"It's not locked," said Kelile.

"To me it is, and it's safe, and I have my own private guard."

Kelile acknowledged that crossing into foreign lands was not easy. He'd crossed the border many times into Eritrea during the war with his small surveillance team. The borders kept shifting as the war moved back and forth, and he soon realised the boundary concept was man-made.

"I began to feel safe everywhere," he explained, "the mountains were mine on both sides of the border, like this hotel room feels secure while you're here. You don't even think about who was in here last week, do you?"

Camille gave him her quizzical look.

"I'm only out of danger when I'm playing my violin," she said, "with everything in my control."

"What do you mean by *control*?"

"Ask Edith, she understands me."

"I prefer freedom," he said, "my happiest time is when I fly my falcon and we're both free. It's something I need to share, when I have no control over the sound of the winds and wings. My experience may well be the opposite of yours, but we're trying to achieve the same thing."

Camille felt her mind grapple with his explanation, but the pictures disappeared before she understood them. She said that when young she used her violin as a weapon to keep her father and mother at bay. She would play complex musical passages and hide her composing from her father.

"The violin as a weapon is interesting; the harmony of weapon and human is deep within our self. With total control of an instrument, the violin and violinist become synchronised. I suspect you have a true martial spirit when playing, but family support is vital to our being as well."

Kelile said that being close to his family was his biggest joy. He found it hard to understand why Camille's family did not support her dreams.

"So did I, and I still don't understand. There was no loyalty," said Camille.

"It may have been misdirected."

The sandwiches arrived with almond biscuits still hot from the oven and Camille felt special sharing them with him. The ease of this new friendship had taken her by surprise. It was not this way with Michel, who seemed to have a hidden agenda. She'd never had a boyfriend. One had never materialised in her limiting circumstances and her experience was reserved to a few moments with one or two male members of the orchestra. That inside knowledge of her private life would have been unfathomable to countless concertgoers. They all thought her stunning, and enjoyed her exuberant on-stage smile and persona. They would have presumed she was well settled into a lasting relationship.

"Nature's sustenance," he said, telling her how with pockets of almonds and roasted coffee beans he could stay out in the wilds for long periods. Camille mentioned her good friend the Inspector in Paris who ate his almonds one by one.

"Earth's food," he said. "Eating them one by one shows great respect."

"Yes, he is respectful."

"What do Ethiopians believe in?" said Camille.

"Well, I believe in what I see and touch and taste. Please play for me," he said, "so I can believe in what I hear."

Camille began to explain that her J.F. Pressenda violin might not be the best one for the size of the room, and he told her the best violin was the one she was playing at the time. Camille stared at Kelile for a long time before understanding, and told him about the Dubai impromptu concert.

"Please play that same music for me."

"It's called *Motherlands*," she said, and played.

Kelile sat listening, mesmerised. It was so different from anything he'd ever heard before. He was amazed that the same Camille he'd observed these last few days could compose and play such startling and beautiful music. He was upset with himself for making such a hasty judgement on this Parisian, and resolved to learn the lesson never to make superficial assessments.

"It's incredible. You must set your music free, it's time to lose all fears, and time you stepped out of all your shadows," said Kelile. "I would love to hear it again. It brought so many images rushing to mind that I was confused at first, but soon everything calmed down. Though it's not what I'm used to, my body seemed to understand the patterns. The listening put me in another world."

"It might confuse you. It's about a different motherland to yours – it's about France."

"Motherlands are similar for those living inside them. I'll take my chances. The world is different all over. We have the coffee, Eritreans have the sea, and Paris has the most remarkable violin player. Now I need to get you out of this room so you can go back home to release your fears." he said.

When the door closed Camille went to the window and looked out, smiling. She wanted to talk to Kelile for the rest of the day. He seemed to know everything. She decided boundaries needed to fall, but she was not sure which, or even if she had any. She knew for certain her only hope lay in Edith's puzzle concept.

"You need to work out your self-puzzle," Edith had said, "decide who you want to be, are capable of being, and be that person. You have to try." Edith had promised to remain at her side no matter what, and she'd said that loyalty came before love; loyalty was forever. Camille knew she was not equipped to deal with her own issues yet, let alone know what they were, so what chance did Lacey have during the therapy sessions? That was a question worth considering. The enigma of Camille's personality was far from being solved.

The analyst did not enjoy the concept of freedom. He charged his patients in Paris exorbitant fees knowing most would never dare to question his rates or credentials. He also charged massive fees for his online products to a web of secret buyers, buyers tied up in the nth level of the Net – the level of decadence and depravity. Whether of psychotropic drugs or hard-core films, the analyst was a major supplier to wholesalers who moved his products around the world. On the same day that Michel arrived back in Paris, the analyst made a dark and inspired decision. He would go up against local street-drug dealers with his own psycho concoctions. He would build a sales team in Paris. He'd pick from his most corruptible patients to build ring after ring around him, direct selling to disturbed locals.

He'd hide behind the cloak of secrecy and fear. The Paymaster and the Stalker were hooked and making him money. It was time to go to deeper and feed the madness of the streets around them.

17

An hour after her final morning of course preparation, Edith had returned to the hotel in high spirits. She remained mesmerised by the timelessness of the coffee ritual, and impressed by the passion of the participants. The whole affair was steeped in culture, and the simplicity and dedication she had witnessed went a long way to showcase the fine traits of the grassroots Ethiopian people. The ceremony reminded her of the unloading of the catch when fishermen returned to port, and the respect shown to the sea and fish by her father's peers. She went to the hotel bar to enjoy a quiet whisky by herself, time to assimilate the strange allure of coffee at one extreme. The whisky, a Laphroaig ten-year single malt, was quick on the palate. Edith languished in the moment; it tasted rewarding.

Swaggering towards her, Hank's approach was as welcome as an axeman's, and the look from Edith froze him in his tracks. He veered off and disappeared, making gestures with his arms as if tumbling off a cliff.

Since undertaking the course, she had renewed respect for Michel's belief in the fine traditions of French pâtisserie and boulangerie. She would pay attention to his passion, support

111

him as a friend, hoping he would not continue to disappoint her. She would confront him on that matter; those from France could never afford to neglect the finer things French. He needed to get the wild-oats thing behind him.

This trip was not turning out as she'd imagined at the Paris meeting, yet she felt that for her, it was far better than expected. She was bemused by Camille's need for comfort, wrapped up in her room. *Each to their own*, she thought.

Edith knocked on the door.

"I need to talk," said Camille, "but I'm not sure what about."

"Let's wait for the tea. First tell me the one thing that matters the most," said Edith, "and we'll start from there."

They laughed at their situation, original Coffee Society Founders having tea in the heart of coffee country. The Kenyan tea was as excellent as the room service waiter had said it would be, and she waited for Camille to begin.

"Kelile visited and helped me. He made everything a bit clearer and reaffirmed my music as timeless. He said my music has an eerie stillness woven into the movement. I remember that, but I'm not exactly sure of anything else he said, it was like a dream, but it was crystal clear at the time."

Edith kicked herself for never having attended one of the concerts, and confessed to her limited knowledge of classical music.

"That doesn't matter. Listening is easy – especially if that's all you're doing at that moment."

"Well, you can achieve anything that inspires you."

"That's what Lacey would say."

"Your therapist, can we discuss that sometime?"

"No, there's no point. It's personal."

"So, what's changed here to make you so upbeat?"

"I played *Motherlands* to people at the Dubai airport and everybody loved it. I also played it to Kelile and he was impressed. I think it's a breakthrough. I felt natural."

"I see," said Edith, who paused and frowned. She wondered if the change in food or water had got to Camille, which would explain her strange delusions of playing at the airport. She thought about the death threat in Paris, thinking Camille must have suppressed it completely.

Edith left Camille's room, and was glad the final ceremony had been postponed until her travel companions could attend. She felt a flush of loyalty and decided it was time to think of ways to neutralise the writer of Camille's death threat. The Inspector had his hands full with murders. He would not have time to help, and she could trust no one in Paris more than herself. She would find out who was the author and add them to her list, alongside the Stalker. She was a fisherman's daughter, and they didn't want to be on her hit-list. She remembered the words *I will kill you, slowly* and thought just how vulnerable her friend was. There was no turning back for anyone involved. She would ask Camille about the *concerto* that was mentioned in the note. She was sure Camille would have some notion of who would want to *be with her forever*. Was there someone who gave her weird looks? Was it an orchestra member?

After a long shower, she enjoyed lazing in her room, wrapped in the hotel's white towelling gown. She called room service for a pot of coffee and a toasted cheese sandwich, and wondered why tourists in French hotels stole so many gowns.

She set up her laptop at the desk and, in sympathy to Camille, Googled violin soloists, classical music careers and composers. Her search ended the instant she found herself watching a YouTube video of a violin solo, played in the

Dubai International Airport. It was Camille, playing that same music she'd dedicated to Arianne. She was upset she hadn't believed Camille. Her friend must have thought her disinterested. There was a long way to go before she would know Camille well.

Edith ran down the hotel corridor, laptop in hand, despite a number of guests presuming she was making off with the hotel's bathrobe. She and Camille were soon watching the video, over and over again. It was extraordinary, and the sound quality was adequate. They discussed the implications of the video for Camille, and when Edith left the room she did so with affection, leaving her friend feeling elated and confused.

Is this freedom? thought Camille. The video had one hundred and twenty three thousand hits. The numbers were growing fast. Why was it called "Find the Violin Angel"? Agitated, she vacillated for at least eleven minutes before deciding between wine, coffee, tea and cranberry juice. She chose the latter.

The Stalker opened the box of CDs and DVDs from Camille's apartment as if it were a gift from an admirer. With trepidation, she inserted the first disc into her computer.

Some violin shit, she thought, disappointed that it was not correspondence to and from Edith. She tried three or four more discs until she opened the vodka bottle and sat down on her bed. No documents, emails, porn or anything interesting. Trying again, she skipped a few and loaded the last one in the box. She was angered to find the documents were an index, and brief descriptions of the music. Camille must have ripped this music from the Net. She would ditch the lot before the Paymaster found them and twisted some bullshit or other out of her.

All her efforts had led to nothing. She wrote 'violin music' on the whiteboard in red. Perhaps it was the music that attracted Edith to Camille? If it was, she needed a way to compete. Once again, she went through her photos looking for clues to Edith; once again, she came up empty-handed.

Damn her, she thought.

The Stalker looked at the empty space where one of the violin player's photos had been. It was the one she'd taken when Edith had coffee and tarte with Camille, and there was still a torn-off section of the top right-hand corner left stuck in place. A shudder ran through her body at the memory of the beating she had suffered, before he had ripped the photo down. *Damn you too, you bastard, I'll choose my own pain.*

When she'd finished eating, she opened her file on the Paymaster and started doodling in the margins. Life had been much simpler before. The analyst had been listening to her fixations; the talk and tablets may have helped her, but now he'd changed the rules. She was being paid as a camera operator, but where was this going?

The Paymaster seemed to have no other interests except bars and his pocket book. Despite the few days the Stalker spent secretly following and monitoring his life, all she could write was *loner, seems psycho, delusional, drinks alone, very tense.* She watched him finish one or two drinks per bar and leave as tensions rose around him, which they always did. He had that effect on people, yet she felt he was avoiding trouble. *Must be the money*, she thought, and watched him make his way across Paris during the day, visiting cemeteries where he drank from his pewter flask and read his book. At night she followed him to the bars and clubs, which he trawled without interacting with anyone. She discovered where he lived, but no sooner had she done so, he'd upped and moved to a new lodging around the corner.

Watching Addis surge past the car window, Edith was confronted by construction. Street after street had buildings going up and people moving about without discernible patterns, rivalling Paris for sheer numbers. The pace seemed frenetic and Kelile assured her that the people on the streets each had their plan for the day – they all had to have one, to survive.

You move or you die, thought Edith. *Much like home.* The concrete coffee building appealed to her: square, functional, not dominating the skyline like most of the new builds. At the main entrance the security guards sat around. They stood up with reluctance as she approached; yet her smile elicited such a warm response that she thought this could not be the scene of Camille's debacle. This was a country she could do business with, and she resolved to fly in alone when she next visited. Kelile showered her with coffee industry information; it had an edge she could thrive with.

18

Officer No.1 knew he had dynamite in his hands. He was not sure how or where it would detonate. He showed the photo to the Inspector, who stayed silent. The Inspector sipped his Brazilian coffee. His mind was working fast and he forgot to pause to taste it; he sipped again. Then he did something he'd never done before: he handed No.1 a few almonds. Seven of them, he set them down in a row in front of No.1, and turned the third one at right angles to the others.

"Time to think," he said, before going silent again.

The photo of the financial advisor's wooden office door in Berlin had a large '7' scratched on it. It was at least three hands tall, with the slash across the upright, loud and clear. The Inspector stayed quiet a moment or two longer.

"This is solid. Was this taken before or after he abandoned that office?"

"A day or two before."

"So who carved it, I wonder?"

"There were seven parties in the litigation against him," said No.1. "We've a team of four, together with their own backup, scouring Paris. They're checking all the adverts, the advisors, and the whole investment industry for the man in the identikit picture. Nothing. I don't know who carved it, but our German colleagues are talking to all seven of them."

"Unfortunately, I feel we might have to remember my second law of complex crime," said the Inspector.

"What seems to be, will often not be."

"Yes, find that advisor, he must be the puppet-master of our killer. Find out where he was before Berlin, and take our people off the baking apprentices, they're all off our list."

"I have."

"Good work, No.1. It's time for powerful purpose, so powerful that we stop these people in their tracks."

In Paris, in the family home, a tired Michel was amused by the formal approach his brother adopted for their meeting. A beer in a bar had become the norm after their father's death, but not today. His brother had not put his cards on the table and there was no formal agenda. Michel waited with interest. He'd obtained a cash-flow report from their accountant, and there seemed only one unusual payment, a large one. His younger brother had some serious explaining to do.

The Lumière baking business was of the finest order, and through both good and bad times, such was their reputation, there was always a profit. Traditions were important to the family, and Michel noticed his mother had set out three cognac glasses for afterwards, and provided the canapés in his absence.

The brother announced the meeting could be kept simple. The company was showing a slight profit, which was acceptable in these recessive times. Cash flow was negative as customers were slow to pay, and volumes were down.

Michel pointed out that a large unauthorised payment to his brother's wife was the cause of the cash problem, and demanded answers.

"Well she's given advice to me for no fee, it's justified."

"She hasn't done a damn thing," said Michel, and asked why any question of payment couldn't have waited until after his return. It had been a waste of time and money having flown all the way from Ethiopia; his brother could have the bill, for his personal account.

The brother insisted they should change with the times. They needed to revisit their business model. He and his new wife never got either the chance or sufficient funds to take a deserved holiday, perhaps even abroad, as Michel was enjoying.

"We don't mess with the business mix," said Michel. "It's always worked, and your wife has nothing to do with our business."

"Well I think she should be involved."

"You're a selfish bastard," said Michel, "wasting our time again. If you want a holiday, do some work to justify it, and don't interrupt mine. I actually needed a break after all these years carrying you."

"And you're stuck in the bloody past, your travel bill is cheap at the price. I need to explore the possibilities."

"Investigate all you want, and come to the next meeting with something real, not fresh air, and nothing about our product is to change. Have your wife repay that money tomorrow."

The cognac rounded off the meeting and was served with prepared snacks. Their mother had included the traditional Palmiers, laced with extra-salted Normandy butter. Michel invited her to dine with him that evening, and she was pleased to accept. The brother suggested it might rain later in the evening, and she would be wiser to stay at home.

"The rain never bothered me before and it won't start now. I look forward to dinner with Michel," said Mrs Lumière.

Michel and his mother savoured the dinner. He chose a Château Cos d'Estournel 2005, Saint-Estèphe to go with their lamb dish, and they ended their meal on a high note sharing a chocolate soufflé. It was as light as a feather, and rich in the dark flavour of cocoa butter. Escorting his mother to their home after dinner, he mentioned that he was going to meet friends, and walked into the night.

To impress Edith, he went to le Musée de l'érotisme to test the erotic side of her theory. He rushed through the ground floor exhibits to get upstairs, and out of sight. Shocked, he discovered the exhibition was arranged with a dignity that added weight to Edith's view. It reflected a spark of real life. Michel immediately felt at ease as most French people would, and he marvelled at the breadth of the historical erotica.

Back on the ground floor, he studied the exhibits, before drifting out into the night to get a drink. A beer or two would go down well and he knew just the spot. There were quite a few hours to kill before check-in for his flight. He decided to walk. It was raining; his brother had been right about one thing at least. A moment before dawn he hailed a taxi to swing past home to fetch his carry-on bag. He could sleep on the flight. It was time to get back to the Society trip. He had girls on his mind.

The intermittent drizzle calmed the man dubbed the Wolf by the Inspector's team. He walked along the Left Bank of the River Seine, counting his steps, stopping to look down at the puddles for his reflection, kicking at the water with his boots. He loved water, and crossed to the Right Bank. He turned to continue along the embankment, hearing the echoes of his own wet footsteps following him, walking under the eyes of Paris's finest.

The flower stalls were empty for the night and had been for some time. It was not his intention to goad the nearby law enforcement agencies. He felt special being in this area with the water moving, and darkness hogging the space between one streetlight and the next. He wore the hoodie again, pulled over his head, and a sharp eye could spot where he'd unpicked the logo of The Doors. It was not cold. The dark scarf he'd thrown around his neck gave him comfort, and a barrier to hide behind. The hoodie shielded most of the drizzle, but the gusting wind had the ability to drift the wet onto his face, and coat the tinted glasses he wore tonight. He turned a full circle, searching for any pairs of eyes that had locked onto him. He did not spot any, and he was not sure if this was a good or a bad sign. There should have been eyes on him. For the first time, he felt uneasy, and yet still gave no thought to the task ahead. He felt disconnected from reality. It was already well after midnight and he wondered whom he would encounter in the grey hours of early morning.

He had the inscribed 'Limited Edition' €100 in his wallet, and continued on his slow way, trying to recollect the last killing. No wonder Natalie had fought back – who wouldn't fight? Natalie had followed her instincts, but she had gone for his gloved hands, which was a mistake

He was at the Right Bank exit ramp, a stone's throw from the water, and when Brisette turned onto the bridge he felt the killing rush: a strange new feeling that enveloped him. She was talking on her mobile phone and that pissed him off. An uncharacteristic lurch was his first move; his feet seemed to hesitate and drag behind him, and he thought of aborting the attack.

Brisette was recording observations on Parisian nightlife, the information required for the report commissioned by a magazine. Her first thoughts were that the man was targeting the mobile phone and, with her last recorded word being "Hey," she rammed the phone into her jeans pocket. Had she jabbed it in his face, her nighttime survey might have seen the light of day. There was inevitability about this looming stranger closing in on her, as his right hand went under his coat to fetch the ligature. Her second mistake was thinking he was a flasher. With the side step she'd perfected for flashers, she ducked right into the leather noose, and doomed herself.

"What's the hurry?" said the Wolf.

The moment he snared his victim, he turned hard on his heels to walk side by side, the noose tightening with every step. She never went for the gloves. She was wiser than that, and slammed a right boot down his shin. He felt nothing; she slammed again, this time onto the bridge of his foot. His leg buckled and the noose tightened. He was a big and heavy man. Brisette went hard at his eyes with her left hand and missed. He panicked, putting his full weight into the throttle causing a hangman's fracture in her neck, and she went limp. He stuffed the €100 into her hand and scrawled on her right hand with the black pen.

Without arranging the body, he yanked his hoodie down further, repositioned the scarf back around his face and fled. The evil floated away from his mind as fast as it had arrived. This should have been hit and run, but his subconscious feared he'd left more than his mark at the scene.

19

Thoughts had a way of swirling around Camille's head, settling down in sequences that made sense to her in a way she could understand. When composing music, similar thoughts fell into magnificent patterns, which the violin interpreted. It was aroused music, full of intense and angry movement from discarded theories. The solitude of her hotel room allowed new primary thoughts to creep into Camille's mind. They affirmed the originality of her compositions. She could take the music out to the world as a vast new collection.

Pacing around her hotel room, staring at the furniture or out through the windows, an ever-shifting slice of the hotel's life crept into her more conscious self. The activities of guests, visitors and staff, as seen through the windows of her room, increased and decreased at different times of day. It was the colour of the sky that impressed her most. It was a hue of blue she had never seen before. She imagined Kelile's bird flying these skies, and realised that since crossing the borders of France she had not composed a single note.

Kelile's words came flooding back to her and she could still hear the caring timbre in his voice.

"When my falcon locks onto a target, it folds its wings and dives, making slight adjustments here and there to keep on course. It never fails in its purpose. You need to lock onto your own dreams, and for that, your dreams must be clear in your head."

It made sense now, perfect sense, and he'd hit the right note.

France is my homeland, she thought, *where I compose and where I'll have to be buried. When I'm home, I must lock onto my dreams.*

She sensed she was beginning to understand travelling; it was changing her perspective, and not without danger. She knew she needed to discover how large her investment fund was when she arrived back home. She had to take charge; changes were around the corner.

The Inspector's progress was shattered by the more brutal third bridge murder. With so many bridges to cover, his team had focused on the Left Bank. Pinpoint accuracy was the nature of this beast. That the killing area was so close to a massive police presence defied logic, taunting the authority's existence. It took the Inspector less than thirty seconds to see that this murder was botched, and realise the Wolf would need prove to himself that he was in control. The Wolf fitted the profile of killers who believed they were infallible, and the Inspector knew such belief was dangerous.

Another bridge killing would not be allowed in their city. His men had been distributed over the area using a vulture-grid pattern. Some team members were granted licence to weave in and out of the pattern randomly, to remain unpredictable. A vulture can spot a carcass from many kilometres, and although his team were equipped with night vision glasses, they hadn't seen a thing. A carcass is static. Their killer was mobile. The net was closing and the Inspector mourned another wasted life.

The team secured the €100 note in a plastic folder, and he knew what was written before glancing at the message. He'd been correct with his Mercury assumption, even predicting the bridge, which was amongst the four he'd named. Mercury was the messenger of the gods: was this auspicious? Time was of the essence, and it was hard to wait for another message. The bastard had shifted to the Right Bank, throwing their main focus out of kilter. It was not good enough for the victim.

The dreaded call to report to HQ at 08:30 for urgent discussions came through, and he thought if the meeting was so urgent why wasn't it called at 05:30? With the team combing the area, he decided to go and eat a meal before facing the firing squad. These HQ discussions were always the precursors to top-level panic, and the Inspector needed a private food and coffee break to think over his responses.

He jotted down a few notes knowing full well that the confidential inter-departmental reports had a way of getting into the hands of the press. He picked his words with care. After two hours of HQ discussions, which wasted time, the Inspector left with his eyes set a little harder. It was about to get worse. He'd instructed his team to have Michel located for serious discussions, and was furious to learn that Michel had flown out on the 07:40 Turkish Airlines flight to Addis. He immediately called for CCTV footage from the airport, particularly to have a good look at Michel's face. His killer may well be marked this time.

Flying out of Paris with a renewed purpose, Michel was confident he'd held his brother at bay. He was glad to have dined with his mother, moments that helped him keep his balance. He was now armed to revisit the erotica discussion with Edith in his own good time, a discussion that might well disturb that balance.

The Embassy car pulled in with a delegation to inform Camille that the security company had no evidence of misdemeanour. They now withdrew the accusation and apologised for the misunderstanding. She needed to stay within the hotel grounds until the docket was closed, which was a mere formality. At her insistence, they agreed to leave the guard as compensation for her previous loss of freedom, and for the first time Camille beamed.

Feeling a new surge of self-confidence, she knew she'd soon be able to throw open her apartment windows. She laughed at herself, a stifled laugh, and decided to go and surprise Edith. They could go off later for dinner and wine, lots of wine, French wine. She got ready for an excursion, and when she told the guard to order some corridor-service on her room account, she made a friend for life.

She looked beautiful.

The Paymaster couldn't resist the temptation to take out Camille's photo for inspection. He could visualise every square centimetre, yet her aura kept sucking him in. He knew he understood her even better each time he looked. This was a new experience for him. Though folded, the photo's creases did not touch her face. He wished the blond woman wasn't in the background. The one missing corner annoyed him intensely, and he would have words with the Stalker about that, when he saw her. This blonde woman had a crease right across the bridge of her nose, which at first amused the Paymaster, and then infuriated him. He was angry today, and he tried to remember which of the medications he'd taken. He'd ask the analyst for more of these soon. They were good for him. He liked anger. He liked to dull it with drink. He felt he knew Camille a little better each time he saw her photo. *This woman wants to be mine.*

He folded the photo again, and placed it back in his pocket-poet book, as always, in a different page, like shuffling cards.

He would talk to his girl through the night, not the dross that people in the bars talked. He would discuss emptiness and the midnight river, and later he would watch as her magic arms played her violin. He balled his fists as he thought of the analyst. Money was needed to support dreams, and dreams would be his soon, he would wait.

"Keep your focus on our project, there will be consequences if you deviate," analyst Zuppin had said. The Paymaster decided to start planning those consequences himself. He felt his knife, resting against his thigh, and he let his thoughts drift.

20

Camille wandered around the hotel complex looking for Edith without success. Once she'd learnt from the concierge that Michel wasn't due back from Paris until the early hours, Camille decided to sit in the foyer and have some tea. She remembered a film, set in Africa, where there was much sipping of tea. The actresses had also discussed intimate relationships and consumed volumes of alcohol. It was a fun and dangerous time, and she decided that she would begin that marvellous side of the trip tonight at dinner. They could take advantage of the quiet days before the paparazzi discovered her. She wanted to wrap her arms around Edith again, rather like she'd hugged her parents in the days before violins. She was happy knowing Edith would return the warmth.

It was inevitable the dinner would be a success. The girls were both relaxed, and their lives seemed to be full of promise. Camille arrived ten minutes after the elected time to find Edith seated and sipping a French cabernet, chosen with loving care. Both the original Founders were in excellent form. Edith told Camille she'd launched a new business venture that, despite digging deep into her savings, had potential.

"You mean your investment fund," said Camille.

"Something like that."

It was the first time they'd enjoyed being together in such a casual way; the evening flew by. Their table received admiring glances, which neither of them cared to notice.

Edith eased up for the first time on the trip. Every business has a start-up moment and she felt confident there was adequate place in the market for another specialised player. It would be a fresh-roast business, delivering top-quality Arabica beans to café and bistro outlets in Paris. She'd phoned her family, she had their full support.

Over after-dinner drinks Edith had the opportunity to share the finer details of her coffee business. She was surprised that this time Camille took a genuine interest. Edith broached the subject of Camille's death threat, and was disturbed when Camille said not to worry. She had no troubles whatsoever, now that her obsession was fading. Life from here on would be great.

"And the letter?"

"Forget it. It'll go away."

Babe in the woods, thought Edith. *That type of threat does not self-destruct – it festers.* She knew the Inspector had two murders on his hands already, and only hoped he had time to investigate the letter. She did not want Camille added to the list of the dead. She'd do whatever it took to prevent that.

At 01:00 when Michel's flight landed in Addis there was no one there to meet him. He knew they would be preparing

a surprise welcome back at the hotel, and so searched for a cab. When Michel finally arrived in the early hours, the party started to break up almost at once, and the would-be suitors who'd hung about submitted to defeat.

Michel intended saying nothing to Edith about his visit to le Musée de l'érotisme for some time. He'd consider it only when back in France, or perhaps when she noticed his improved application of *l'art d'aimer* – the art of love. His every intention lasted an hour or so, and once he had Edith to himself he launched forth.

"I visited the museum."

"What museum?"

"The erotic one."

"Oh?"

"Yes, I understand it all now."

"You do?"

"Yes, let me explain..."

"No Michel, if you need to explain, you've missed the point."

"Why?"

"Well, after countless visits with my tourists, I'm learning that erotica is unlike the simple reactive impact of porn. Erotica has layers, it can exist with love and emotion, and that's its most simple explanation. I suspect neither of us will get close to a deep understanding of erotica in our lifetimes."

"I believe I might. It's cut and dried."

"No Michel, porn is cut and dried, erotica is open and endless. Anyway, I'm not interested in taking this further; this is where it ends. I'll leave you to work it out your way, and, keep it to yourself."

"Another drink?" said Michel

"Thanks, but it's time for me to sleep."

Michel sat and mulled over her words. He was now convinced that Camille was the only woman for him. He would try to explain erotica to her from a baker's perspective, if he could remember the subtleties. Perhaps Edith would write it down.

The Founders called it a night, agreeing to meet mid-morning and poolside for a day of sunshine and swimming. Edith acquiesced, and decided a pool day would be fun; she needed time to relax.

It was a magnificent and sunny day in Africa. The morning kicked off with a huge English breakfast and fine Sidamu coffee. Needing to chase the coffee with something as respectable, French champagne was called for. When the girls requisitioned Michel to apply their suntan lotions, they both noticed the firm, controlled application. They thought that bakers had useful attributes, similar to kneading the bread, or applying the final touches to the King's Cake.

The stark contrast between Camille's black bikini and her ivory skin attracted significant attention. It was the feline stature and grace of Edith that set France apart as the first talking point of the day. In the water Edith had no peers, and the years of swimming off the beaches in the South of France had gifted her an effortless style. As the people around her splashed their way across the pool, even bronzed men who'd plunged in to try and look the part paled in comparison. Edith had the figure of youth, not cut and trim, but natural. A girl who lived, rather than thought about living, and who'd found in her mid-twenties the perfect recipe for life, without the pain of searching.

With a second bottle of Bollinger topping up their glasses, Michel found his land-legs. He offered a toast to the three Founders and their achievements: Camille for her freedom, Edith and her new venture, and himself, for having foiled his brother's coup – or so he thought. Had it not been for Edith's timely intervention, he came close to tossing his empty glass into the pool. Ordering mojitos for everyone nearby, he began to regale the story of Camille's arrest to one and all. This included a French travel writer who was never slow to earn a few euros sending copy to Paris. Edith marvelled at the embellishment of the story, and Camille soon admitted being the unknown violin player they'd heard, playing from her room in the hotel.

Camille conceded to popular demand to fetch the violin for photos at the poolside, and was soon cajoled into playing. The poolsiders mistook her carefree look as an appreciation of their applause, and so doubled their efforts, and the impromptu concert went on and on. Camille never quite got her feet back onto the ground that evening.

While the incognito journalist took photos, she recorded many a quote from the effervescent Michel. He was firing on all cylinders, and all the while another video was being filmed of the live performance. Camille wore the traditional black of an orchestra player, and although what she wore deviated from the Orchestra norm, in her bikini she impressed even Edith. The Founders were on top form and Edith, who'd never deviated from her mission, enjoyed the banter.

Such is the modern way; a Parisian daily newspaper ran the story 'French Violinist Freed in Addis'. The pictures were sensational. They raised eyebrows amongst the orchestra community, and pulses around Paris. The other papers had to chase the story. Michel was in the photos for all to see, and his picture raised a smile on his mother's face, and a scowl from the brother's wife. When the photos were taken, Edith had retreated behind the photographers. She later slipped away in the melee unseen, wanting to prepare herself for the following day's ceremony.

As the evening dimmed into what might be regarded as post-pool melancholy, the baker and the violinist's discussions drifted between relationships and marriage, and almost put them to sleep. Democracy reigned as they voted two to nothing that being single was the best solution, although they had different images in mind as they did so. Michel suggested there may well be nightlife of some note in Addis. He would ask for insider details from someone with connections. Camille responded it would be easier to ask Kelile, who might agree to show them the city by night. As if on cue, Kelile arrived at the hotel with news that the paperwork from the authorities would be completed the following day. Camille was cleared of all suspicion.

What suspicion? she thought.

In Paris the orchestra committee called an emergency meeting. They invited the visiting conductor (who was not one of Camille's favourites) to participate. *Perhaps*, the wisest amongst them thought, *he could be the much-needed decision maker.* The committee had to present a united front to the press and queries emanating from the morning's headlines were coming in thick and fast.

One brave soul broke ranks to suggest Camille was bound to be innocent, and as reported had been a victim of circumstance. Another member said she was one of their best musicians, with a rare flair and individuality. The majority felt she was guilty of bringing disrepute to their good name. They would need to deliberate further on their stance. In the meantime a consensus was reached that all requests from the press should elicit the response of 'no comment'.

It would seem to the press that questions about the violinist were getting the brush-off. She had no family they could hound, and her neighbours had little to add, except that she threw all-night parties, and played her music.

The Paymaster was the one exception. He was getting answers. Walking in Paris – as was his habit – he was glancing at the front covers of newspapers at a newsstand when the world stood still. Once closeted on a café corner with a copy of the paper, he stared for some time at Camille. He soon learnt she was a violinist of considerable talent and furthermore, she was across the border and out of the country. He had a moment of concern that she might have suffered at the hands of her accusers, and a second moment where he went blank. He took his own original photo out and compared his photo to that in the newspaper. There was no doubt, same violinist, his violinist, and he knew he would need to plan the way forward. He had not finalised the outcome of their liaison, and he would have liked Zuppin to prescribe something stronger to settle his thoughts.

The Inspector walked past some eight metres from where the Paymaster sat, and for a few seconds his flesh crawled. He took a moment to scan the surroundings, but was unable to focus on anything specific. He often got especially bad feelings in this area. He was tempted to sit down for a coffee and flush out the source, but he was in a hurry. He was carrying an unread copy of a daily paper in his left hand, and had received a mobile message from one of his team. It was about developments in the bridge murders, and it was garbled.

When Paris was dark that night, the Paymaster would be one of the first fifty thousand to watch the second Violin Angel video on YouTube, and his flesh crawled. There were minds messing around with his woman, heads would roll.

There would be death. He found her home address through the newspapers, which was easy. He would visit; she was coming home. He'd searched for Addis on Google Earth.

21

Inspector Vasseur was metres from his HQ when he did an about-turn and reached for his mobile phone. Paris was bathed in sunshine and only the occasional brush of wind managed to keep the streets sane. The Inspector needed to order his thoughts, and knew a kick-start of coffee at his favourite bench by the Seine would do the trick. He called the department war-room and requested officer No.1 to meet him there armed with a clear head, two strong coffees, and full details of the latest developments.

"I can do better than that," said officer No.1.

"Surprise me."

The Inspector felt at home on his bench. If he found it occupied, he'd mastered the art of standing so close that the incumbents would usually move on. It was all for the good cause of justice. During daylight he felt invigorated by the flowing waters of the river and the stream of tourists enjoying the area. These tourists deserved the security of safe passage, and also remained under his surveillance. The movement around him focused his instincts.

"How are your family?" the Inspector asked, taking a real interest in all he heard. "Now tell me about what you've got."

The officer took out his mobile phone and played the Inspector a copy of the recording made by victim No.3, Brisette. The mobile phone hadn't stopped recording when she'd stuffed it into her jeans pocket.

"Ah, we now have audio."

"We have his voice," said the officer, "indistinct, but of use."

They played the segment over and over and it was almost impossible to fathom. The Inspector requested it went to the audio specialists as soon as possible.

"They have a copy," said the officer, "I'll get the assessment to you the moment it's out."

Vasseur sat staring at the Seine for a full five minutes replaying the voice in his mind. It was male, but he couldn't tell what it was saying. There was only one short phrase. He found himself holding his breath, and let the breath out. Taking five roasted and salted almonds from his left pocket, he flicked them one by one with his left thumb up into the air. He caught them between the thumb and index finger of his right hand, before placing each one in turn into his mouth, to crunch and savour.

Of course it's male, he thought, *we'll be onto him soon, his pride will sink him, it's become personal since the last attack did not go to plan. Now he might become killer and strategist. That will be ugly.*

The brother's meeting with the co-operative went well, so he thought. They would even receive an extra payment for allowing co-op members the right to use their Lumière name.

"Take it or leave it," the co-op negotiators said, bolstered from the Paris headline photos showing Michel entangled in some messy business or other.

"You have twelve hours."

"It's his own problem if he wants to go gallivanting," said the wife, being her own true self. "Your mother is so old school. You can set about slashing the staff numbers and production facilities at once."

"You're right," said the brother, "Michel will be proud."

"Who cares," said the wife. "You're the boss now, and when Michel is back, we'll go on a shopping trip to New York."

He signed the deal on the basis that Michel was in the air somewhere, and he was running the business. It was done and dusted, with only the family name issue needing sign-off.

"A mere formality," he'd said, despite knowing those rights were vested in the family members, and not the business itself. Their late father had said the Lumière name was sacrosanct, and could never be sold out of the family.

It was the day of the coffee ceremony. Before the sun settled into its early morning journey across her hotel room, Edith was on her way to the outskirts of Addis. She was with Gabra, going to hand-cut fresh grasses for use at the ceremony. They'd breakfasted on the spongy *injera* bread, cheese and honey, and had ordered tea in deference to the coffee they'd serve later in the day. Edith told her mentor of her days of coffee drinking, well before the morning light came up over the water, at sea with her father. They'd pour from flasks prepared by her grandmother and use the black plastic lids as mugs.

"We'd save the last round of coffee for when we were tied up back at shore, and he'd put a tot of rum into the mugs, our sacred welcome-home brew."

"That's like the grasses we spread on the ceremony floor, to welcome the good spirits to our gathering. We scent them with frankincense in honour of all present, but I think our ceremony is less risky than being at sea with your father."

They wrapped multi-coloured cloths around their white dresses while cutting. The grasses went onto the car's back seat, and arrived at the Benyam family building an hour or two before Kelile went to the hotel to collect Michel and Camille.

"This coloured belt is for you to wear around your dress today," said Gabra as they arrived at what she called their rooftop village. "You will notice some of the hems of our dresses have colour woven into them, as does life, and this is a gift to you from the girls to recognise that you are at one with us."

"I'm honoured, thank you all so much," said Edith.

The assistants had swept the larger of the ceremonial-day huts for their arrival. Once the grasses had been spread around the area, the frankincense was sprinkled over them adding to the aroma in the air. They washed the utensils, the black clay *jebena* kettle, and the pestle and the mortar to crush the roasted beans. The round flat roasting pan was washed five times.

"This washing blesses the five elements, and we include the spirit as the fifth element, the one which binds the others together," said Gabra. "I will wash and prepare the green beans myself, while you join the girls to prepare the fire."

There was to be no rushing any part of the ritual. They discussed Edith's trip with her as they helped her build the charcoal fire on a raised open stove, adding each new set of coals only once the previous layer was burning well.

We need to build a fire that holds its heat constant. We first roast the beans, then boil water and the coffee grinds together, taking our time. The fire is the centrepiece of the ritual, and must be as strong as our friendships, Edith remembered.

Edith was unaware that Michel and Camille had arrived on the rooftop with Kelile, who'd informed them they could only go into the ceremony area once they were all invited.

When the charcoal fire was declared perfect, Edith lifted the roasting pan by its long handle and began to roast the green beans over the coals. She shook the pan continuously to even the roast, while two of the girls set up the small ceramic cups on a tray for the serving. Gabra joined Edith, and the beans changed colour, getting darker and darker from their light-brown hue. When the oil began to line the surface of the beans, they stopped the roast, wafting the coffee bean smoke around the room. The youngest girl lit incense, and summoned the guests to attend.

Michel was entranced by the rich smell of the roast and humbled by the hive of activity around the preparation. The guests were offered peanuts and cooked barley as a snack. Michel watched as Gabra discarded the very darkest beans, taking turns with Edith to pound the roasted beans in a mortar, using a wooden pestle to crush them down. The grinds needed be as even as possible to be suitable for brewing. Camille stared at all their white dresses and thought Edith looked wonderful. With the overwhelming odours mingling in the room she looked forward to tasting the coffee. She realised the tiny cups might be a reason they would have three servings. It made sense to her now, but a mug would have been easier.

The grinds were sieved to remove the larger bits and put into the *jebena* kettle. The water was added and brought to the boil over the coals. Once drawn to Edith's satisfaction, they stirred the coffee and put the kettle onto the grasses to settle. Edith then placed incense at the door, and thanked the spirit of earth for the gathering.

The girls put a few drops of coffee into each cup and ceremoniously emptied them onto the grasses. Edith lifted the kettle to pour all the coffees in one long uninterrupted flow from three hand heights above the cups. She ignored any that spilt between them. When she'd finished pouring in one movement all the girls clapped for her.

"Why did she pour like that?" Camille asked Kelile. "She messed the tray."

"It is so the grinds stay on the bottom of the kettle and don't get into our cups."

"Like the sediment in a wine bottle?"

"Exactly like that."

The first cup was presented to the eldest in the room, and the second to Camille.

"You're honoured," said Kelile, "we drink it black with sugar or salt."

"Sugar please," she said, "I'd prefer that."

Edith tasted her coffee the way she remembered the Inspector had, with deliberation. The brew reflected the harshness of Africa, with a bold strength that warmed her heart. It was magnificent, and for a brief moment she wished the Inspector could be here with her. That thought lingered with her.

News reached Addis that Camille had achieved minor celebrity status in Paris, thanks to the poolside story. The samples incident was now closed and filed behind locked doors, and there was a scramble at the Embassy to be the one to deliver the good news to her. Now that she was untarnished, she would sit well at their dinner table, and the wives had begun to inquire after her. As befits such times, it was a more senior member who claimed the honour. With his small team in tow, he set forth to be the bearer of tidings. The concierge informed them Camille had gone out mid-morning, in high spirits.

That he'd advised her to stay within the confines of the hotel caused the senior of the French contingent to lose face. "She needs be taught a lesson, who the hell does she think she is?" he insisted, before instructing the team to hunt her down or else. After brief consultations, they split up city areas between them, and agreed to meet up at a later stage. The hunt was on.

The Stalker replayed the CD that had haunted her for last twenty-four hours, and added the music to her iTunes library. Expecting the Paymaster to arrive sometime with details of a new assignment, she knew it was time to return the box of recordable CDs. She'd bin the empty bottle of Château Latour 1996, compliments of Camille's father, which had proved too much of a temptation.

A sharp air of conspiracy circled the meeting room when the orchestra committee re-convened. No members had excused themselves, and the conductor had extended his own previous invitation. There was no discussion of compassion or compromise. For some in attendance this was the coup d'état that would remove Camille from the orchestra. In future there would be no place for her kind. For others, she was just too knowledgeable for their liking, and for the committee spectators this was good sport. They had seen the pictures of Camille adorning the daily papers. One member even suggested her skimpy black pool attire was a deliberate attempt to mock the traditional black outfits worn by the players at concerts.

"There was some lout hanging all over her."

The meeting went ominously quiet when one of Camille's supporters retorted that Michel was one of the finest bakers of Paris and from a most respected family. It seemed to the supporter's mind that they were having fun. On that note the ice was broken, they should bring in some pastries and coffee for sustenance while they deliberated. The spirits of the hunting pack rose again and it was as well that the room had dim lights to hide the smirks on their faces as they sensed a kill.

The two or three faithful Camille supporters had arrived prepared to take up the fight where they'd left off the previous meeting. They presented a memo signed by the majority of the orchestra in Camille's favour. They were caught off-guard by the committee senior. He stated that he had inside information from a reliable source that there was more to this Ethiopia business than met the eye. He had been asked not to divulge what he knew; expressing that it was confidential.

None of Camille's supporters had the nerve to challenge him, which was just as well for his dignity. His source had been the online version of the same article they had all read. In mitigation, perhaps the web version seemed darker and more ominous than the print version. Or perhaps those sites he visited having seen Camille in her bikini were themselves darker and sleazier, rather like the decor of the committee room. Camille was to blame.

"This is not about her case in Ethiopia, this is about her taking leave for a family matter at short notice and requiring the orchestra to adjust. She in the meantime wallows in a swimming pool, semi-naked with God knows who, and not her family."

"That's strange," said one of Camille's supporters, "she has no family that I know of."

"Exactly," said the senior, "case closed and time to vote."

They voted two against the motion to dismiss Camille Laroche, and eight for the motion. So ended her contract with the orchestra with immediate effect. The result of the vote was written in the minutes. It was something Camille would have known about, had she been at home, as a letter went winging its way to her apartment that morning. After the celebratory lunch, the senior was horrified to see that Camille's leave request had actually cited 'Founder matters', and not 'Family matters'. His secretary also reminded him that Camille's investment fund was a most significant annual benefactor to the orchestra. He was furious that she'd posted the letter immediately he'd signed it, as per his instructions. He decided the best course of action was no action. Perhaps the fund advisors would overlook the issue. They would be his type of people. Funds and intimate relationships were all-important, and he looked forward to experiencing one of each.

22

The analyst worked on his local drug supply project, computing the numbers, pencil on pad working out the best-case scenarios. He demanded the best or heads would roll. The Receptionist sat in front of her computer, her codebook propped adjacent to the keyboard. She moved the fourth digit of the code to the front and the third digit to the end of the sequence, inserting the two key symbols of the day into their places. This opened the encryption key to a remote server. She began sending out the day's film orders to those who had pre-banked the funds. By agreement, the clients had three days to watch the films before the content would delete itself from their computers. She had an hour to distribute the latest film collection before the code sequence would invalidate. It was second nature to the Receptionist and soon complete.

She then sealed the courier bags and called the company to collect and distribute the 'medicines'. After a final document check, eighteen parcels whose contents were subject to massive mark-ups were on their way. They would be delivered within the next twenty-four hours. She typed the final code into her computer, which locked the encryption – a cryptographic system protecting their lair. The code also switched on a time lock, which would activate and wipe the machine should a new daily code not be punched in within forty-eight hours. This emergency key, while not foolproof, protected clients for a few days should the analyst be forced to abandon ship. The computer would notify clients with a warning signal. An alert interested party using reconstruct surveillance would have had little problem intercepting their system.

With the administration complete, it was time for patient appointments and her favourite pastime. The analyst justified her presence as observer. The challenge was to extract the most intimate sexual details and fantasies from patients, to act as a precursor to their own trysts.

Winding down, Edith booted up her laptop, and browsed the Parisian press 'Addis pool' stories. She sent the family another combined email giving the real story of the goings-on in Addis. Judging by the coverage on other French websites, it was obvious that a storm was brewing over this incident. The papers had been supplied copy and photos from someone at the poolside the previous day. She accessed YouTube and located Camille's video from the Dubai Airport concourse, and was astounded to see it going viral. Three hundred thousand more hits in a week, and a second video had been released, 'The Angel Violinist Poolside'. It was surpassing the first video's viewing numbers. Camille looked gorgeous.

Edith watched as the hotel poolside came alive in the video. Camille played music with a strange magnificence, against the background of clinking glasses and splashing water. The patio vibrated with excitement. In a matter of hours the written press would link the Addis incident girl and the viral violin videos together. The story would grow exponentially, and had spread to the international press. Edith downloaded the new video and went looking for Michel and Camille. This would be a night to remember.

Michel and Camille were nowhere to be found. The concierge informed Edith he'd called them a taxi about a half hour before, and they'd gone out. On spotting Edith in the lobby, the hotel manager came rushing across and thanked her for all the bookings.

"We're full," he said, "what with all the press people coming in tomorrow. This is great for the hotel's publicity. We're sending champagne up to your rooms with our compliments."

Edith smiled and said thanks. She decided that a drink was called for after all, and went to the more intimate bar, where she ordered a beer and joined the other guests. At midnight enough was enough, and with the exciting travel stories now on their third telling she went to bed. It had been a great day.

Grappling with sleep, Edith realised they could never have predicted the outcomes. For Camille, these could be far broader and more meaningful than any of them had considered. Of concern, was that she was appearing in a growing number of articles on the Internet, and lead pages of Paris newspapers. She was becoming a sensation. There would be consequences and Edith realised this could turn into a dream or a disaster for her friend. She also knew she could get sucked into this whirlpool herself and might inherit the roles of shadow mentor and shadow psychologist. Camille lacked street-wisdom in every sense, and what nagged at Edith's sleep was loyalty; she could never abandon her friend to the wolves. None of them were briefed to face the press here or on arrival in Paris. It was just as well they would be flying out. Edith suspected that Camille was tougher than she made out. Music takes hard discipline, but managing the limelight would be another issue. The answer lay in whether Camille had enough raw steel inside her to temper her naivety. Edith would bet that she did.

It was the Patrón Añejo tequilas that bounced Camille into the all-night mood. Under strict supervision from Michel, she sipped them, without salt, to savour the flavour as they slid down. She ordered the taxi as a surprise for Michel.

"Free," she said, "to go drinking in a foreign land."

Camille and Michel were only warming up, and were already storming the venues in Bole Road. There wasn't a coffee in sight. They had whiskies in hand and their thirsts were growing.

Whether it started at the Cotton Lounge or Club Illusion she couldn't remember. Later at the Dome Club she noticed photos being taken of her and, thinking it must be the dancing, she doubled the effort. Earlier in the evening, the two of them had been coached to eat *injera* bread in the traditional way. They tore strips off the flat bread from the sector nearest them, and used that to scoop up a chunk of one of the many spiced accompaniments. They drank a few glasses of the local *Tej* honey-wine as their dessert.

For the second time on the trip, Michel realised he'd stood Edith up. Camille shrugged her shoulders and said their friend could catch up with them later.

"She's hereabouts."

Walking hand-in-hand like a prince and princess into the buzzing atmosphere of the Dome, Michel felt on top of the world, and protective.

"Feels like home," said Michel.

"It's an assault on the senses," said Camille, and dropped his hand.

Marko Segura and his sister had visited the pawnshop in Paris two days prior, after closing time. She had pointed out the violin case through the shop window.

"That's what you owe me."

"So this is the payback," he had said, "then I'm forgiven."

"By me, yes. Not by my cat."

The violin had been played in numerous concerts and while its condition had not deteriorated in any way, its price was yet to be determined by its new keeper. The case was old and creased, perhaps worth about €30. He hadn't bothered to open it; the youth pawning it had claimed it was his brother's, who lived in Nimes and needed the money, usual story.

Two days later at midday when the weather was hot, Marko entered the shop and ambled around.

"I need a guitar, for next month, I'm saving," he said.

"Nobody's saving, nobody's buying," said the attendant.

"I'm not nobody."

"Keep looking then."

Marko's sister entered a few minutes later and, ignoring her brother, went right up to the attendant's desk, "Remember me? I'm back alone."

"Yeah, looking for that *special* discount," he said, "Right place, wrong time, come back when we're closing."

"That's a bad time," she said "it's supper."

"Are you a little kid?"

"Fuck you, it's not my fault you've got another customer in your shop."

"It looks like he's gone," he said. "He needs to save money like you all do, there's nothing much for free."

"Later then," she said, and was gone before he could stand up.

Three streets away the brother and sister bought a fresh baguette and went to the park to eat, Camille's violin in his hand.

"And now?" he said

"We deliver the violin to its owner. It'll be good karma for you, you need it."

"Let's finish eating first. Can I look at it?"

"No, it stays in its case."

"Are you sure about this?" said Marko, "She won't think we stole it?"

"I'm sure, trust me."

"Why now?"

There was a sense of foreboding as they walked up the stairs to Camille's apartment, and when they reached the fifth floor the Paymaster had beaten them to it. He was sick of other people in his woman's life. They were carrying a violin. He'd take that for a start.

"Students?" said the Paymaster, "Who are you?"

"Not answerable to you." said Marko.

"And who are you?" the Paymaster repeated, taking out his knife.

"More armed than you," said Marko, pulling out the Glock.

The Paymaster backed off. He knew all about the odds here and he had bigger dreams in mind. In any case, there had been no answer to his knocking. Perhaps they weren't back from their trip yet. He would bide his time.

"Why did you need the gun to visit the violinist?" asked his sister.

"Instinct."

"Well your instincts were right, now promise never to carry it again. You're an artist, not a gangster."

"So father's a gangster, not a builder."

"No," she said, "he's just got a past."

23

The Embassy team in Addis had scoured the more seedy dives of the city for hours. They were blending in, and hours later winding down their search for Camille. The senior member decided to go upmarket on a hunch. He visited the Dome only to catch the fugitives red-handed on the dance floor. He ordered in a drink and called for backup. Within half an hour the entire team were eating out of Michel's hand, and queuing for a chance to dance with Camille. The French were united in success.

Camille was sleeping the sleep of the almost famous, oblivious to the workings of the world. Two weeks or so of the trip had taken its toll, and her mindset changes were tiring, whether she understood the process or not. Going to bed, she had felt it was time to go home. Had she woken, her feet would have ached as much as her head. The guard warned people in the corridor to keep moving along or show their room key. It was the same short shrift Michel had received when escorting her home earlier. He too had been moved along.

Michel was settling into the lounger when a waiter announced an international call holding for him. He requested it be transferred to his room and felt a dull thump in his chest as he rushed upstairs, hoping there was no bad news about the family.

"Great news," said his brother, "we got the best deal possible."

"So how is mother?" said Michel, "and the wife?"

"Thrilled with me. I signed the business up to a co-operative and things are looking good. We're cutting overheads and there will be better profits. The remaining staff will be delighted. There could even be bonuses."

"Hold on," said Michel, "go back a step, I'm not sure I like the 'signed', or 'remaining' bits. Go through this with me from the beginning, every detail, every clause. I'm all ears."

The younger Lumière, with the wife hovering and waiting to go and celebrate, explained the deal in full, answering every prompt from his elder brother detail by detail.

"You signed on the dotted line, in what capacity?"

"Chief Executive," said the brother who felt uncomfortable with the loud silence on the other end of the phone.

"How did you describe yourself on the contract?"

"As Chief Executive… are you still there?"

"I'm still here," said Michel. "Now, listen to my every word. You're on speaker phone and I'm recording this on my mobile," he continued. "I resign from my positions in the company, and activate my sell-out clause as per the shareholder memorandum. Go to the bank and start the process to have my funds released. I'll be back in two days."

"The sell-out clause is not for Chief Executives," said the brother.

"Yes," said Michel, "but I'm not the Chief Executive now. You are, as you demonstrated on signing that agreement. Goodbye, and regards to the wife."

He left his room exhilarated, and went poolside. His brother had sold them out to the devil. He ordered a bottle of Gran Patrón with four tequila glasses and a bowl of limes.

"Please keep the snacks coming," he said, settling down comfortably in the sun.

Michel inspired conversation from strangers; he welcomed it like cream to strawberries, or in this case, like champagne to caviar. He had vague flashes of swapping glances with some of the faces now relaxing in the sun. Memories might surface later, but now he felt a need to wallow in the grandest of feelings – freedom from his brother's stupidity and laziness.

"How's your wife?" was their opening line, which took Michel a few seconds to fathom.

"To the best of my knowledge I'm not married."

Debbie and Julie, impressed with his linguistic skills, ordered drinks for their own account.

"Oh, we watched the girl you were with at the club. She has a great sense of rhythm. So, she's not your wife."

An hour or so later, Debbie wrapped smoked salmon around her index finger, and inserted the morsel into Michel's mouth.

"Next time with lemon, it adds the spark," said Michel, washing it down with a shot of Patrón. The girls swam a few times, even dragging Michel into the water. Back in the sun, he worked his magic applying lotion to their bodies. As the heat built up after midday, Julie suggested they go try out room service. Michel gave them his room key.

"I'll see you there."

"Hurry," said Julie, "or we'll start without you.'

"Unfaithful bastard," said a woman on a lounger nearby, "and such a talented wife."

Amused, Michel smiled, swam two more lengths of the pool, and dried off. Taking the bottle of Patrón, he walked through the hotel up to the room, relieved the waiter of the drinks tray in the corridor, and knocked.

"Room service."

"It's open."

Michel went in and climbed into bed with them.

"In Paris," he said, remembering scenes from *Last Tango*, "we start slow". He turned them both face down and began massaging their bodies.

"Did you lock the door?" said Julie.

"No."

"Good, in case your friend comes to join us."

Not a good call, thought Michel.

"Not another word."

About four hours later, Edith tried Michel's door, having had no response to his room phone. The guard had assured her he was there, so she went in. They were all sound asleep with the empty tequila bottle between them.

Strong bodies, she thought and went to the bedside, *let's not waste this.* She picked up a half bottle of champagne from the ice bucket, and moved the do not disturb sign from inside the door to the outside. Smiling, she walked back down the corridor. *And about time too, Michel.*

At eight o'clock Edith asked Camille to come to her room as soon as she was ready for dinner. She was there seven minutes later, the tone in Edith's voice having brooked no argument.

"I have news for you," said Edith. Camille was shocked by the second YouTube video and the number of views. She read some of the articles in the French press, and remained confused about the Facebook "Rescue this Girl" page. She gave up trying to understand.

At nine o'clock sharp all three Founders were seated with Kelile and Gabra at the dinner table. Michel was dressed to kill, the dinner jacket not at all out of place in the circumstances. There would be many toasts that evening and when Gabra presented Edith's certificate, Camille was emotional.

"I'm so proud of you," she said "I could never have done that, white dress or not."

Yes, it's over, thought Edith, *and now I think it's time for a man, a challenging man,* She lifted her glass and toasted the thought.

Later that night the Stalker would sit with officer No.4 for the second meeting in the bar where they'd first met. She'd hold his hand across the table as her iPhone recorded more details of his last few illicit affairs. She taped his thoughts on his colleagues, and his great success in combating crime. She would look into his eyes as he spoke, unnerving him somewhat, hearing little of what he said. She'd think rather of his wife and the time they'd spent alone at home after drinks in a bar. She still felt the afterglow, the sensuality. She would have to concentrate on the officer who held the bigger prize, the information why police were watching Edith and her travel companions flying out. She'd need to get the answers, still desperate to connect with Edith.

An hour or two earlier, in the company of the Stalker, Yvette – the officer No.4's wife – had phoned her husband. *He was still in the meeting, he'd said, and suspected it would be a late one again, after midnight, out of his hands.* Yvette told the Stalker he wouldn't be home for hours, but the Stalker already knew that, she had him sitting in a bar waiting for her. *Here comes sweet revenge for women*, she thought. *Let the bastard stew, I'm with his wife.*

Yvette had seen the Stalker rub her own neck and press the pressure points on her temples. Watching her she felt a warm feeling in her belly, an excitement. She'd never had sex with a woman, but something about the Stalker made her interested, she had no idea what. Yvette led the Stalker by the hand; she told her to sit on a stool, massage was her speciality. Peeling the Stalker's top down off her shoulders she started to rub, in long slow circular movements with her fingertips. Her thumbs remained on either side of the spine. She moved up onto the neck, with the same slow touch, pausing with pressure where she felt the tension. Yvette leaned into the Stalker, loved the deep red shade of her long hair, which curled in loose circlets around her neck, she loved the smell. She shifted the hair to one side, and kissed her lightly on the nape. She felt the girl shudder, wondered how she'd come into her life so recently, and why she felt so relaxed with her.

"How does it feel?" said Yvette.

"Starting to help, I'm still tense, a long day."

"Leave it to me. I've been home all day." She slipped her thumbs into the top again, pulling it down to the Stalker's elbows, and moved the massage from her back to the top of her chest. She cupped her left hand over the left shoulder, resting it there, while her right hand moved in bigger and bigger circles on the Stalker's chest, first past the edge of her right breast, twice, and soon over the whole breast. She pushed the top even further down in the front. Yvette felt the nipple as her hand moved across it, and leaning forward again, dropped her left hand onto the other breast, her thumbs between and over them as she caressed. The Stalker turned her head to look at her, and their mouths met, gently at first.

It was an hour or more before the Stalker left, in no hurry, glad that Edith and friends had gone on a trip.

For the first time, it dawned on her: she liked who she was, what she did, and there was no need for the assistance of any analyst.

Arriving at the bar some forty minutes after she'd left Yvette, the Stalker saw No.4 on his mobile again, a near-empty glass of beer in front of him. She sat down next to him, and once she'd made the iPhone recordings of the conversation that followed, it was time for business. She had all the ammunition she needed, she'd get the answers. He needed no coercing.

"Were you calling the wife when I arrived?" the Stalker said.

"No, a girlfriend," he laughed, "the wife's boring, she's asleep long since."

"How's your dangerous job? Working on rapes and robberies?"

"No, bridge murders."

"What bridge murders?"

He told her, astonished that she hadn't heard.

"Too busy with my own life," she said, "Do you follow the suspects?"

"At times, I followed some to the airport last week, the man was connected to the bridge victims."

"He escaped?"

"No he'll be back soon, we're monitoring him."

The Stalker upped and left without a goodbye, unnerved herself. She had the violinist's CDs in her room and prayed she hadn't left fingerprints in either of the girls' apartments. She didn't want to get sucked into any murder investigation; this was too close for comfort. Did Edith know she was travelling with a murder suspect?

Back home, she wiped the discs and box clean and disposed of them in the ground floor bin. Upstairs she poured a vodka; they'd empty the bins soon enough. She needed to think. With their previous film stint rained off, why hadn't the Paymaster rescheduled their third filming session?

The Paymaster realised he'd visited this bar in the Latin Quarter too often of late. *Not a wise move.* He picked three pills from his pocket and ate them. Two were bitter; the beer washed the residual paste away and he felt his mind was nearer to a truth. He needed Camille back in Paris. He should have carved the kids on the stairs, and knew if it weren't for the Glock he would have. The violinist would have felt proud, protected.

He took out his photo of Camille. She was so beautiful, his Camille, so beautiful. He knew suddenly that patience would feed his passion; it was time to move, time to shift bars. He took his knife from between his thighs and put it in his jeans pocket. Not a soul in the bar saw him do it, but everyone felt an instinctive relief, magnified as the Paymaster departed down the cobbled street.

24

Sauntering through the VIP boarding channel a well-seasoned celebrity, Camille felt relieved to be going home. Her problems were history. *Gone forever*, she felt.

Edith managed to get seat upgrades for herself and Michel at the check-in counter using tour guide credentials. Though she did enquire for Camille, only those present were eligible. In any case, they only had two vacant seats. They boarded the plane some time after Camille with a relative air of calm. Michel waved goodbye to all and sundry as best he could. He clutched his cabin bag and boarding pass in one hand, and his Ethiopian baking book in the other. The proof of the pudding would be in the reading, which he intended to attempt on the flights.

Dubai after midnight was somewhat familiar to the Founders as they ended the first sector of their home flight. Camille felt a sense of resolve; she would miss the availability of Kelile's wise words, yet knew she'd have her Society compatriots with her in Paris. She resisted the temptation to re-enact the scene of the first YouTube video, and instead chose to eat. With fond memories she traversed the concourse remembering she had a handful of dollars to spend. She would go shopping, after a meal. There were no foreign travellers begging for a recital, yet the déjà vu feeling prevailed. She carried the violin case, feeling a slight rising panic at the unknown world ahead. She considered the option of resigning from her own future with immediate effect, like Michel said he'd done to solve his business problems. After a double cheeseburger and chips, which she thought worldly, she resolved to face the future with power. She looked forward to bringing her compositions to life and decided to finally score her music for orchestra, a priority on her return. She couldn't wait to play them with accomplished musicians in this new light of freedom. There was something about the mid-point of her journeys that influenced her, and she was comfortable between borders.

At Charles de Gaulle the midday madness was brewing. Edith declared her new Taytu handbag at customs and they waved her through. Michel and Camille had only memories to declare. With the press flashlights popping despite the time of day, questions were shouted at Camille from all sides. With total calm she declared Edith to be her manager and Michel her bodyguard. She turned down an invitation from a TV network for an end-of-week interview, knowing she had other plans to make.

Michel's family driver ushered them through the throng in his professional manner, which Camille noted for her must-have list as they drove to the inner city. Edith wondered if this whole newfound fame was a nightmare in the making. An ominous sense of doom was rising on the tide.

A twenty-five minute drive took them to Camille's apartment. With fond farewells and promises of a get-together, Camille lingered over Michel's hug. It did not occur to her that she'd allocated him bodyguard status no more than thirty-five minutes or so beforehand.

The Inspector met with officers No.1 and No.2 from the bridge murders team. They walked along the pedestrian path, talking in soft voices. There had been little wind on the nights of the first two murders, and it was gusty the night of the rain killing. Today, the air seemed stiller than still.

"We have revisited the signatures," No.1 said to No.2. "The 'Limited Edition' reference could refer to the seven litigators in Berlin, or seven planned killings. The scratched 7 on the Berlin door, and those on the victims' hands, tie in. The Inspector has a theory, and one we need to move on fast."

"We now know," said the Inspector, "that the finance advisor was of medium height. The killer, or Wolf as you call him, is tall. Our assumption was correct, there are at least two people involved. The €100 notes are linked to the advisor; the probability is the limited edition inscriptions are his message. There's also a ninety-odd per cent positive match with samples of his handwriting. The advisor himself scratched the seven on the Berlin door. The Germans have witnesses to that."

"And the Venus, Mars sequence?" asked No.2.

"We'll get there. We have a problem with the limited edition, and a theory. This could be a warning message to the investors he stole from in Berlin. Seven investors, a nominal

€100 repayment, and a body for each investor. This is one sick financial advisor. He's not surfaced among the Parisian financial circles, but we know he's here. There's no trace of a Kurt B. Huber in our city, so where is he, and who is he now?"

"The first priority," said No.1, "is to find the person doing the killings. He's not a professional hit man, that's a certainty. Whoever he is, we need stop him. We believe he's new to killing. We presume the cosmic references are his personal messages directed to us. An alert, even subliminal, giving directions to the next attack venue."

"The next killing, " said the Inspector, "if he sticks to the current cosmic pattern, will be on the Pont d'Arcole or Pont au Double. Our top priority is to cover both bridges, stop the murders. What we have to go on is a leather belt or strap, a nebulous taped sound, and the cosmic clue."

"We need a miracle," said No.2, "a magic break, or we need to force something."

"All dangerous concepts," said the Inspector. "Let's stick to the cosmic clues, keep looking at their relationship to earth."

Eight minutes after they'd dropped her off, Camille made an emergency call to Edith. Edith and Michel arrived much like a swat team to the rescue. Seeing the look of angst on Camille's face as she waved a letter, Michel was uncomfortable and, as she wasn't injured, he'd be on his way.

"The bastards," said Camille, "they've fired me. I'm not a second violinist, first violinist, concert master or anything. I'm stuck in this cage again."

Edith said nothing, but sat with her, and waited.

"To hell with them," continued Camille, "it's the first violinists, I scare them, they watch me. They know I can see through them, even the cellists. I scare them too."

Edith read and reread the letter, the parts about decorum, the violin, the swimming pool, and the photo in the newspapers. It was hard to comment, especially the part about leave for family reasons, which she queried.

"You Founders are my family, besides I never wrote that."

"Thank you, and if you're not a second violinist then what are you?" said Edith

Camille walked around the apartment for some time before flinging open the balcony doors. She walked out, unprompted for the first time in her life, and for the first time in Edith's presence. Edith stayed inside, and remembered her luggage was still in the boot of the Lumière vehicle. She made a mental note to phone her parents as soon as possible.

"I'm a violinist and composer," said Camille, "and I'm liberated."

"Well that's a start. Let's take your bags upstairs."

"Why not? You'll be the first visitor to my private space."

"The first family member," added Edith, and they laughed.

Upstairs the real disaster of the stolen discs swept other problems aside, and Camille's tan paled white. Edith watched her turn and turn in circles, take off all her clothes and walk in a trance to her bed, where she clambered under the duvet. There was not even a whimper, only a silence that blanked out the sounds of surrounding streets, beating back even the most inquisitive of dark notions. Edith went downstairs, fetched a bottle of the Balvenie and returned to the bedside. She drew up a chair and started stroking Camille's hair, over and over. Not a word was uttered. There was nothing to say. Edith thought of those times her grandmother had stroked her hair on the occasions when Edith had worried about her father at sea in a storm. He always came back, so too would Camille.

She could weep for her friend, but there was no time for that. Her loyalty would drive her to seek solutions, obvious ones, or necessary ones, and she'd implement them no matter the personal cost.

First she decided to tell Camille to get rid of all the barriers to her real self. *Kovchenko* must go, out of her existence and memory. She needed Camille to make her own choices, to be herself. She would need to discover her new self, and would be free to do that. She was not caught between borders, as Michel seemed to be. Camille was now grounded in Paris, her home, and while she was a genius, that did not make her wise. She would have to learn wisdom if she still had time. The axis of consequence was shifting; there was no turning back.

Eighteen hours passed before Camille resurfaced, and Edith was still in situ, although she'd been downstairs two or three times to search for food. She'd switched the whisky for wine.

Edith had contemplated the status quo. She'd committed to Camille as a friend and, in return, was welcomed as family. There was no point in reporting this break-in. Too often the investigation itself caused the dumping of stolen goods. Losing Camille's entire collection of compositions was unthinkable. Loyalty had no boundaries, and Edith knew whatever it took, she'd get the CDs back.

"What do I do about my music?" was the first question Camille asked.

"Can you reconstruct the works?"

"Why?"

"So you can play them,"

"Given time, yes, why?"

"You should think about that 'why'. I'm going to buy us some real French food and then we'll feast and celebrate your new career."

"Why?"

"Because I'm hungry."

It was another ten or twelve hours before Edith returned to her own apartment, and the streets were dark. Within minutes, she'd discovered that she too had received an uninvited visitor in her absence. Her security had foiled the break-in attempt. She punched in the override code on the hidden keypad and noted the video button flashing, which indicated activation. She phoned her father and mother in Marseillan without mentioning the attempted break-in. She talked about the trip and how she looked forward to their next family meal together. They offered to send her oysters and she accepted.

She checked the apartment. There had been no entry.

Right, she thought, *let's have a look at you, let's see your face.* There were three hidden cameras in the lobby, strategically placed to get the best overall view of a potential intruder. They should have taken a photo of the face of her intruder. One camera had been disabled, but the other two had worked well.

You're not quite clever enough. Sitting in front of her computers, it took about four minutes to have the unsuspecting intruder on her Mac screen. Edith had expected a male, but printed out both colour and black and white photos of the female, who appeared well organised. She looked like she had a tool belt under her jacket, early thirties, attractive, with curly red hair. Judging from the camera angle she was shorter than Edith, but taller than Camille.

What the hell did she want? The girl was well groomed. This was not the norm for a break-in, and she had no memory of seeing this face before. She phoned Michel and gave an update on Camille's situation, asking if he could visit her to lend support. She suggested he focus the conversation on future opportunities and not on commiserations.

"She's tempted to wallow," she said, "she needs to move on. This is good for her in a perverse way, a taste of other realities."

"A touch harsh."

"Yes, that's life."

Michel arranged to have Edith's luggage delivered in the morning with a little something he'd made that evening. For the first time he mentioned her coffee ceremony, "It was awesome," he said, "it's only just struck me how awesome. Let's have the next meeting soon."

At the end of the call, Edith thought about that statement for a while. She decided that both Michel and Camille lived so far from the present that their lives must be one long spatial challenge. Even so, she welcomed his request for a discussion about their future business.

"You're right," he'd said, "there are strong synergies between coffee and pâtisserie. We can create a special place and bring the ambience of the production to the public. It's been done before; we'll do it better."

Edith checked her upcoming tour schedules and, as the days sped past, spent some time drawing up pro-forma itineraries for her clients. She got a notification from Kelile that her shipment of green coffee beans was being assembled in their warehouse. It would soon be trucked en route to the port of Djibouti. He said he'd update her with a confirmed sailing as soon as the nominated vessel left port.

Her father had offered to arrange all the import formalities and she had accepted. He would arrange warehousing at a friend's facility near the port of discharge, and they could ship piecemeal up to Paris, when she needed stock. He'd said it was about keeping business in the family, and Edith wondered on how large a fisherman's family was in reality. She knew her father counted his many friends as family and she felt that was the way it should be.

She required a small commercial roaster for the green beans, and a suitable packing method, glad that green bean shelf life was long. Once roasted, her beans would only be ground when about to be used. She'd have a small number of customers for whom she'd roast and deliver on demand. Collecting cash on delivery would keep the administration cost minimal. The rest she'd sell to the public in the new eatery they planned to open. Michel's skills were legendary and her product was world class, so it was only natural that would be the best starting point.

Over the coming weeks, while Edith and Michel tackled the setting up of the new businesses, Camille continued to worry. In trying to resolve life's options, thoughts spun in her head. She wrote down six vague ideas on six equal squares of paper: *sue the orchestra, burn the violins, get Kelile to visit, cancel the orchestra stipend, become a tour guide, become a conductor.* She folded the pieces of paper into smaller and smaller squares and threw them as far as possible. She opened the one that went the furthest. Having read it, she phoned Kelile in Ethiopia. He was delighted they'd all settled back in Paris, time had flown, and the team in Addis missed them.

After the call she tried to recollect the conversation word for word, but failed. She knew she'd offered him an air ticket to Paris, and accommodation, desperate for more advice. He'd refused the ticket offer, saying he had intended a trip soon to discuss Edith's business plan with her. He promised to be on the next suitable flight. He'd joked about VIP boarding, but she missed the humour completely. Camille was grateful he was coming, that's what mattered to her. Looking at the next furthest square of paper she phoned the fund managers who were relieved to hear that she was safe and sound back in Paris, and would action her request at once. The balcony doors were wide open and she walked out with an opened bottle of water. She'd try the fisherman-style drinking, from the bottle, that the others had reminisced about. She could do it. She could cross borders; after all, she had crossed a few already.

A while later her phone beeped with a reminder for orchestra practice. For a moment she panicked: what were they rehearsing? She relaxed, and sat back at her desk, violin near, and continued the challenging task of recreating and scoring her compositions for orchestra. She was making headway. From somewhere deep inside she gave a sigh, a sigh of freedom, and a sigh for the women and youth of classical music, whether they wanted it or not.

On the other side of the Seine, the Paymaster also gave a sigh, a different sigh, whether she wanted it or not. He took his book out from his pocket and stared at Camille's picture, and he opened another beer to wash down more pills. He'd discovered in the press, well after the event, his girl was back. She would be missing him, he'd wasted too much time already.

25

With Paris smouldering in the late summer heat, Edith and Michel worked furiously to get their future lives on track. Michel, unburdened from the family business, was free to make decisions. In spare moments he settled down to conversations with old acquaintances in the bars, bistros and cafés. He took the opportunity to meet with former staff, and assure them of his loyalty. He was a different Michel, as if a page had turned.

Edith had eased back to business, taking time to show off the ever-evolving Paris to her clients. Though the new venture filled much of her time, she was conscious that she'd abandoned her friend Camille to her own devices. She felt a post-trip Society meeting might be a suitable tonic for Camille in her state: unemployed, famous and confused.

Camille agreed without complaint.

"In my apartment," she said.

"Always, yes. Keep the balcony open."

"Will you take minutes of the meeting?"

"No, these meetings are short. There's only time for new experiences and memories."

The photographs of the Stalker lay on Edith's kitchen counter staring at her every time she walked past. She worried she'd neglected Camille's stolen CDs for too long, and she'd been walking to and fro for some time, flipping her oyster knife into the air and catching it. She adjusted the grind size on her burr coffee grinder, tasting yet another cup until her body felt the caffeine throb. Her thoughts kept returning to the subject of Camille's missing CDs. She realised she'd had at least five coffees and decided another one might well settle the previous ones. She opted for a coarse grind, a more Addis grind, which she felt would do the trick.

If this woman in the photo was the same person who had entered Camille's apartment, the probability had increased that she might get the discs back. It was a slim chance, but slim chances were more than enough for Edith, who knew exactly what the Marseillan fisher folk would do.

Back on her computer, she opened a folder she had named 'attack', wondering if this girl was also the writer of Camille's death-threat note. She chose two pictures in the folder and made enhanced copies of each in black and white and moved these to one side. She gazed a long time at the colour photos. There was one showing the full face and another with a left side profile. Edith memorised the skin tone, hair colour, eyes and face. She ignored distractions that might change often such as hairstyle, earrings and brown leather neck-thong. She minimised the two photos and opened the black and white ones, printing half a dozen of each, passport size. She put four of them in her wallet, closed the attack folder and turned her attention to the upcoming meeting.

At the Society meeting Edith was only going to serve one type of coffee. It was a coffee from an Ethiopian private estate.

These selected beans were the ones Kelile had presented to her as a parting gift. They had been pre-roasted. She would grind the beans at the meetings, and decided that if coffee was going to compete with après-drinks in the future, only the finest or most unusual would do. In future she would enjoy seeking them out, hoping to generate many interesting discussions. Coffee was powerful enough to stand on its own feet, and she would encourage participation by future members in the rituals of preparation. On reflection, she decided all meetings should begin earlier in the evening, with three coffee tastings, followed by food and drinks. Edith would suggest it to the other Founders. Democracy needed to thrive. The oysters from her parents had arrived and she made a mental note to fetch them on the way to the meeting.

Edith keyed in the alarm code, closed her front door and went out onto the streets. It took her little over an hour to become aware that once again the Stalker had settled into following her. Taking care never to make eye contact, she led the woman around the neighbourhood as she greeted friends more effusively than usual. She needed to keep the Stalker on the trail. She needn't have bothered as the Stalker was well hooked.

Edith returned home, keeping a safe distance between them. She opened the file and noted down her observations. The Stalker had carried a small black and grey backpack, was younger than her photos reflected, and a lot prettier. What little of her hair you could see was a vibrant red, swept back off her forehead, and tucked under a dark green bandana. Under the 'why' column in a file on her computer she typed a few question marks. If the girl was gay and wanted a relationship or sex, why didn't she just come on to her?

She'd have to accept Edith's 'no', and perhaps that possibility scared her. Money wasn't a motive. If she was responsible for Camille's break-in, why wasn't anything taken apart from the CDs?

When Edith had ordered a beer at a bar, the girl had taken a table and ordered a coffee, good choice, and not once had Edith been able to catch the girl looking at her. Professional? Police? Lawyer? She closed the file, then started working through her emails from the newest backwards. At least some of them she would soon be answering.

Gabra's email detailing the flight and arrival time of Kelile's trip to Paris had caught Edith by surprise. After a moment's reflection she knew his input into the business model would be invaluable. His trip would suit her. It also occurred to her that Camille was in need of all the attention they could give. Thinking about his presence in the city triggered the early makings of a plan, which she typed up in her new Stalker file.

Camille had come back to a lonely home and was further deprived of the orchestra players' company. This concerned Edith. Having no family was so foreign to Edith that she had no answers for her friend, barring Camille starting her own new family in the far distant future. First she needed a life. She often adopted such a detached attitude, and seemed so removed from things around her. Perhaps she needed the more professional help of a psychologist, rather than the student analyst Lacey. There were renowned practitioners in the area. Edith would discuss the subject with Michel.

The email from one of her regular and wealthy American tourists caught her interest. It was an invitation to attend a fundraising gala at the Louvre, the second ever of its type to be held as far as he knew. He expected the finest of dining; an orchestral concert he hoped would be under the glass pyramid, and interesting company. She accepted by return; it was her chance to learn about orchestras, a beginning.

The only positives the Paymaster attributed to analyst Zuppin were the pills he dispensed, and the Receptionist about whom he fantasised in a love-hate manner. She sensed an antagonism, something milder than his violent truth, and she usually disappeared into the back room at the first opportunity. This enraged the Paymaster even more as he sat in the clinic waiting room.

Fucking General, he thought, *sitting in his room all day dispensing drugs. The bastard is sicker than us, planning lives from prescription to prescription, watching his films, drinking his herbal tea and whiskey.*

He loathed the waiting room. The counting of pills irritated him, click, click, one by one into a plastic pillbox, and the typed dosage instructions he never bothered to read. Once summoned to the consulting room, he became a puppy, and he hated that too. He acquiesced and started talking all sorts of garbage while the analyst sat staring at him. He suffered when there were long silences and filled them with any random words that spilled onto the wide desk. Some were jotted into the analyst's journal, which added to his suffering. He'd steal the journal soon, he'd steal the whole dispensary, steal the Receptionist and whatever else he wanted.

That's it, he thought, *what I want,* and his thoughts immediately went to the photo of Camille. He had no idea what he wanted except that he wanted to leave the consulting room and get away from that space. He found himself telling the analyst that he was beginning to experience different emotional responses again, but the pills either dulled them or mixed them up. Sometimes he felt opposing emotions at the same time, like empathy and violence. How was this curing him? He glanced up at the mirror behind the desk and all he could see at first was himself. He looked blurred, as did the painting on the wall behind him depicting the French revolution – all killing and mayhem. The men morphed into the analyst and the women all became Camille. He froze. He did not like her in the painting, and he'd steal that too, and cut out the analyst's face.

More of a drug dealer, thought the Paymaster, who knew he was too deep into this research charade. There was no turning back. He needed the pills, any pills, and he needed the money. Then he realised he was still talking about the Stalker and her private fixation on some woman. The pusher just sat at his desk writing notes.

"She's regressing, she's doing her own photography. She's stalking, putting your project at risk," said the Paymaster.

The analyst nodded, stood up and paced around the room. He held his hands behind his back as the tape recorder on the desk kept recording their current conversation. He let the Paymaster ramble on and on, let his own silence force his patient to keep on talking. Some of this voice recording could serve as a background to the second project film. The re-release was still a work in progress.

Analyst Zuppin was a perfectionist, and as disappointing as the first film was, devoid of responses and emotion, the second was more than encouraging. He was editing it again. He needed to prove that his psycho-stimulation drugs worked. He could spice it up with words and sounds. In fact, it would make a good base film; the ones to follow would ramp up the action and emotion. Imagine how superb the final film would be. He'd send a trailer of the film out to his pseudo-analyst clients worldwide, and they'd demand more. They could sell his drugs exclusively to their patients. This idiot was correct; the Stalker was a potential problem. She hadn't handed the third film to the Paymaster, and he needed these films. After intense editing, they were the proof the drugs were effective, that they enhanced emotions exponentially. The drugs were the key to future earnings, above and below the counter.

The Paymaster felt the clammy sweat rising, felt a nausea punch into his abdomen, and carried on talking.

"Tell me about the first episode," said the analyst.

"Again?"

"Every detail, every thought, what happened, afterwards how you felt in your head, everything."

"It was filmed, you can see it all,"

"She can't film thoughts, I need to hear them."

"I waited until evening, I took your pills. I activated the hypnosis trigger exactly as you taught me, and I presume it left me in a neutral emotional state, much as you'd explained. Then I went out. Looking back, I can't remember thoughts. I felt like a robot, nothing happened. I felt weak, not strong. I almost went back home, some fucking cure." The Paymaster felt his arms tightening, and soon his shoulders and jaw, the same sequence as usual, and he forced them to stop.

"What must I do about the Stalker?"

"She's my patient, leave her to me, just fetch the third film from her and I'll pay you the advance on the next one. Stay away from alcohol like I told you, at least until the project's over."

The patient stormed out of the consulting room. He felt like punching the Receptionist then and there. He left the clinic and went instead to a local bar, ordering a double vodka and a beer before settling down in a corner. He faced the crowd and hoped the Receptionist would pitch up after work – he needed a distraction. He took the photo of Camille out of his poetry book and stared at her, deciding he would take all the photos of her from the Stalker's wall. He had never seen a more beautiful woman, and how congruent they would become. He looked at all the other drinkers around him. None challenged his gaze, and after a few minutes he realised for the first time that he had no control over his feelings about this woman, his woman. He needed the right pills to give him back his own emotions, the ones he'd enjoyed in his youth. He should feel something about his girl other than ownership. He would think about that. His body relaxed and he started smiling, a cold smile.

The head of the orchestra committee took an urgent call from the Louvre gala organisers despite the rule that meetings should never be interrupted.

As he exited to take the call, all eyes and ears followed him, and not a word was heard from the collective, rather as if the call was on a hotline direct from the Kremlin. He left the door ajar to emphasise that the call was to himself, in person, by name. He would bring home the prize and bargain hard for all their sakes. He turned on the speakerphone for full effect, the committee needed to hear this. They'd realise why he'd not taken a pay cut, as they all had.

"The orchestra is definitely available, yes, I will shift dates around as this is for charity. Yes, we'll keep the fee to a minimum. Our committee will meet to discuss suitable works to perform." He requested a time to approve the suitability of the venue, and insisted on all the rights to record the performance.

"One special request please," said the caller, "about Camille..."

"Ah yes," he interrupted, "no need for your concern, we've cancelled her contract with immediate effect."

"Hold on, we wanted her seated next to the Concert Master. We hope for a full live performance of *Motherlands,* and other works. She's the talk of Paris."

"I see, well in light of..."

"Wait, thanks for your time, we'll reconsider options under the circumstance, we'll give you a call if we need you. Stay with your current schedules meantime."

He returned to the committee meeting room where they expected him either to tender his resignation or throw the customary tantrum. They knew from past experience that he plunged into situations and viewpoints without thinking. He held the power, so they acted along, hoping one day this idiot would get his comeuppance. Instead of choosing this time to rebel and vote him out, the majority voted that Camille would have learnt her lesson, be full of remorse and ready to return. They would grant her a second chance. The committee at last felt they had a compassionate side; in fact, they were going to be well known for it. They felt vindicated.

Once again the committee head left the door ajar, phoned Camille and broke the good tidings. He outlined their gesture of understanding and reconciliation, saying that it was her chance to make amends. Perhaps a place on the committee as the second violinists' representative might be in order.

"No thanks," said Camille, before returning the phone to its cradle. She was enjoying working on her music; it kept her focused, and soothed her thoughts.

26

The Society meeting was a raucous affair from the outset. The trip was now a distant memory, and had cemented their bonds. Kelile was welcomed with open arms. He and Edith served a coffee brewed with such passion and precision that it emboldened the bean. Camille requested an encore. Michel in turn confessed to having handpicked the pastries from forbidden competitors, all traditional in the finest sense.

"Worthy competitors, Normandy butter."

Without a moment's hesitation, Camille accepted the challenge to play for them, and the piece she played, *The Still Wind,* resonated deep inside them all.

"Extraordinary," said Michel.

At midnight they opened the first bottle of Bollinger. Edith shucked four dozen oysters before they'd finished their first glass. She spun her knife into the air after each half dozen, and with the confidence of a doyenne caught it, ready to tackle the next. Kelile watched in amazement, and made the decision that if he ever went to war again, it would be shoulder to shoulder with Edith.

The Stalker remained outside the apartment block using the street's many awnings as cover. She hoped Edith would leave before dawn and she could connect with her. It didn't happen. She couldn't afford to miss an opportunity, even if it took all night. It gave her time to think through what her first words to Edith would be; once again she rejected every idea. Edith's appearance alone on the balcony made her stalker's mind race. *What had Edith just done? What was she about to do?* She shivered, and took a drink from her flask – vodka, something to ground her – and was soon back on track.

This time Edith was one step ahead and had the Stalker's number. She was playing with her, letting her take all the line; she'd set the hook in the morning. She knew it was time to confront this woman. Edith went back inside and put a quiet proposal to Kelile who, having considered the matter, accepted. The attack would launch soon, not with malice, not with any purpose other than the return of Camille's masterworks. It never occurred to Edith to continue questioning why she was being followed. All her life people had taken an unusual interest in her well-being. She had that side covered.

The Paymaster waited outside the Stalker's apartment door. Hard knocking had convinced both him and the neighbours that she was not at home. He could wait.

At 04:00 he could wait no longer and walked off into the night. He'd be back.

As requested by Edith, Kelile rose early and avoided the apartment balcony, and any fervent watcher's eyes. The two had coffee and croissants in the kitchen while Michel slept on. Up on the sixth floor Camille was playing one of her violins. On the fifth they discussed their morning strategy.

Edith left the building and returned to her own, where she showered and changed into jeans and a light sweatshirt. She checked her email and then made her way to a favourite bistro. She was greeted by the staff and positioned herself at one of the outside tables, ordering the gâteau au chocolat and a café glacé. Kelile sat at the back, away from the street, giving himself a clear view of patrons at the tables. He had a local newspaper which he couldn't understand, a glass of water and a coffee. In his pocket he carried a GPS system, with the Paris map loaded.

My bold detective, thought Edith.

In less than an hour, the Stalker had a fix on Edith and entered the bistro, sitting close to Kelile. He recognised her immediately from the photo. The Stalker managed at least two new photos of Edith. Kelile used his newspaper to good effect. He noticed her deliberation over her choice of subject; she must have photographed at least ninety per cent of the patrons.

Not an amateur, he concluded.

Edith paid her bill some fifteen minutes later and meandered back to her own apartment. He had prepaid his bill, and tailed the Stalker with the ease of a professional.

Different from my time in the mountains.

Once her quarry was off the street, the Stalker hung around for ten minutes before turning and heading away herself. She was tired, and never once watched her own back.

Kelile followed her to what he presumed was her home. He waited an hour or so outside to be more certain, before seeing her close the red curtains. He decided she was about to rest. He messaged Edith the address, took a few photos of the building and checked all the exits. He confirmed the apartment number, five. With the position marked on the GPS he returned to Edith's apartment.

There was significant activity at Camille's apartment. The security team that had equipped Edith's home were at work shoring up the entrance and fitting a high-tech system. Stronger than the Bastille, they advised, which in turn made her consider how strong she was herself, and which part of her in particular. The public violinist was fine, controlled, and passionate even. She could write evocative music born out of nowhere, both dark and sensitive, and she could play the violin as well as anyone in Paris. The other side of her was a different matter. She could be confused by her own shadow. She remembered Kelile's advice: *You've got to step away from your own shadows.* But thought, *How do I do that? How important is strong? Do I have to face that question again?*

She resolved to have a session with Lacey as soon as possible, but with so many people around it would not be easy. She had a private back door to the trade staircase from the sixth floor; she'd use it. *Strong* and *shadows* needed some serious thought.

At her own apartment, Edith did not linger over her plan. She had the address, the door number, and she'd studied the photos. She slipped her oyster knife back into the blade sheath, dropped it into the pocket of her jeans, subconsciously patting the pocket – she had her friend. Kelile insisted he'd go with her as backup, and she acquiesced. She wanted to move while her Stalker was in residence. She would leave the Inspector out of this; petty theft was hardly something he needed to worry about. There was more serious crime about.

The Paymaster returned to the Stalker's home some forty minutes after Kelile's departure from the area. Camille's apartment had been easy to break into for the Stalker, and so in its turn was the Stalker's for the Paymaster. A shoulder to the door was all it took. He left the door a centimetre open to facilitate a quick exit if necessary. The Stalker was inside and alone.

"Now what?" she said.

"The third film," he said, "where is it?"

"Here, why? We haven't used it yet."

"Yes we did, days ago."

"It was raining so hard, how could I film? I've been waiting for you to re-schedule."

"You fucking idiot, I took the drugs, I was there, who cancelled? The analyst's expecting the film, he's holding my next session's money."

He felt a huge desire to humiliate her, attack her for all his own emotional psychosis. He could save the analyst the need to punish her, he'd do it himself. They could find another camera operator: who needed this unprofessional bitch? He'd warned her. The analyst might even pay him a reward. He, for one, had followed his orders, taken the damn cocktail of pills and followed all instructions, interacting with people in the rain.

He'd cable-tied her wrists behind her back before she had time to think of consequences.

"And?" she said

"First, some questions. That girl in the photo: where's her file?"

A blank stare from the Stalker.

"First question again." This time he stripped out his belt. He looped it around the top of her head as a tourniquet and twisted it tight. It was so tight her eyes started bulging and she felt a blankness that preceded the rush of pain. She tried to speak, but nothing came out. The Paymaster bent closer, and loosened the twist.

"Edith's… friend…" she said, and kneed him with her right knee flush in the face. She felt his nose give and then saw the blood spurt, first from one nostril and then from the other. He looked strange, mad and confused in the moment, and it dawned on the Stalker what he intended to do. She tried to knee him again, but he turned the tourniquet viciously and using it as a grip, slammed her head twice against the wall of photos. Dazed she lay on the floor, trying to shake her mind clear. Death was too close and there wasn't another option.

Co-operate, she thought, and with her hands behind her back she went into a foetal curl, lying on her left side.

The Paymaster took the Böker Kalashnikov knife from his pocket.

"Here's the final memory aid," he said, and shoved the black blade into the waist of her jeans. With one firm stroke he sliced the denim down the full length of her right leg and out through the hem, exposing the leg. The flesh already looked to him like part of a carcass. He clasped one hand over her mouth, and ran the blade hard right down her shin, gouging into the bone. Her body arched and sagged, and when she bit into his hand he slammed the blade through the top of her bare foot, just above the toes and deep into the floor; pinning it there. She vomited.

"Last time," he said. "Who is Edith?" She glanced over at the wall and he nodded, "And where does the violinist perform?"

She looked up at Edith's photos on the wall. Her head felt strange, and she mouthed, "I'll take you there."

He shook the knife in her foot, turning as he heard a noise on the landing outside her front door.

The building's main door on the roadside was open, and access would be easy. Edith and Kelile had approached with circumspection and purpose. He had explained that the apartments in the building seemed small, but not much smaller than hers. Edith told him she would go in, say her piece, get the CDs and leave.

"I'll come with you."

"No, let's not complicate issues."

"I understand," said Kelile, "but life isn't logical, it's complicated. I'll be right here, and if the curtain moves I'll be up. Have you thought this through?"

"I'll play it by ear."

"Not wise. Take a moment to think this through, visualise upstairs. What if there's more than one person there?"

"I'll ask for the CDs I lent her, and leave."

"Is this about attack or defence? What's your approach?"

"Attack."

"Physical or verbal?"

"I'm not sure."

"Be sure," said Kelile. "Being sure saves time and lives."

She looked at him and hesitated.

"Watch the curtain."

Once inside the building Edith had second thoughts about what Kelile had said. *He's right, I'm sure she's not sitting there waiting for my lecture.* She was comforted by her oyster knife; she could defend herself against any woman and most men – guns excluded. She had no prior knowledge of stalkers. *What the hell did they want?*

For a moment the air in the building seemed to freeze, Edith outside the door, the Paymaster inside.

The Paymaster inched closer to the door. He sensed a presence, but he wasn't in full control of himself. The Stalker lay still. She tried to scream, but nothing happened. She was scared of chasing the visitor away, and shut out the pain. The worst was the pain in her head, which felt smashed. She looked at the hilt of the knife, trying to focus, and heaved, but it hurt. The Paymaster looked back at the knife. *Stupid,* he thought, *I need it now,* and realised the belt in his hand would do. There was no explaining away this situation. He smeared the blood from his nose over his face as camouflage – the less identifiable the better.

Edith took a step closer and with the door a fraction ajar she went in, and took in the horror. The Paymaster took a step back, to entice her in further.

Attack, she thought.

"Hello Edith," he said, which stopped her, and in that instant he went for her. He was quick for a man of his bulk. He swung the belt in an arc, the buckle aimed at her head. She stepped into him and without hesitating threw a straight left jab at his broken face. In the second before the impact with his nose, she dropped her right shoulder and hip. Using all the power of her momentum, she plunged the oyster knife into his inner right thigh. When the guard hit flesh, she turned the blade as if opening an oyster, and twisted the guard plate down, deep into the wound. The buckle arched over her shoulder, glancing off her lower back with little damage. He went down on one knee and stifled a scream, his hands grabbing at the knife; it hurt. As Edith turned to continue the attack, he lurched up and out of the door, fleeing the scene.

Edith slammed the door shut and jammed a chair up against the handle.

"He's not coming back in here," she said to the comatose body on the floor.

She dialled Kelile on her mobile.

"The stalker's been attacked. The man is covered in blood, follow him. Be careful, when done, go to Camille's. I'm calling for help here… yes… fine."

She called the Inspector to send medics fast. She cut the Stalker's hands free, leaving the knife in her foot, and tried comforting her. The Stalker kept mumbling about a violin girl, and dry retching. Edith looked at the photos strewn across the wall, shocked that most were of herself. Two were of her and Camille in the café, and between those, an open space and pin where a photo had been. She stared in realisation at the blank space.

"You both," were the faint words of the girl.

"That'll be his last mistake," said Edith, which sounded like an echo to the Stalker, who was losing her battle for consciousness.

Kelile waited for the man, and when no one exited through the front of the building, ran up to apartment five, knocked on the door and called. Edith scanned the room without seeing CDs, and told him to check the bin downstairs. She would see him at Camille's. Downstairs he could see a splattering of blood. He avoided trampling them as best he could, and followed out the back door to the service yard. The man was gone. He searched and found waste bin number five, rummaged, and withdrew an envelope and box of CDs. He was away minutes before the Inspector, two or three of his team, and the ambulance crew arrived.

He'd failed to notice a curtain on the first floor shift, and had he done so would have caught a brief sighting of a bloodied face peer down at him.

27

The Inspector went up the stairs running, the same way as Kelile had, a few steps ahead of the medics, relieved that he had given Edith his contact number.

She's not the type to stand back, he thought.

The ambiguity of the patterns being woven around the murders made no sense to him; there were too many wheels within wheels. He was desperate for a connection. He had a strange feeling about Edith. At their meeting following Natalie's death, Edith had struck the Inspector as a girl he could climb mountains with, trusting she might feel the same way about him. He tried the door, spoke to her, and she let them in. The medics went straight to work.

Wise girl.

He had more time to survey the scene than Edith had, she'd locked it down, touched little and given help to the victim. He took his time, surveyed the photos, and the notes on the whiteboard.

"What happened in here?"

"I don't know. I came to confront this girl who I suspect has been following me around for weeks. She tried to break into my apartment –my system caught her on camera. I think she broke into Camille's too. The door was ajar when I arrived, a man had been beating her, he had a smashed face. He attacked me, then I hurt him, and he ran off."

"I saw blood on the staircase. Describe him."

"Tall, dark hair, big, like Michel. His face was covered in blood so it's difficult to describe. He said my name, but his voice wasn't clear. I stabbed him."

"Stabbed him? With what?"

"My oyster knife. I shucked oysters at Camille's home last night and I had it with me – his unlucky day." Edith described the knife with its short sturdy blade and steel guard plate.

"It stuck in his leg. It's sentimental and I want it back, my mother gave it to me."

The Inspector looked around the room, seeking patterns in the photos, asking Edith to explain them to him.

"They're taken from a fair distance," he said, "were you ever aware of her?"

"I sensed someone, wasn't aware of this woman in particular."

"Perhaps the stalker and the attacker were working together."

"Perhaps, but they don't seem to like each other. The bastard has removed a photo of Camille and me from that batch. I won't accept that."

"Yes, the famous violinist, the whole of Paris knows about her. You're out of your league here; he's left his mark, the girl will tell us more. Stay close to your friend; we'll have someone near. Watch your back. This seems all too professional."

The medics had stabilised and moved the Stalker to the ambulance. Edith left. Her body was shaking. She stopped at a bistro and ordered a shot of whisky with a coffee on the side, and attempted to think the incident through. She called

Kelile on his mobile. He asked how she was, told her to come to Camille's home, where he'd have another whisky ready.

"One's enough," said Edith.

Camille came on the line and said she had a surprise for her. Edith didn't need any more surprises. She paid her bill and crossed over the Seine.

The Inspector liked little about this; that Edith was safe was the only positive. The team started taking the scene apart piece by piece. The Stalker was identified as Catherine Peress. She was dispatched to a secure hospital where medics advised they expected her to be comatose for some while. The bleak feel of her apartment sent signals to the Inspector. He ordered one of the team to secure and check the bins, and to get first comments from the neighbours.

"There were two of them that went through the service area. The first one was limping, he went straight out onto the street. The second one came afterwards, he searched number *five's bin*, and then he also left," said one, "he looked like a foreigner."

The officer made notes, contacting as many tenants as possible; the doors to apartments two and eight remained closed, nobody at home. He logged a note to revisit them in a few hours. If the occupants were absent, there seemed little point. They could not have seen or heard the day's events.

The Inspector emptied the contents of the Stalker's file drawers, putting the paperwork to one side, while officer No.3 started stacking files. These files, together with the computer, were sent to head office for detailed examination. The walls were photographed extensively, and the photos taken down and sent in for reassembling. The Inspector's preliminary on-site examination revealed in-depth analysis of a few females, and a file on a male called the 'Paymaster'. They also discovered seven and a half thousand euros in cash, and enough camera equipment to support at least two photojournalists.

The Paymaster had fled to street level and instinctively went out into the building's central service area. He was in no state to go public. The pain from his puncture wound made his head throb. It was unusual as pain went, as if something inside him had become disconnected. She'd missed the artery, hit into the bone and ripped the flesh where she'd turned the blade. He needed pills, to regroup, and work the knife loose and staunch his wounds. A blood trail followed him and he slowed to a walk. At the trade exit on the street he paused to pinch and hold his nose to stop the blood. He looped around and back into the building's front entrance, just as Kelile knocked on the door upstairs. He avoided apartment one near the entrance, turning back to confirm there was no blood trail. He knocked on apartment number two.

When an elderly man opened the door, he pushed his way in. The Paymaster shut and locked the door, indicated for the couple inside to go to the kitchen and checked all four rooms. They were alone. Mr and Mrs Debauve stood and stared with blank faces at the bloody apparition that had come in from the heat, and neither of them said a word. He worked fast, gagged and tied them to their kitchen chairs, found the medicine cupboard, and took what he needed to the bathroom.

Inspector Vasseur gathered sufficient forces to work the neighbourhood. A big man covered in blood and limping would leave an impression somewhere. Street smokers, shopkeepers, café patrons, someone would have another piece of the picture. The direction in which he was heading would help. They had the blood samples en route to the lab. The word on the girl was not positive. She was in a shock-induced coma and the medical staff wanted to prolong that, to keep her on a ventilator. He confirmed a twenty-four hour police guard had been posted at her door.

The Inspector made the call: his team had tightened their guard on potential bridge-murder locations. He pulled two or three of his undercover team back from bridge patrol to HQ. He reassigned them to hunt and pursue duties on this new case. They needed to stop this sadistic bastard, who by a hair's breadth had failed to become a killer himself.

The Paris heat was getting to people. He requested the team leader meet him at his favourite café and brought along one of the Stalker's files. Unusually for the Inspector, they sat at an inside table. The Proprietor had seen this before. It heralded bad times. The Inspector took out his notebook and pencil and read through the file. There was nothing sinister in it: stalking without intent to do physical harm, lots of details, habits, movements. He ordered again, flipped through the notes and wrote a list:

The Connections: Michel, bakeries, Edith, stalker, photos, attacker, society, violinist, threat-letter, bridge killings, €100 notes, Berlin, limited edition, financial advisor, male killer, pre-dawn, symbol 7, Venus, Mars, Mercury.

He paused to phone HQ, and asked them to provide the violinist with a guard, and take notes of all the comings and goings from her apartment.

When his colleague arrived he said, "Talk to me. I'm missing something here."

"We hope for prints from the knife in her foot. He's a vicious bastard. The camera equipment seems excessive for a stalker. She was equipped to take video footage, but why?" said No.1. This was not a typical stalker's mode of operation.

"We're searching for the films she must have taken. They're not on her computer and there's no sign of her uploading them to the Internet, so they must be elsewhere. All she has are blank digital cards."

The Inspector opened the file again, and this time looked through the filming instructions she'd made, section by section. The word '*bridges*' stared out at him, and while he knew this was Paris, and thousands of people took pictures on the bridges every day, only one had their shin sliced open to the bone.

When he'd listened, he thanked his fellow officer and asked him to get someone to check the hospitals and clinics, and to put them on alert for inner thigh puncture wounds. The officer assured him that this had been actioned.

He then added to his list: *Murder team, dissension, missing photo, stalker files, blood trail, cash, links, film equipment?* He ringed *violinist, threat-letter* and *missing photo*, before writing *connections; interview Peress asap.*

He turned to the Proprietor.

"What was it you once said about a world of connections?"

"I said something like '*moments are all connected, the trick is to search for the integration*.'"

"That's it," said the Inspector, "*search for the integration*."

First the easy part, he thought, *a small circle within a few bigger ones*. He then began to draw a mind map linking sections randomly and adding thoughts as they occurred. *Who the hell was the Paymaster? Search for the integration.*

He surmised that if there were links, they were close to him. If it was random coincidence, they ceased becoming random once connected. What else lurked behind this strange facade? He thought about the coffee Society members – where was their bridge connection? A baker who knew two of the victims. He phoned the undercover surveillance man at Camille's block, informed him they were going to post a uniformed guard there, and assigned him to watch Michel. "I want to know his every movement."

His man reported that both girls and a foreign-looking man were currently upstairs in the apartment. Inspector Vasseur decided an uninvited visit was called for; he needed to set his instincts free in their company. He was also concerned by the intentions behind the missing photo. He would make that a priority question to the girl in the hospital, as soon as she could communicate.

The Proprietor placed a third cup next to the Inspector. He put a slice of rich chocolate cake on a white plate next to that, and the bill with a large red 'Paid' stamp across it.

Edith, her composure regained, stopped on the bridge on her way to Camille. She ignored any advice to watch her back, and took some time trying to understand the connection to the Society. This rogue virus in some way touched them all.

She walked down the steps from the bridge and onto the walkway that ran along the river, and had no reason to suspect a male on the bridge was photographing her. Her proximity to the water made her nostalgic. She phoned her father and told him she would email him that evening as life was currently complicated and she needed his input.

"Is it the coffee import?" he said

"No, and please don't involve mother, let's deal with this one ourselves first."

"It's difficult to wait till evening. Should I come to Paris now?"

"No, you'll just have to wait. I'll explain... everything is still under control."

When Edith arrived at the apartment, an ecstatic Camille greeted her, holding her box of CDs.

"You got them for me. I'm alive again. I'm so glad you're not hurt."

"So she'd binned them, I wonder why?" she asked Kelile.

"And we got this envelope as well."

Edith took the empty envelope from him while she hugged Camille, saying she was so happy for her.

"I looked for the man, followed his blood trail to the street and it stopped right there, by the pavement. Blood doesn't just stop like that, he must have climbed into a vehicle. There wasn't one outside a minute before. I checked her bin and left. About the envelope contents…"

The arrival of the Inspector caught them all off-guard.

"Camille, my congratulations on your newfound fame. I look forward to hearing you playing in person. Your security system is impressive. What else is new since our last talk?"

"Thanks, I've been learning about travel."

The Inspector introduced himself to Kelile and asked where he fitted into this happy gathering. He listened to Kelile's answer, liked the unwavering eye contact, and felt an unusual strength about the man.

Dignified and accomplished, he thought.

"I hear this establishment is famous for its coffee," he said, breaking the ice. "Michel told me all about it."

He accepted Kelile's offer of coffee, freshly ground and roasted.

"Only if you all join me of course, thank you."

The Inspector glanced at the empty addressed envelope Edith handed him, folded it and slotted it into his notebook. He thanked her and asked to inspect the box, which he studied.

"They are out of their sleeves," she said. "This is the index disc, which has been touched, by Camille, not by us. The rest are music, and the DVDs are live orchestra performances." He asked her how she knew they'd been handled, and accepted her explanation.

"I'm afraid I touched them, I've been busy making copies," said Camille.

"I'll need the index disc to check for prints of people other than yourselves," he said, "and the rest you can hang onto, they're compromised already. I promise you a copy of this one will be delivered back here tomorrow." He asked her to play him one of the others, saying, "We deserve that you preserve these works."

He warned them to report break-ins, and Camille said that she did not want more strangers wandering through her home. He said he was no longer a stranger and requested she show him where they were taken from.

"How did she know they were here?" he said
"No one in the world even knew they existed," she said
"And nothing else was taken?"
"No."
"Enough of business,"

They went downstairs. Vasseur went to the balcony, phoned an assistant, provided him with sufficient details to conduct an urgent background search on Kelile. The coffee was served in Ethiopian cups, a set of which had been presented to each of the Society members by Kelile on his arrival.

"I'm not expecting to be disappointed," said the Inspector as he bent down to test the aromas. He breathed in through his nostrils, holding the breath for a few seconds. He then released the air. Camille laughed, Kelile frowned, and they all found themselves leaning forward in empathy. Lifting the cup, the Inspector closed his eyes, and with a quietness usually reserved for after midnight, he took a long slow taste of Kelile's brew. They watched.

"Fantastic coffee," he said, "Extreme, in fact," and he tapped on the table three times. "What exactly is it?"

"A Society secret," said Edith.

The Inspector requested an application form for the Society, hoping to relax them, perhaps put them off guard. He confirmed he would submit the form as soon as this mess was sorted out, and asked that, if he was accepted, they call him Jean-Luc, but only during meetings. He then asked Kelile and Edith to join him on the balcony for a debrief, and listened as they went through the details. He appealed to Kelile to keep close to Camille, which he agreed to do for the next few days.

"For the sake of international relations," said the Inspector.

"Exactly."

The men shook hands; the Inspector then shook Edith's hand and bowed to Camille. He was looking forward to buying her music, whenever she decided to record it.

"I'm a vinyl collector," he said, "release vinyl versions. By the way, where is young Michel?" Without waiting for an answer he made his departure, telling his new man on watch to record the timings of all their coming and goings.

"Oh, I forgot, there was a feedback letter and invoice inside the envelope," said Kelile to Edith, "from a counselling analyst named Zuppin. I haven't looked at it yet, but it's on the side table."

"Zuppin," echoed Camille, staring out the window.

"We'll have a look," said Edith. "The Inspector has enough on his hands."

28

Swallowing a handful of painkillers from the bathroom cupboard, the Paymaster set about repairing his face. With limited resources, he stemmed the nosebleed with ice and paper towels, and turned attention to his leg.

Fucking girl knew what she was doing.

The puncture wound would have been a lot simpler had she not twisted the blade and left the knife wedged into the wound. It had missed the artery. Though the pain was intense it was bearable, and the bleeding had all but stopped. He worked the guard and blade loose from his skin, looked at the hole in disbelief and poured surgical spirits into it, gritting his teeth. Using a nylon stocking that had been drying on the towel rail he bound the wound. That would do for the present. He pocketed the knife – a lousy exchange for the one he'd left behind – and promised himself that he would give it back to the Edith character, blade first.

Having showered and dressed again, he checked the mirror and decided he looked like a street fighter, certain that no one would bother him.

Picking up the chair with the old man strapped in, he moved him to the entrance hall facing the front door. Without a word uttered he moved the old woman in her chair next to the old man. He tied the man's left wrist to the woman's right and re-secured their other hands to the chairs.

That will stop them tumbling over to make a noise.

In the kitchen he made himself three eggs, which he ate with bread, drank half a bottle of the wine he'd found open, and waited for darkness. With dusk, quietness had settled over the building and he returned to the couple with two plastic shopping bags. He placed these over their heads and bound them tight around their necks with tape. Neither of them moved.

"You've got two minutes of oxygen left," he said.

Collecting his jacket, he moved the chair from under the front door handle, opened and closed it, and was gone in under a minute. Night was about.

And now I'm a killer, he thought.

The Inspector sat outside the Proprietor's café at his habitual table.

That's more like it, the Proprietor thought as he ground fresh beans. Vasseur laid seven almonds out in a row and turned the third and seventh at right angles. He took out the photos he'd taken months ago from this table, and stared once more at the Stalker's right hand. It clutched a small camera held way down by her right thigh. Having taken three quick photos himself, he could see that she'd aimed and shot a picture in that split second. It was the same second his instincts had led him to press the shutter. Evidence indicated the Stalker had taken some of the photos on her wall.

Her camera's at the lab by now, he thought, and picked up his notebook to write. With a long slow breath he relaxed back into his seat.

"The usual," said the Proprietor, laying it on the metal top.

"And a beer," said the Inspector. "Today this looks a special coffee. I'll savour it with the respect it deserves. I've time for the beer afterwards to celebrate my day off. The team's hard at work."

"A beer? You must have met a woman."

"Yes, a fine woman. Bring two beers, we'll celebrate."

"Of course."

Ten minutes later the assistant arrived carrying a file and was not invited to join the table. He handed Inspector Vasseur a document with positive feedback. He reported that all seemed quiet on the bridges. The Inspector opened the incident file and read the various reports. When he read '*no answer from apartment numbers two and eight. Occupants of number two usually at home, except Sundays*', he knew Kelile's observation on the blood trail's sudden ending was on target.

Smart one, he thought, *dangerous bloody smart one.*

The Inspector phoned his officer No.1. "We still securing apartment five? Good, move an incident team there now, secure number two, back and front, don't go in, I'll meet you there."

"Hold the beers, I'll be back." he told the Proprietor.

Vasseur arrived a minute after the team. Following a brief discussion, they decided to breach the door, and go in fast and armed. They did.

The sight of the couple tied hand in hand and heads in plastic greeted them. The Inspector's worst fears were coming true. The team secured the rooms while the Inspector went to the bodies. "Evil shit," he said, "he's feral, very feral."

When the plastic heads turned towards each other, the room froze.

"Alive, get them off," announced the Inspector. "Childproof… call medics and counsellors."

An hour later, after tea, biscuits and gentle sedation, the Inspector said goodbye to the elderly couple and left them in good hands. The attacker had a few clear hours or more on them. He would be well away. As a precaution, Vasseur ordered a neighbourhood sweep and a guard on the apartment.

"Until we smoke these bastards out."

Officer No.3 took out his own notebook, a clone of the Inspector's, and wrote *'bastards'? perhaps more than one.* He decided to read all the files again. He wanted the title of Inspector one day, and he too wanted to read between the lines. He'd learnt that the Inspector shared only what he thought necessary to the investigation. He'd heard him say "too many minds blunt the edge" on more than one occasion, and that should he die, to "check my notebook".

The Inspector had made his way back to the Proprietor's café. The first Heinekens were consumed in silence, *to wash away doubts.* They lingered over a second before the Inspector turned his mind to the madness creeping ever closer to the Fourth Society.

"A cognac and one for you," he said, "Hennessy Paradis." Vasseur opened the notebook. Even in the quiet it was grounding to have the Proprietor sitting with him, chatting or not.

Camille gave Kelile a map of the area and declined his offer of a walk to clear heads. He went onto the balcony to clear his own, he would go out later. She stared at the phone and ignored its ring for the third time in as many hours. This time he wasn't there to prompt her and she did not have to offer an excuse. She decided that four was becoming her lucky number and would answer the fourth time it rang.

"Yes."

"Camille Laroche?"

"Yes."

The organisers of the Louvre charity gala were requesting her to play at their event and apologised for the short notice. They proposed a fee, and assured her the full co-operation from an alternate Parisian orchestra. They confirmed a thirty-minute appearance. It could be longer if she wanted. She would be the star attraction. Camille asked for time to discuss it with her management team, thanked them for their interest and insisted that if she accepted her fee was to go to their charity.

"We'll reserve you a table for four," he added.

"Amazing, thank you."

A few minutes later the phone rang again and a Chicago-based organisation proposed a USA tour.

"I'm rehearsing for my Paris show," she said, "my time is tight, thanks for your interest." She gave them Edith's email address and asked them to leave the details with her. She then took the phone off the hook, deciding Edith would be the first person she'd share the news with.

After the call, Camille went upstairs, chose the Lorenzo Storioni violin and, for the first time in her apartment, played with an open heart. None of the neighbours complained. Having played, she called Edith on her mobile and asked to meet.

"Here, please."

Was that a 'please'? thought Edith. *Progress.*

The Paymaster tried to shake the sense of doom with tablets, swallowing those the analyst had told him to hold back for the next experiment.

Too bad, I'm not an experiment, I want them now. He decided to chase the handful with vodka, it always helped. He took out Camille's photo and his newspaper clippings.

She's perfect for me, no one else deserves her, and if I can't have her...

He could take her back to Zurich where they could be completely alone, no one to disturb them, or even better, to a different continent where he wasn't known by anyone. He decided to test his feelings first.

He located her address, which he'd written into the back page of his poetry book, and found himself walking through the bustling streets to the Marais. The drugs masked the pain. The air looked clear and felt calm. He reached for his knife, which was gone, and felt that deep anger rising up. He hated most women, why should this one be any different? He especially hated Edith.

Sensing Camille needed space to herself, Kelile decided on a random tasting of Parisian coffee, and left for that 'walk'. Camille had many decisions facing her. They'd talked of obsessive behaviour and her music at length. She told him that as long as she took a violin with her, it acted as a talisman and gave her courage. At last she felt positive that she'd beaten the phobia. The belief of loyal friends and the crossing of borders seemed to have shaken her through it.

She knew it was time to revisit Lacey and ponder closure therapy; time to set new rules and targets. She waved goodbye as he prepared to leave. She had scheduled another violin practice upstairs.

"For the neighbours."

The Paymaster found the building once again and went up to the fifth floor; it was all too easy. He felt strange, vacillating between ecstasy and rage. The air swirling up the staircase was ominous, a hot breath where none should have been. He had signed the guard book as 'delivery service'. He'd ask Camille for Edith's address. He felt for his pocket-poet book, he'd write it somewhere in there. There was unfinished business with Edith. Her days were numbered.

29

Edith could not escape the mental image of Camille's photograph in the hands of the monster she'd encountered at the Stalker's apartment. She walked home via a different route from the one that was her custom, and the sight of Kelile sitting at a pavement table took time to register. His firm wave snapped her back to the present and she joined him for a coffee.

"Tourist in Paris?"

"A concerned tourist," he said, adamant that she voiced her concerns to the Inspector.

"The Inspector cautioned me to leave it in the hands of professionals, but my instincts drive me to do something about it."

"Err on the side of caution, I prefer you in one piece.

The call from Edith took the Inspector by surprise. They agreed to meet at La Mosquée on the Left Bank where they spent a few minutes together.

"We're working your description on both banks, and the entire area from the third arrondissement to the sixth, and all hospitals and clinics. The man who attacked you faces the further charges of the attempted murders of the old couple. He'll surface. We need to ensure his strange interest in that photo doesn't make you or Camille the next victim. He may be the person behind the threat letter to Camille, and now has a score to settle with you. We'll pin him down, we'll get him."

"And the bridge murders?" said Edith

"That's another matter completely," said Vasseur. "We have a large team on that case. Our communities all want a result by yesterday, and I can't blame them."

She left satisfied the Inspector was handling the case.

The Paymaster remained lost in limbo. The capsules he'd swallowed were a random choice. There was no way to predict the outcome. The explanations of the analyst had long gone out the other ear. The analyst had called his mobile three times in the last hour and was disturbed by the lack of response. The Paymaster had no way of knowing that concern, and would not have cared in any case. The daily papers had reported the vicious attack on Catherine Peress who was now in intensive care. Analyst Zuppin had stayed away from his own rooms as a precaution, sending the Receptionist to a nearby café to watch the entrance. He was unsure of the Stalker's state of health, and concerned at what she was telling the police. He had no time for the law, except to be one or two steps ahead of them.

There seemed no limit to the speed at which the days rolled by, and it was soon apparent to Camille that she needed to share her Louvre concert ideas with people who cared about her. The team were the only ones who fitted that bill. After practice, she opened a bottle of sparkling water, poured a half glass and sat to wait for their arrival. One of her own CDs was playing, and for the first time she felt a sense of pride in the music. She refilled her glass, and added sliced lime.

The music from Camille's apartment kept the Paymaster pinned by the door; it was hypnotising, and he was oblivious to the new cameras recording him. His hoodie hid most of his features, and cameras or no cameras his identity would not be compromised. His emotions were racing between anger, compassion, and a meld of the two. This Camille person hungered for him. It was in the pictures, that faraway look, wanting to be somewhere else. He knocked on the door, just once, and by instinct his hand went to his knife, his new purchase – the damn Stalker had the other one.

What a waste of a good knife that was, he thought, and hoped that maniac friend of hers was not here visiting. Too bad for her if she was.

Camille didn't hear the knock. She was lost in the moment, thinking about the music she was to play at the concert, and the support musicians for each piece. She looked forward to the rehearsals almost as much as the concert. If ever there was a live test on the originality of her work, the rehearsals were it. She prayed that none of the musicians would ever relate her music to movements from other works.

The true test, she thought, *it had to come.*

Footsteps echoing up the block's main stairwell took some time to penetrate through the Paymaster's focus, and followed hard after his second knock. His reaction kicked in, and he froze a moment before coming eye-to-eye with the Spaniards for the second time. Marko was carrying the violin in its case.

"You again? A delivery?" said the Paymaster, before squeezing past the Spaniards and going down the stairwell. These kids had guns.

Camille answered the door, even checking the monitor before opening.

"I'm glad it's you," said Camille, "I needed to thank you."

"No need. There was that man here at your door," said the sister, "he said 'delivery'. He left nothing. The same creep pulled a knife on us when we came to bring you the violin weeks ago, before I knew you were away."

"There's lots of creeps around, I'm learning that," said Camille.

"We found the violin at a pawn shop, we stole it back," said Marko, "my sister said it's what you do, a busker."

"Something like that. I love this violin. You didn't steal it, you repossessed it."

"Rock music is great," said the sister, "Marko is an artist."

"What art?"

"He can tell you."

"Well, tell me all about it."

"I shot her cat," said Marko

"Why'd you tell her that?" asked the sister.

"It just came out, I can sense the cat in here."

"There's no cat here. We all say strange things," said Camille, "especially me."

Marko told Camille about his art, his passion for graphite, the feel of his pencils as they followed his thoughts. He told her what he saw, he could sketch. He preferred more simple lines that burst with the look of what he wanted. Camille leaned forward to hear each word. Marko had moved into her shadow, and she was aware of her own distant thoughts reflecting back at her, with more strength than she could have imagined. They talked for hours, and Marko's sister was amazed she'd heard none of this from her brother before.

"Are you that interested?" he said.

"Totally."

"You never said."

"I thought you knew."

"Will you draw my cat? I need to see him. He speaks to me, like a voice inside."

"What's he tell you?"

"Stuff."

"What's your name?" asked Camille.

"Danna."

"What's it mean?"

"No one can judge me."

"Not quite," said Marko.

Camille heard more about street life in Paris from the Spanish than she'd ever heard before, it began filling in tiny pieces of her lost youth. She asked to take them to lunch as a thank you.

"I already said, no need. I'm starving, so yes, if we can show you the city one day," said Danna.

Kelile spoke to the police guard outside Camille's apartment. One delivery man and two kids had signed in; the kids had a violin in a case. The guard had checked that.

"There's the delivery man leaving," said the police guard.

He saw the limp, insisted the guard call Inspector Vasseur, and kept his eye on the disappearing figure.

"Yes, follow," said Vasseur, "but don't interact with him except self-defence. Warn Camille to lock herself in."

Kelile told the guard to contact Camille, and went after the man as he limped towards the Seine. Closing in on the unsuspecting Paymaster, he slowed to a suitable trailing distance.

The untouched tartelette au citron put Michel in a fine mood, relaxed, contemplating his new life. He ordered a crème to go with it. The call to Edith seemed a natural extension.

"Lets talk about business, I have ideas."

"When?"

"Now."

"I'm on my way to Camille's apartment. I'll come and have a quick chat on the way."

"The pastries are first class, I'll order more." said Michel.

"Good habit, thanks."

His proposal made more than sense to Edith. He had space in the Pâtisserie-Café for a glass-walled *coffee-roasting room,* in full view of the customers. If Edith wanted to run her roaster there as an interesting sideshow for customers, she could use it rent-free. He'd install industrial extractors and she could roast, pack and supply from the glasshouse. He showed her plans. They'd sell 500-gram packets of fresh roasted beans to his café clients, as well as use them for the in-house coffees.

"It's a generous offer, I accept. I'll train a roaster to put on a show."

"Deal done, then," said Michel. "Strictly business."

"Does business have to be so strict?" she laughed, and Michel kicked himself.

Kelile watched the Paymaster go into the building and exit a few minutes later, having changed shoes, and wearing a different leather jacket. He carried a backpack that looked well stuffed. The Paymaster had decided it was a good time to move his cash stack to safer quarters. *Stay one step ahead.* He would return for the rest of his things, especially his photo of Camille, which he'd washed free of blood after the attack, and was not yet dry. He'd leave it until his return. *Better safe than sorry.* He'd carry his now scarred poetry book with him. He had seen a guesthouse that looked innocuous. It would do at short notice.

This must be his home, thought Kelile, and realised he was not the only one watching the Paymaster. There was another who had been there before they'd arrived, and though the other man had his back to Kelile, his interest in the Paymaster was obvious. This one was shorter and older than the Paymaster, and Kelile knew it was not his place to interfere. This was France, not Ethiopia.

He watched the Paymaster go towards Saint-Germain-des-Prés, and made his own way back towards Camille's. Not for the first time he wondered what he was doing here in Paris.

At this moment Addis seemed a long way away, and he was all the more nostalgic for it. The original call from Camille had nothing to do with this maniac who'd attacked Edith. Nonetheless he'd decided to stay for her concert, and stay he would. He called the Inspector and gave him the address of what seemed to be the man's residence. The Paris police would have to do their job; the Inspector seemed capable. He had his own family and his own business waiting in Addis.

The analyst Zuppin had not spotted Kelile outside the Paymaster's lodgings, and by some miracle had himself not been noticed by the Paymaster. Hiding outside the lodgings ten minutes or so later he watched the Paymaster depart. After waiting five more minutes, the analyst messaged to warn the Paymaster that he'd attempted to visit, to discuss the Stalker, only to discover a police raid taking place.

That will keep him at bay for the time I need, he thought.

After the call the analyst gloved up and went inside, broke into the lodgings, stripped the place of documents and pills. He pocketed the oyster knife, which lay on the rickety bedside table, and after a moment's hesitation took the photo and clippings of Camille. The analyst loved classical music and this was the violinist who was getting all the coverage. He felt she had a strange familiarity about her. He was out of the lodgings within five minutes, and called the Receptionist who gave him the all-clear at the consulting rooms. He went back to shred the files.

Staring at the picture of Camille, he wondered how tall she was, and decided the photo was a keeper. He felt an unusual melancholy wash over him. Perhaps it was time to leave Paris for a while, let all the mess settle down. It would give him time to re-evaluate the project, to think of another way to tackle it. The money from the pills and films was coming in thick and fast, and he had a lot more stock to sell. He'd stick it out a bit longer. He needed to replace the Stalker; there were many sordid experiments still in the pipeline.

The people, always the people let me down.

He asked the Receptionist to get two tickets to the charity gala at any price and resolved to treat them both to a royal night out. *We've spent too much time here,* he thought. He would take the Receptionist with him when he moved on. She fitted the bill. Perhaps to Cannes, London, or Moscow? Somewhere interesting with clients loitering on every street corner. First he needed to tidy the mess of the Stalker. It would be no more 'Zuppin' for him, back to the letter A, perhaps a name like 'Audran'. Analyst Audran. That had a good ring to it, or perhaps he could do more investment advising. It was quick and easy money.

The glass of wine in Camille's hand seemed as natural to Kelile as a cup of coffee was in Ethiopia. *Part of the culture here,* he thought, *live and let live.*

He contacted the airline and confirmed the flight home.

"Oh," said Camille, "that's sad."

"My business with Edith is almost done, my family need me home. You are doing well by yourself. You're so busy, and after Edith and Michel's opening I'll go home."

He admired her absence of nerves for the coming performance, and told her he was surprised she wasn't apprehensive.

"I've been practising since I was seven years old," she said, "I'm happy I've scored my favourite music first."

Kelile wished he were as relaxed as she was with everything going on about them. She'd even spurned Michel's offer of a lift to the concert on the night.

After Edith's arrival at the apartment, they discussed their concerns over threats received, but Camille shrugged them off.

"I always walk to and from concerts. It clears my head, prepares me. I like the sounds of the streets."

"And if it's raining?" said Edith.

"I walk, and I'm not changing my rituals now, you should know that. I got rid of my one major fear, and I'm not going to take on more."

"There are times for caution," said Kelile. "This seems one of them."

"It doesn't worry me," Camille said, "I'm not a stalker, you and Edith are here. He can get as many pictures as he wants from the newspapers anyway. What's the issue? He might like my music."

"If he sent the threat letter, it was before your music was on the Net." said Edith.

"Maybe he came to concerts like Michel."

"Do you know a Zuppin?"

"Lacey does," said Camille, "He's a therapist. I think the girl who stole the CDs must be his patient, after all, she got that invoice."

Disappointed by their concerns, which she felt exaggerated, she used the concert excuse to go upstairs to practise. Again she shut the stairway door, which perturbed Kelile, whose request to join her had been refused.

"Then practise down here," Kelile had said, "I'd love to watch."

"Thanks," she said, "I need to do this part alone."

Camille laid her violins out on the bed and chose. The seventeenth century Roggerius would do well. She stowed it in its case and returned the others to their resting places. She selected a compilation CD of her shorter works and set the player to repeat mode. She put on her black hoodie, and went out the back exit. In the bistro she sat at what she now considered *her* seat, violin case at her feet.

"Will you play for me one day?" said her bistro friend.

"I think I'd love that."

"Then today the wine will be on me, and we'll feed you like a queen."

"Are you expecting anyone?"

"The usual: Lacey," she said.

"Then I'll leave a place set. Does she drink wine?"

"You know she does."

Camille thought about Kelile's leaving, it was days away now and his company had been a huge comfort, much like the guard at the Addis hotel. Kelile must have thought her crazy having no time to talk, but how could she explain that? She hoped Edith would be her official advisor and move into the apartment – that would help, that would be a simple way to integrate into the world. Ethiopia had been uncomplicated, she could manage the same here in Paris. Had her obsession masked other issues? Perhaps she had a touch of something else? The anxiety-therapy manual might explain all that. She drank more wine and ate the food, forcing herself to think through the alternatives. The wine helped for certain; solutions presented themselves at times like these.

"Thanks, the food was special."

"And Lacey?"

"Oh she's been and gone, goodbye."

Her friend looked at her as she walked away, and shook his head.

Touched, a little bit touched, the Marais madness.

Camille walked along Avenue Victoria before deciding she'd take a new route home, and hesitated when she realised that the way ahead was wide. The trees dominating both sides of the avenue lifted her gaze above the greenery. She discovered she could see into the far distance in Paris. Even here on street level, the view stretched much further than from her apartment windows. Looking down this street was not restrictive; it brought back memories of Addis. From her hotel she could see for miles, deep into the everyday lives of the people living in the area. Addis was not her city. While Edith had warmed to Addis, Camille knew her roots were tied to these streets. She needed to know them so much better; they were an extension of her home. She could walk around the pavement tables of Paris with a smile, step into the street if necessary. That would annoy her in Addis, at almost any time of the day or night.

She focused on the lamp posts and their lamps, all unlit in the sunlight, and they beckoned her in a mysterious way, called her to walk into the future. The doors at street level that she passed seemed so haggard, so inviting. She'd need to open some of these doors, go down a few of the half-hidden passageways, explore this new Paris. Perhaps she would ask Marko and his sister Danna to come with her. Fate told her there was a need to be brave, and she longed for a moment of bravery. It would guide her to freedom, as the shapes of these lights guided her home, one by one, and Camille wondered what new excitement awaited her back at the apartment.

30

The Paymaster knew the police raid had upped the ante and given away far more of his personal details than he cared for. He was not scared of the challenge presented – he knew he would have to change his habitat and identity as many times as needed. There was no way he was going to get himself arrested for attacking the Stalker, and for killing the old people. He had other plans for his future life. At present he was working on instinct. He was reliant on no one and he had enough cash for the time being. He could react in a heartbeat, keep moving, and keep ahead of the law. They'd have to play catch-up. He'd arranged his possessions so the next move would be simple – lift his bag and go. He'd purchased an innocuous black canvass holdall, and his important things fitted into it, with room to spare.

He made a list of everything left in his old lodgings that might compromise his ID. On reflection much of it would incriminate the analyst. Especially the instructions on the psychotropic drugs, whose testing he knew was illegal. He wanted his photo of the violinist – with the girl who'd attacked him – and her damn knife. Those would confirm his link to the assault at the Stalker's home He wondered if they'd discovered the old people's deaths.

Calling the hospital, claiming to be family, he was advised to his relief the Stalker was comatose. He knew the violinist's friend would find it difficult to describe him; he was covered in blood at the time. At least he'd the foresight to shift his cash and identity documents. He was almost home free. If it weren't for his violin girl, he'd be long gone already.

The Inspector was fishing for information, and had little to pinpoint the whereabouts of the Paymaster. He sent an advance team into the building who found nothing of particular use, although they took more DNA samples. The sight of the Cardinal beers in the fridge made them thirsty – the weather in Paris was hot. They left them untouched; they had sufficient prints already, and advised the Inspector. The prints would be clear. The team set up a strong presence around the lodging to ensnare the man on his return; unaware the analyst had come and gone beforehand. The police launched the visible raid the following morning when it seemed their man had fled. The attempt to trap him had failed. Unknown to the Paymaster, the raid had not been successful; the analyst had done an expert job of clearing the decks long before the police went in.

Two vodkas helped the Paymaster. He was annoyed he had not taken all the pills with him, along with the cash. He would stock up on his next visit to the rooms. He needed the analyst only for pills and cash, and certainly not therapy. A raid on the analyst's rooms was an option, but if there was no cash that meant trouble, and he would have burnt his bridges.

Breaking into the clinic and getting out of the EU would be a wiser option than staying around; better to start a new life. Galvanised by that thought and the many others rotating through his mind, he decided on action. He first visited a barber and had his head shaved clean. He booked an extended session at a tattoo parlour, explained what he wanted and went next door to the bistro. He needed to eat and pass time while they prepared. If he was going to South America, he should toughen his act, eat more, drink more, and change his appearance. Perhaps that would help the shooting pains in his head and the depression that engulfed him. He ordered two more pork chops, more sautéed potatoes and two beers to wash them down, and waited.

He was called for his session. As the hours ticked by his snake design came alive, mouth gaping, with fangs beneath his left ear. It wrapped once around his neck and the tail slithered over his right shoulder and onto his back. As the snake-man he felt better, stronger than the Paymaster. He felt the future getting closer. With day well smothered by night, he looked in the mirror, nodded, and counted out the cash in high-denomination euros. He wrapped his blue and brown Krama scarf around the dressing on his neck, and left the parlour.

The long hours under needle had helped him relax, and he proceeded with the plan he'd developed during the time. As the next business day woke, he booked two one-way tickets on Air France to El Dorado International in Bogotá, Colombia. There was a stopover in Barcelona, and he thought that if he failed to bond with the violin girl he'd get off there. Her surname eluded him so he used his: Meyer. That part completed, all that was left was for him to tell her, and to control that faraway look she wore. He'd visualised their escape together, and in the visualisation things worked out the way he planned. She would be relieved, she was a genius like he was. They needed to move to better towns and new beginnings. If she refused, he'd have no option but to deal with her, then kill himself: *double suicide,* he thought. She'd appreciate the touch, the clarity.

Sitting in the living room, Kelile grew concerned over Camille's many disappearances to her private quarters. He fielded two or three phone calls from interested press and music people, and gave the answer she'd requested – "…in a meeting, please email details…" – a response she'd learnt from her ex-orchestra committee. Kelile had visited Paris earlier than intended, a result of her plea, yet in Paris she was too busy to engage. She had issues, and it was not his place to delve into them. He was an acquaintance, Edith was her best friend, and Edith was by far the more sociable of the two girls. He decided to go and join Edith, left Camille a note, and went out.

Her two scheduled works and a potential encore for the concert had occupied much of Camille's thoughts these last days, and she played the pieces over and over. The old fear rose inside her midway through the playing, but each time she soldiered on to the finish. She was finally playing the works of Camille Laroche.

This time was reality; this time she was going public. At the slightest suggestion of plagiarism she would destroy all her work, she would have to flee somewhere. The thought had tempted her in the doubtful moments since the concert offer; escape might be the best solution. She could go back to the hotel room in Addis and contact the guard once more. That would be a bold solution, or go somewhere else, east or west, and disappear forever. Make the odd request to the investment fund. They had assured her that there were enough funds for her lifetime. She stopped herself – this was not the solution. She needed to purge thoughts of *Kovchenko* once and for all.

It was all action at the pâtisserie-café. After weeks on the project, workmen were putting the finishing touches to the site, which lent the décor a simple, yet traditional, quality. The equipment tests were underway in the kitchens, and final adjustments had been completed in the coffee roasting room. Michel's mother was there to lend a hand, pleased to meet his new acquaintances. Kelile went straight to the glass-walled roasting room and rechecked the extraction equipment and the '*master roast controls*', as he called them. These he used to set and adjust temperature and timings for accuracy and roast consistency. The first major roast was undertaken, which he monitored. A few seconds were often the difference between success and disappointment. Once the roast was completed and the beans were cooling, there were demands to test the result.

"Far too soon," said Kelile, "perhaps in one to two hours."

As usual, visits from Inspector Vasseur were unannounced, and his visit to the renovations was no exception. Once he'd left, Michel's mother described him as "utterly charming, a solid and good man".

"I hope so," Kelile said, "he protects your streets."

The Paymaster had every reason to shift lodgings for the second time in days. The whores at the guesthouse were no real problem, he could deal with them, but he'd spotted sketches of his old self being shown around the neighbourhood. Sooner or later they would happen upon the barber or tattoo parlour. He decided a French beret would help. He purchased two or three more Cambodian Krama scarves, and a new dark jacket. With money in his pocket he entered a bar a hundred metres away, looking different from the man who'd sat there an hour earlier. An hour or two later, he returned to the guesthouse with the jacket, more hats, two more hoodies and a long summer coat.

While hunting new lodgings in the area, he switched from the Left Bank to the Right Bank. He secured a room down an alley with a window giving him clear sight of the entrance, and another window, which doubled as a back exit. The red curtains were a bit ominous, but he'd be out of there soon enough. As a tourist from Hamburg, he paid for the new lodgings up front in cash for six nights, before returning to the guesthouse to collect his shopping bags and other belongings. The cash was stuffed into the holdall again, and things no longer needed dumped in a bin two blocks away.

He deserted the guesthouse with a night in credit, knowing they'd soon have new guests in the room to cover any of his traces. He'd kept the whores at bay, and smiled. He regretted his actions killing the old couple. Murder would keep the police on his trail; assault was one thing, killing was another.

Camille sat in the bistro in the Rue des Lavandières and waited for her therapy. She put her head in her hands, made a conscious effort to slow her breathing, and waited. Her 'friend' as she called him had seen this all before, many times, and went to choose her wine. That was the first need. Food could come later. Camille intended to work through *Red Winds* in her mind, note by note, in anticipation. She thought she sensed the start of an anxiety spell creeping upon her, so willed it away. Looking up, she ordered. "The usual, please."

Her friend nodded and she thanked him.

"And food with your wine?"

"You choose for me."

"And are you expecting anyone?"

"Yes, always, that's why I'm here."

He paused and nodded, thinking *still touched poor girl, so sad.*

"Of course, shall we start to prepare your food, we can serve it when it's ready… at its best?"

"Yes, thanks," said Camille, before getting lost in her music. The wine was of exceptional quality, and the food cooked with the greatest care and talent.

Three hours later, relieved and confident, Camille walked straight up to the police guard, filled in the book, and strode on into her apartment block. Not having seen her go out, the guard considered the situation and decided that the best action was no action. She was home, and secure. He checked the note in the logbook, which showed the time of her entry. Under the 'From' column, she had written 'Rue des Lavandières'. Two hours later there was shift change, and the matter was not mentioned.

Camille, finding Kelile had not returned, decided to map the best route to the designated Louvre musicians' entrance for her concert day walk. She needed to check the approximate time it would take. There could be no mishaps on the night, and as her father had said, "To walk is the finest ritual Paris has to offer, together with an abundance of food, wine and ambiance of life." She understood parts of that. It was time to enjoy listening to some music at home, later she could go out the back way, carrying a violin case.

She laughed. She was becoming skilled at going out onto the streets; they felt welcoming.

<h1 style="text-align:center">31</h1>

There was a vitality and new sense of purpose about Michel. He seemed to be everywhere at once, discussing the alterations and lending a hand to the workmen where needed, all getting ready for the opening evening. He'd arranged the event a few days after Camille's concert, not wishing to detract from her moment.

The Inspector watched the way Michel acted and moved. It had been many weeks since the third bridge murder and there was a need to revisit all lines of enquiry, to search for a chink in the killer's armour.

What if the murders were paid hits? thought the Inspector, the profilers agreeing with the possibility of that contention. *If the third killing did not go according to plan, would the killer change routines? What then?*

The bakery connection had regained momentum. The team had uncovered an article written by journalist Brisette a month before her murder. Entitled *Baking: the Art of Dying*, the article outlined the slow death of fine baking in France. Inspector Vasseur needed to halt the killer. Why Michel might object to the article made little sense, surmised the Inspector. Michel should have lauded it. Many a death occurred through misguided principles, and many more would continue to. He took out his notebook and reread the account of Camille and Michel's meeting, resolving to spend time chatting to Michel's mother. She gave the impression of being old school, wise and solid. He wondered how she viewed her son.

"A man of principles," she said, "bakes like his father and lives for it, not too much time for the right girls yet." While the comments gave no direct inkling of darkness, the word 'principles' rang an alarm in the Inspector's mind. He decided to interview Michel about the journalist's article and her death. It coincided with his brief trip back from Ethiopia. His mother's comment on the subject of her evening with Michel raised a flag: "... then he went out gallivanting." Vasseur decided a few stiff drinks with Michel might well peel back layers and open the doors to his movements after that dinner.

The Paymaster was relieved the electric spasms in his head, withdrawal symptoms from the earlier psychotropic drugs, were dulled by this new batch of pills. These drugs acted in unusual ways. He'd given up taking them in the order the analyst had prescribed. What the fuck did that idiot know? In any case, what was the 'to be taken with water after meals' shit? *With vodka and beer 'when you feel like it'* made more sense. He might visit the clinic again if the shocks came back, but he feared he'd blown his arrangement with the analyst. If the violinist insisted they kill themselves, rather than fly to Colombia, the shocks in his head wouldn't matter one way or another. Perhaps he should force her to kill him first, as his show of faith. He trusted her. They'd need to find a clear moon for that. He wanted a moon.

He'd seen the press concerning the gala and her quirk of walking to concerts. She had his permission to play this concert; he'd changed his mind. Edith was the new target. Edith had to die, and soon. He'd let Camille know about that in a note he'd deliver with her air ticket, to put her mind at ease. Crossing the bridge, he traversed the streets from Rue de Rivoli up to the Marais, working backwards from the Louvre to Camille's apartment. He'd avoid the police guard, and would need luck to predict her exact route, but he was a lucky man. There were too many possibilities to leave to guesswork. He purchased a tourist map and pencil, and sat for half an hour at a café working out the potential routes from Camille's apartment to the gallery. He was uncertain which entrance she would use so he took a guess. Despite not tasting the coffee in front of him, the slight caffeine jolt seemed to trigger the pills, and things became a lot simpler. The words he'd use to explain their South American trip to her came to him and, as in his dreams, there were natural links between disconnections. She was a genius; she would be able to connect it all. Of course she'd understand. She'd be relieved at meeting him, applaud his boldness. It was all so simple. Had the Paymaster been facing the reflective glass of the café, he would have been surprised by the smile on his face. That smile had been missing these past few years. Satisfied things were going his way, he ordered a second coffee and hoped to remember to taste this one.

In Marseillan, Edith's father's support was as expected. They'd discussed the threats to Camille in detail.

"Psycho," said her father, "the worst type, unpredictable and cruel. You did right by your friend, but call the law, that's why we have them. Help where you can, but please be most careful. Keep in touch."

In the early morning Edith went to the sea, and swam out into the waves. She valued her long swim on the coast, embracing the water she'd missed for so long. At family dinner that night her grandmother held court with stories none of them had heard, and Edith felt their strong familial bond strengthen further. Her heart went out to Camille, considering her lonely childhood. She resolved to be an even better friend, to try to get close to her and stay that way. She would return from her lightning-quick trip in top spirits.

The clients attending the Louvre gala arrived in Paris and Edith met them in good time, escorting the wives on a tour of the more fashionable couture houses. They were disappointed she would not be at their table, understanding her wish to sit with her friend, the star of the night. She made a promise to introduce Camille to them. Edith was impressed that a grand institution such as the Louvre set so fine an example by housing an event such as this. It represented France at its finest, and she made a mental note to put her feelings in writing.

Michel had arranged the car and driver for Camille's guests, and gave instructions for champagne on ice in the limousine. The pâtisserie-café venture, 'les Amis de Michel', was less than a week away from opening. With all on track, Michel and Kelile returned to the apartment to offer Camille moral support. Signing the apartment police logbook, Kelile noticed a reference to Camille's return a few hours earlier. He realised he must have been at the apartment when Camille had left; somehow unaware she'd slipped out. He expressed the concern to Michel who said, "Well she's a big girl and we've been through this with her before."

The reference continued to nag at Kelile, and he vowed to broach the subject with her once more. These were dangerous times. Unable to attract her attention, they ventured upstairs to her suite and discovered the classical music haven. The upstairs shed a new light on Camille, and reflected a mindset different from that which she had created on the floor below, with its mishmash of style and clutter. Kelile also noted the exit door, and his instincts told him to keep that information to himself.

"She's gone again," he said.

"Perhaps rehearsals," said Michel, "or that walk to the Louvre she's been threatening."

They decided to look for her, and Michel, a son of Paris, knew her likely route.

As the second coffee was presented to the Paymaster, his eyes lazed over the strollers-by and he was shocked to glimpse what looked like Camille. Violin case in hand, the girl was some thirty metres beyond the café, heading in the direction of the Louvre. He hesitated a second, deciding to leave money for the coffees rather than risk a ruckus. He slipped a €100 bill under the cup and left, mind bursting to recall the chosen words, but his memory remained blank.

In that moment she'd turned into a shop, delaying their meeting. She was only in the shop for five minutes, which was more than enough time for the Paymaster to have passed in pursuit. When he reached the first section of the gallery without seeing her, he decided to retrace his steps. He was furious she'd evaded him.

Camille enjoyed the walk, relieved that her works had been lauded at rehearsals. There were no indications of plagiarism in press articles concerning her two videos. Quite the opposite; all of them were praising the originality. She felt vindicated, and decided to abandon her search. Her practised repertoire would need to increase if this concert proved a success. Judging by the viewing numbers of the Internet clips, genuine interest was gaining momentum.

The supporting musicians had appreciated the work. The conductor, not known for compliments, marvelled at the 'defined complexity'. He offered her introductions to the classical music world, people she was in awe of. "She has a vast treasure trove," he later remarked to associates.

Ten minutes into their search, Michel was slowing down. Kelile moved ahead. Whether hunter or the hunted, Kelile's instincts remained sharp. While he only knew the vague direction of the Louvre, he felt confident. He had no idea when Camille had left the apartment. She had failed to sign out again, and only if she were at further rehearsals would he assume her safe.

During his army days in the mountains bordering Ethiopia and Eritrea, he had trained his peripheral vision to search the extremes. This ability had been of significant value on occasions. His wide-angle sight was greater than that of the average person. It took a second or two for the man in the beret and the chequered Krama scarf to sound Kelile's warning bells. The man had changed his appearance. The bearing, walk and facial features were enough for Kelile to identify him. It was better to follow the attacker then to search for Camille. This way he had her threat in his sights and she was safe.

He paused and re-confirmed the sighting. The limp, though reduced, was still there. Kelile wished he'd brought his camera; the man's new guise needed circulating. His mobile's camera would have to do. It would at least give Vasseur's team some idea. He couldn't apprehend the man – that had been made clear, so Kelile took four photos while following. He sensed a new tension in the man's bearing and glanced down at the man's hands. They were empty, not armed, and he decided to remain tight on him.

I'm following in the footsteps of death, he thought.

The Paymaster was focused. He'd pictured Camille in black, violin case in hand, strolling down the street with her trademark tense expression. It took a few seconds to react to this smiling girl, who did not match up to expectation. Words, he was thinking of what words he might say to her, and with a morbid sense of acceptance he made a snap decision to keep it simple and hand her the air ticket and note. The name 'Camille' was printed on it, and though the surname he used was his own, it spoke for them both. She was his, she would understand. She would be in the same space he was.

When the Paymaster reached into his pocket for the ticket, Kelile closed the gap with speed, changing the outcome only after paper appeared, and not a weapon. Camille was oblivious to the episode, lost in thought. When the man moved into her space, holding something out to her, she reached out by instinct and grasped the offering the moment Kelile stepped between them. The Paymaster at first presumed 'police'.

The Paymaster swivelled on his heels, shrugged, and walked off into the crowds.

She'll understand, he thought, but not before Kelile had glimpsed the head of a snake tattoo as the Cambodian scarf shifted. He had no recollection of seeing any tattoo the last time he'd tailed him.

"And what was all that?" said Camille, holding the envelope.

"The danger we've talked about, raising its head again."

They sat at the bistro, opened the envelope and both stared at the contents. An airline ticket in the name of Camille Meyer to Bogotá, Colombia, and another hand-written note in the same format as the note she'd received before the Ethiopian trip.

"He mistook me for someone else," she said, "Meyer? Perhaps he wants me to play a concert there?"

"I don't think so. He's the man who attacked Edith. It's a one-way ticket."

"Strange."

"Yes, like the back door to your apartment."

"Oh" she said, "my favourite door, it disturbs no one."

"I can see that. At least tell me when you're next going to use it."

"I'll do that," she said, "where is Bogotá?"

part four: play your violin at the concert, I will watch your dream. I will kill your friend when the applause dies.
part five: when we are together she will be the sun.
part six: we will be together soon, forever.

"Another cryptic message," said Camille. "We've had one before. This one scares me. Is he writing to me? What should we do?"

Kelile phoned the Inspector.

The Paymaster remained on a high. He rationalised the man's interference as positive. He hadn't remembered what to say, but with the other man there, he'd been vindicated for not saying anything. She had taken the ticket, so she'd accepted his offer. She hadn't stopped smiling, though he preferred her scowl. She could begin to think more about being together. Next time she would not be surprised to see him. He'd check his own back. He'd been so good about that a while ago, and was not sure why his guard was now slipping.

He went to his lodging and changed appearance again: lost the beret and scarf, and went instead for high polo neck shirt and medium-brim black woollen hat. He swapped the jacket for a trench coat, applied yet another layer of self-tan, with care working the colour over his face, neck and scalp. Now it was up to her.

<h1 style="text-align:center">32</h1>

The notebook and pencil rested on the café table and the Proprietor was pulling a coffee for the Inspector. He observed the Inspector eating his almonds absent-mindedly, and felt a moment or two of concern. Having watched him eating them one by one so many times before, Vasseur seemed to be ignoring his own rule. The Inspector answered his mobile on its second ring and opened his notebook, twiddling his pencil in his fingers. He started writing. He scrawled: *beret, scarf, snake tattoo, air ticket, note.* He asked Kelile to put the ticket and note back into the envelope and refrain from handling them further. He would have it collected from the bistro by one of his team. The Inspector dialled his team room.

The team had people on the street within three minutes and knew they had one shot at this before the Paymaster changed his look again. They had the note copied and delivered to the Inspector within twelve minutes. Within twenty minutes they'd located the tattoo parlour. The artist regretted that his "unusual customer" had refused permission to have the tattoo photographed for their portfolio. He had also taken the sketches away with him.

"Bizarre person," the tattoo artist said, "kept getting shooting pains in his head, seemed to get relief from the needle." He never mentioned that the head was shaved, or that the client had paid in €100 notes.

The Inspector turned the pages in his notebook to the page headed 'Paymaster'. For the umpteenth time he re-listed the latest look the attacker had adopted. His men advised they had the air ticket in hand. He told them to trace it and a minute or two later they had details. Two tickets were bought, with the surnames Meyer, one for Camille, and the other for a Mr Gustav. A walk-in client who paid cash bought them at a travel agent in the Latin Quarter. The agent couldn't remember any other details; she'd wanted him out of the agency as soon as possible.

The Inspector wanted this man on three counts of attempted murder. His team were already doing a broader Interpol search for a Gustav Meyer. He remembered the Cardinal beer.

"Try the Swiss people again", he told them, "They must have something." He needed to question Ms Peress, the Stalker, but the doctors insisted her head injury was too serious to take chances. The Inspector added 'films' to a new list. The Stalker's video camera had been used. They'd found no used memory cards.

A copy of the note given to Camille arrived at the table and Inspector Vasseur read it to himself. As he'd predicted, the man had now turned his wrath on Edith. *Psycho revenge time, ego shattered*, the Inspector wrote in his notebook. Once again, he'd have to shift men – this time to watch over Edith. He wouldn't tell her about them. He'd use one of his best, get her to the café, and his man could follow her when she left.

He turned to his 'Michel' page and had nothing to add except *can't connect, copycat?* He underscored 'copycat' two or three times, before he noted down '37'. There were thirty-seven bridges over the river and decided he needed to condense the search, get results. They would cover all those bridges nearer the two islands in the Seine, the Ile de la Cité and Ile St Louis. Based on their prediction they'd triple the watch on the Pont d'Arcole and Pont au Double. It was some time since the third murder, and experience reminded the Inspector not to allow complacency to creep in.

His team desperately needed a harder lead.

The Proprietor had abandoned the delivery of the first coffee, which he drank himself. Seeing the Inspector shut the notebook, he made a fresh one. The Inspector closed his eyes and swayed an inch or two either way, thinking to himself.

Another murder threat in such a short time, two separate killers?

'She will be the sun', he read. Of course, the planets: Venus Mars Mercury, and then the fourth, based on distance away from the earth, the sun. Same damn killer, there is no Wolf. Now we'll get the bastard.

He leaned back in his chair, threw four almonds into his mouth, and called officer No. 1. The Inspector then clasped his hands behind his head, looking up at the sky. After a minute or two, relieved, he turned once again to his 'Michel' page, crossed out 'copycat' and added 'unlikely', which he circled twice. He then added three 'murders' to the Paymaster list, under the attempted murders.

Tired, thought the Proprietor, *perhaps he's lost the woman.*

Vasseur opened his eyes and looked at the Proprietor.

"Jacques," he said, "I sense it concerns you, I'll call her in a minute, these are worrying times for me."

"And how did you know I was thinking about her?"

"Your thoughts are all over your face. Now for your fine coffee."

"Mexican," said the Proprietor, "wonderful depth and flavour. I knew you'd come in, so I had them roast some a touch longer, the way you prefer."

"A-ah there you go, you too sense things."

The Inspector called in officers No.1 and No.2 and explained the *sun* analogy, which in all probability connected the bridge killer as the Paymaster. Edith could be the targeted victim number four.

"We need close a ring around her and the violinist. This Paymaster, your Wolf character, seems to be circling them. I'll call to warn her, and get her here. When she leaves, have one of your best men tailing her 24/7."

Edith had just delivered her tourists and their parcels back to the hotel. She was going to Camille's apartment to offer moral support before her big night when the Inspector called.

"Edith," he said, "this is business and not too pleasant. Please meet me at the café as soon as possible." She declined his offer of coffee, but would come by immediately for a brief discussion. She said loyalty to her friend came first, no matter what, and they'd need to get straight to the point. He did, and she knew his warning was serious. A storm was brewing; it was heading the Founders' way.

She promised to meet him later for something to eat, they could discuss living in Paris. He agreed to sit tight, attributing his unusual glow to the Mexican caffeine.

"Jacques," said the Inspector, "I'm in for the long haul here, this table is HQ for the next few hours."

No.1 and No.2 had their team in place around the café in double time, and while one man would be tight on her for the foreseeable future, the backup team had their supportive strategy.

The arrival of Edith at the table early evening made more than one head turn. As usual she failed to notice, and if she had, it would have elicited no reaction other than a smile to all customers. She focused her attention on the Inspector, and the Proprietor offered a glass of red wine to clients, on the house.

"It must be his birthday," said Edith

"Yes, or his wife's," said the Inspector. The Proprietor pulled out all the stops for the food, and the Inspector insisted that while off-duty Edith call him Jean-Luc.

"When did you go off duty?"

"The moment you arrived."

"Well then, a yes," she said, "but only once all the cases are solved and put to bed."

"There are always more on the way, but I'll make a note of that," he said, "under a new heading."

"What heading?"

"I'll tell you once I've closed the case."

The Chateau Latour 1999 Pauillac, a gift to their table, was a perfect accompaniment for their food. Épaule d'Agneau Braisée aux Haricots, braised shoulder of lamb with beans. This, the Proprietor explained, was what his family would be eating that night.

At 11 p.m., when Edith realised the time, she said goodbye and refused all offers of a walk home.

"I'm sure your men are watching the bridges."

"Yes, but always expect the unexpected."

"Thank you."

Once Edith had left, the Inspector and the Proprietor shared another bottle of red, and talked into the night.

"To a grand Bordeaux," toasted the Inspector.

"To a real woman at last," toasted the Proprietor.

"Yes, and there's some way to go before she can walk alone in our city once more."

"Will your work ever be done?"

"Not in my lifetime."

The new lodgings seemed larger than the guesthouse room he'd vacated, and were much closer to Camille's apartment. He hoped the move would throw the authorities off his scent for a week or so. He'd extend his stay if all seemed safe, however would keep an eye out and move again if necessary. He was still annoyed about the breakages deposit, but on reflection he knew it was a small price to pay.

The only things I'll break are their necks, thought the Paymaster, before finishing the unpacking and opening the red curtains. He'd hidden most of the cash in the space behind the fridge, near the motor and, satisfied with the ways life was progressing, he decided to sleep. Things were going his way.

The mobile's ring woke him.

"I'm getting a new cameraman," the analyst said, "we can fix up a shoot soon."

"Make it soon or you'll be too late."

"Why?"

"I'll be gone, and never mind where. I need more capsules, these are mixed up."

"Bring them in, we'll sort them out, give you the new batch."

"No, get the Receptionist to meet me. I'm not coming in." He hung up and turned his mobile off.

The analyst sent the Receptionist out shopping to choose an outfit for the gala evening, and spent the next hour updating his research project. He knew the data was terminally flawed, and made an academic decision to ignore that for the time being. The clients needed the films; it was profitable business. They made patient fees look like small change. He checked the site for orders. They were still coming in for the new Paris series, while the older film series were selling well. He considered them his classics. It seemed likely he would have to move on soon, but his was a portable business and these films went to club members only; no new members had been accepted for over ten years now. They'd shut the door on that. New members were high risk.

Her compatriots were relieved to discover Camille in great form before the concert. Her outfit was as black as Paris without lights, and she still insisted on walking.

"It's my ritual, like your coffee ritual," she said, and only when they threatened to tie her up did she relent. Kelile insisted he walk with her, saying it was a duty in his family to support the women at all costs. He would be failing himself if he did not accompany her.

"Thanks, appreciated, as long as you don't say too much, it's my private time to prepare myself. We can talk after the concert, I'd like that."

She needed to get to the Louvre two hours before the concert. Kelile had decided to return to the apartment after the walk to change. He would later travel in the car Michel had arranged for them. The walk proved uneventful, and though Kelile felt uneasy, he could never have spotted the Paymaster who'd chosen his position with every care. He was sitting up on a first floor balcony of a restaurant, tourist map and newspaper in hand.

The Paymaster had settled in for the long wait and was reassured to see his future lover walking past unaware, her escort a step or two behind. He nodded to himself, waited until Kelile had walked back as predicted, and went to find himself a better position. He needed a new safe spot with a clear line of sight to the Louvre. He took an hour to assess the entire area and returned to his chosen spot where he sat down. They'd let their guard down after the concert, and that would be his time to take out Edith, to balance the books. He decided to eat, keeping his hoodie on the entire time, much to the annoyance of the staff. The €100 gratuity eased that situation. After all, the table he sat at was not in a popular section.

The Inspector, thanks to the air tickets, now had a name, Gustav Meyer. They ascertained within the hour that the man wasn't using that name to register in any accommodation. The team had discovered his third lodging place that afternoon, and that too was deserted – a few days earlier according to the concierge. It was as clean as a whistle, except for two capsules under the bed. Even the bins were empty. They had sent the capsules for analysis. The handwriting report showed the apartment delivery man and the author of Camille's notes were one and the same person. The odds were shortening, and the Inspector knew he was starting to dominate this man.

The Paymaster knew that new deaths would be reported all to soon, deaths that would dominate the Parisian cultural press. Deaths that would make the bridge incidents seem innocent.

33

The Lumière chauffeur was anxious to drive Michel and his friends. He rejoiced in that a request had been placed for half a dozen bottles of Bollinger, and especially for the late father's favoured flute glasses.

Just like old times, he thought. He'd heard the blond girl Edith was in the party; she brought life to any occasion. If she was, it would make a great change from driving the younger Lumière's wife around all day, shopping.

"Your time of arrival Monsieur?" asked the chauffeur.

"Fashionably on time," said Michel, "we are guests of the star attraction." Michel popped the cork of the first bottle and they drove off on a slow circuitous route of Paris, especially for Kelile's benefit.

"To our honoured guest and your family back home," he toasted.

"And his fine new outfit," said Edith, who thought he wore it with classic effect.

Their table was more or less central, which suited them well, and the place setting for Camille remained reserved for after

250

her performance. A small wrapped box sat at her placing, its card sealed in an envelope. Michel was all for opening it, but was dissuaded. Camille was on stage, and their wine was flowing as generously as it was at tables surrounding them. Edith sat on edge, her heart pounding. She'd seen the vulnerable side of her friend so many times these last few weeks, and thought that for Camille this high roller audience must be daunting. The fact that Camille never flinched and was even smiling led Edith to question whether she knew or understood her friend at all.

Camille took all in her stride, looking in charge as she dedicated the first piece *Red Winds* to those people in the world who find themselves in the wrong place at the wrong time. There was a beauty to her music that melded seamlessly with the girl who played the violin at the front of the stage. Her appearance, stark and crisp, and her movement of the bow, graceful and controlled, captured the movement of the winds over the dark depth of the bass. It mesmerised her audience. The orchestra behind her, though dressed in black, paled in comparison. The conductor rejoiced in the moment, all thoughts of concern for this gifted young composer fading from his mind. He was proud to be a part of this remarkable event. The piece was a fraction under nine minutes long. No one in the audience shifted, reached for a glass, or looked away. They were spellbound. They were witnessing an inaugural concert of a marvellous virtuoso talent.

There was no hiding the conductor's emotion. He later graced their table with his presence and in a moment of generosity presented Camille with his Sarstedt autograph pen. "You'll need this more than I do, of that I'm sure. Sign with a free spirit."

The analyst noticed the interaction and sat at a table for two at the back of the venue, which was not the best position for acoustics. He nevertheless received a clear and balanced sound, which was acceptable. His interest in classical music was not widely known amongst his more nefarious acquaintances. He preferred a modicum of secrecy.

It was obvious to all observers that Camille was born to be on stage. Her second piece, a full version of the majestic *Motherlands,* confirmed the talent. The French amongst the audience took the music to heart, the intricate phrasing mimicking their everyday lives. Camille stayed on stage prior to the encore, such was the applause, and when given the opportunity introduced the final work.

"I composed *The Saturn River* as a monument to things creative, and the seven themes are intended to spin through the work imitating the seven rings of Saturn. This is its first public performance and it's dedicated to all French musicians, artists and filmmakers, past and present." She thanked the supporting players and conductor for their time and willingness. The audience remained enthralled as she played without effort, using unusual forms to breath-taking effect. It was an honour to be present and the warm applause lingered a long time, not a soul left sitting. Michel was in love all over again, and Kelile, observing the reaction, knew he should advise him that a man needs to act his on feelings for a woman, and not bottle them up.

A few select guests felt honoured to have Camille visit their tables, and attention from those surrounding Camille's table did not wane all evening. She agreed to join the car trip home, relieved to hear there were a few unopened bottles of champagne. She made no mention of her performance. She knew this was the start of something wonderful for her music career. There would still be challenges other than music to deal with: decisions, touring, publicity and strange places. These were challenges she did not look forward to. Camille promised to join Edith and the others outside by the car, once she'd said goodbyes, and was heartened by the knowledge the Inspector's men were protecting Edith.

When she emerged from the equivalent of the stage door, she understood why the guard inside had offered to escort her to the vehicle. The throng was hyped and everyone was saying something to her all at once, much like the airport homecoming. She heard none of it, yet did gather from the lady thrusting a gala menu at her that she wanted an autograph. She used her new pen for the first time like a seasoned pro and although the signings continued for some time, she eventually made her way to the team car. The chauffeur opened the door and Michel popped a cork.

"Strange" she said to Edith, "I even signed a picture of you and me eating tarte in Rue Mahler."

"For whom?"

"I can't remember, there were so many hands and faces that I tried not to connect too much, anyway it's not important."

"I hope not," said Edith, "I hope not."

In the wake of the car, the Paymaster stood in a state of fury. He'd watched the analyst and his receptionist hand in hand joining the melee at the exit. That was supposed to be his second contact moment. He was enraged when he saw the analyst holding up his missing photo of Camille to be signed.

The fucking bastard, he thought, *how the hell did he get that?* It changed everything. He felt a fury that eclipsed all those before. *Stuff your films*, he thought, *everything my own way from here on out*. He was shaking and decided to return to the bar immediately, planning to garrotte the bastard and his receptionist. He had been determined to ask Camille to wear the present he'd had delivered to her table. The double-headed crystal snake brooch now rested in her violin case, with the simple note attached, which read 'together'. He'd intended to kill Edith as she joined Camille, but the analyst's appearance had scuppered that plan, for the time being.

The analyst, unaware of the Paymaster's observations, called Lacey on her mobile early on the morning of Michel's opening function.

"It's been some time," he said. "Let's meet, I have something most interesting for you."

"Whatever it is, I'm not interested," she said.

"It's for charity."

He could be persuasive. She dressed in her black jeans, T-shirt, red beanie and the usual scruffy denim jacket, donned her Vuarnet sunglasses and summer scarf and went. At the analyst's rooms, she walked past the Receptionist without saying a word and went straight into his room, leaving the door wide open.

"Close the door," he said, noticing the new white T-shirt with the slogan 'Back to eternity'.

"On my way out?" she snapped. The analyst was playing classical music in the background and she recognised Wieniawski's Concerto No.2.

"Okay let's have it," she said and, without ado, he offered her ten thousand euros to film the Paymaster's reactions to designer psychotropic medications. She'd only have to film him at night in public. There was nothing to it.

"It'll pay your tuition fees," he said, "twenty to thirty minutes only, and we'll keep it private. The research is very confidential."

Lacey stood up and walked to the door.

"I'll text you my answer," she said. On her way out she asked the Receptionist what these films were.

"Interesting works, top quality,"

"And the charity?"

"What charity?" the Receptionist said, and Lacey left.

The Receptionist went into the analyst's room and turned the volume up.

"So do you think she'll do it?" she said.

"Money talks, and once she's made the first film, she'll be hooked like the Stalker was."

"Let's watch them again," said the Receptionist.

"Later. We'll play the game now."

34

Lacey walked to a café on the Ile de la Cité and ordered coffee and pancakes, and thought about the analyst and his lady helper. At least he hadn't laid a finger on her this time. The memory made her ill, but worse still, what was the analyst doing with that signed photo lying on his desk? She sent her text message before the coffee arrived, "No". Next she finished the coffee, ate the pancakes and ordered another round. She then phoned Edith, "I need to talk to you, please, I think it's urgent," and gave her the address.

Twenty minutes later, Edith arrived and was shocked by Camille's outfit: T-shirt, denim, and red beanie?

"Look at you," said Edith "is this the new you?"

"It could be, it's my Lacey outfit."

"For when you go to therapy? I'm confused."

"No, when I become Lacey. She is another *Kovchenko*, a persona for my self-therapy sessions. She doesn't exist; the guise helps me think in other ways, outside of my usual self. It's no big deal; it helps me survive. I realise the *Kovchenko* and Lacey days are over. I'm in over my head with this pretence. I must trust myself."

"Well the change in outfit suits you, you look so young."

"I am young."

She told Edith about the analyst Zuppin, who'd sent the Stalker the letter and the invoice that Kelile had retrieved from the bin.

"It's all too close to home, I don't know where to turn next."

"You need to make choices as we discussed, and you've begun to do that. You turned him down?"

"Yes, of course I did."

"So why tell me all this now?"

"He's got that picture of us I signed, it's on his desk, the photo you said the attacker took off the Stalker's wall. I never focused on people wanting me to sign things at the concert; it was all a blur. Zuppin or his receptionist must have been there."

Edith shook her head, *games within dangerous games*, she thought.

"We need tell the Inspector."

"I knew you'd know what to do."

"We'll stay well clear from them now on, leave this to the Inspector, these people are evil."

Camille bought a baguette from the boulangerie and went home, beginning to think she knew more about therapy then her once potential mentor, Zuppin. She'd cleaned *Kovchenko* out of her life, and now would clean out Lacey; she was almost done.

One last task, she thought. *The hardest, and finally I'll be free.* The thought scared her, but she knew it's what Edith would do in her place, be brave. She wondered whether she'd have a real personality afterwards – she'd like that.

Edith stayed put, thinking about the spiralling situation – it stank. She needed to work out solutions in her mind, to tell the Inspector all the details. He was the professional when it came to crime. The Inspector's man could sense Edith's unease. All was not as it should be. She tried calling the Inspector, and fate dictated that she did not connect. He was focusing all his attention on the hunt for the Paymaster. He was the one on the ground leading the hunt, and there was a vast area to cover. Edith's shadow stuck to his post, following Edith back home. Hours later, he trailed her to the opening of les Amis de Michel. He was a solid officer, a good man, but he hit a snag – '*entry by invitation only*' – and he couldn't blow his cover.

Officer No.4 went to the hospital to relieve his colleague, took one look in at the Stalker and knew it was time to resign. He called the Inspector on his mobile and confessed to a prior personal interest in this woman.

"She asked me questions about the case."

"And?"

"I answered her."

"There are a lot of lessons to learn. We'll talk this through soon. You did right to call me, stay at your post."

Les Amis de Michel was ready in good time for the opening celebration. The invitation list was select, spread across all walks of life with one common denominator: love of the finest in French traditional tastes. After three hours of food and drink, the doors would be opened to the public. When rumours spread of the expected attendance of Camille, the new musical genius of Paris, there was a surge of requests to the exclusive opening celebration.

Kelile had chosen a special consignment of Edith's Yirgacheffe beans to roast for the event, and had prepared a large batch two days beforehand. Demonstrations of roasting would be one of the evening's highlights. Michel checked the pastries chosen for the opening and the savouries to follow. An ample supply of Pol Roger champagne was chilled and on hand to welcome their special guests. He knew it would be a spectacular evening, and the forecast, after a brief shower, was for clear skies. With his chefs hard at work, Michel began the first preparations for the two dishes he'd make himself. To work with the coffee theme, he'd decided on croquettes de marrons, the chestnut and rum flavours would be lifted with a touch of double cream. For the champagne lovers he went savoury, choosing barquettes tosca. He would spread his Parmesan soufflé over the crayfish mélange a minute or two before serving. Guests might detect a deliberate, if controversial, taste of Italian in the topping. It lent a touch of international flair to the night.

The late summer flash storm strode across Paris, as if an army of cleaners were hosing down the streets in double time. The outside temperature dropped to a comfortable level. In the clinic the heat was stifling. With the last of the patients dispatched, the Receptionist stood in the doorway to the analyst's room and initiated their game.

"Celebrations," she said, "cash is rolling in." She sauntered in carrying a bottle of whisky and a carafe of water and placed these alongside the research folios. The analyst set the two new videos and their favourite bestseller to run on the three screens. He undressed, bound the Velcro straps under his desk to his ankles and moved his chair back. She turned the lights right down for better viewing of the screens, and switched the videos to loop.

The electro-pulsar attached to his ankles sparked to life. Zuppin felt the familiar convulsion work through his body and settled to the rhythm. He took one deep pull straight from the whisky bottle and beckoned her over, turning the pulsar up a notch. He stroked her while the pulse moved from his body to hers, and when she was naked, they were hooked by the expectation in the films. The Receptionist slid onto his lap, and leaned forward over the desk. As the films began to replay, he took another hit from the bottle, and looked down at the signed photo of the girls. It was time for fantasy. The analyst closed his eyes and lost himself imagining future film attractions. He'd explored this theme to death, and while her body worked, his mind raced.

The grey cat, an uninvited and recent addition to their clinic, was disturbed by the sounds. Bored by their antics and annoyed by the flickering films, he jumped off the couch, and began a relentless pacing of the room. The damn door was shut, and while the Receptionist was lost in the moment, the cat took three steps towards the desk and leapt up.

The Paymaster read in the daily paper that the opening was rumoured to have the best pâtisserie spread of the year. He welcomed the opportunity to mingle unnoticed with so many. Edith was involved and at openings, crowds caused confusion. This was his invitation, the only one he needed. After his killing business was done, he could celebrate the night with Camille. She'd feel their freedom.

He hovered around the area, assessing the opportunities. He'd had sufficient rest. The random combination of pills today gave him alertness, a sharpness that condensed his ideas, giving him focus. There were two plans still on the cards and Camille was in charge of both.

She makes the decisions, I make the destiny, he thought. As soon as she recognised him, and made her effort to connect, he could arrange for them to meet at the airport before their flight. They would start their new life together. If she did not greet him, they'd die together. It would be her choice and he was certain that she had made up her mind already. She would be expecting him at the venue, looking ahead to their new life.

Camille was not at les Amis de Michel. She had sat at home since meeting Edith, before deciding to go to the bistro to make life choices, still troubled by the photo on the analyst's desk. She had been more assertive acting as Lacey, and would integrate that character into herself at last. The persona had helped keep her on the positive side of sanity. This time she would take all the responsibility for decision-making, as Camille, so as not to burden the ghost of Lacey. She realised she did not need to escape her home; she loved it. It was her private *Motherland*.

The trip to Addis had taught her that. In Dubai she'd felt free for the first time. There'd been no cave to hide in, and that had been a catalyst. Now she'd thrown open the apartment windows and let the world in. The door to her apartment was still locked, and had reason to stay that way. There was no longer a need for disguise; she'd outlived the obsession, the phobia, and crossed one border – now all the other borders were crashing down. It was time to live.

Her father had been wrong; Paris was safe if you stood your ground. She knew first hand the analyst had a rotten side, and the more she thought about it, the more she worked herself up. The pieces were beginning to fit the puzzle, and there was no place in her future plans for anyone so vile. Even the thought of his abusive mind festering near the photo annoyed her, and she determined to rectify matters. She could not allow it; she would make a decision on how to act. Edith was right, it was not time to burden the Inspector; he was hunting killers. She'd stand her ground, as her friend had, and she had the right to choose.

Edith had shown her how true loyalty worked, what real friendship meant. Now she would do something brave for Edith; it was decided. She'd committed to meeting her friends later, and had every intention of catching up with them to celebrate. It was her turn to be loyal.

35

Without deliberation, the Inspector accepted Edith's invitation to the opening. He felt confident he hadn't made it onto Michel's personal shortlist, even though they shared a love of the best Parisian foods. He arrived early and people were already packed in. Michel's reputation was a guarantee of excellence, as his father's had been a lifetime ago. His mother, glowing with pride, took up much of the Inspector's time.

Kelile took a break from behind the roasting glass to meet some of the city's finest. Laughter coming from Michel's mother and the Inspector was music to his ears, following the tense few days.

So, Paris does have a lighter side, he thought.

Michel's mother soon realised that her son was going to miss out on this gem of a girl. Edith was the finished article, and the Inspector had eyes for her. Edith had the capability to achieve whatever she wanted; the signs were there.

As host, Michel was in fine form as he discussed his favourite subjects: traditionalism and food. He went searching for Camille and, not finding her, called her mobile.

"I'm seeing my therapist. I'll be on my way after. I'll enjoy the walk."

From the outside terrace, eyes watched Michel's every step.

Kelile went back into the glass booth leading a small posse of admirers, keen to be educated in fine roasting techniques.

The bubbles were rising to the surface in their own good time. The Inspector needed to bide his time and observe everything in detail. He couldn't miss a trick here. If he did, it would cost lives. Having scanned the area from the bar to the roadside entrance, he looked at the ginger ale in his champagne flute. It looked like the real thing at first glance, much like everything around him, and then he realised he was faced by the identical issue. He needed to see beyond the façade of this killer. He had to rely more on his senses, to acknowledge his special gift.

With Edith so close he was concerned: he needed to concentrate all his powers on investigating, and clear his mind of other thoughts. He was a man, and Edith affected him whether he liked it or not. He knew her comment about finishing current investigations was apt, and was relieved she was busy overseeing the roasting-room launch. It was time to avoid her completely. He needed to focus his mind on this evil. She'd understand after the event.

The Inspector hated to admit it; the blue haze was back, creeping into his mind. Something here was amiss. The dark notions were back. He tried to shake them off, but the feeling was too strong.

Where? he thought. *Where?* He put down the glass, took out his camera, and snapped a dozen or so wide-angled shots of the crowd around him. He wasn't the only one taking photos, and the crowd posed for everyone.

"Ah Jean-Luc, business or pleasure?" asked one of his journalist friends. The Inspector joined him and, under the pretext of admiring the turnout, scanned the crowd again.

Edith held the key to that link. The first opportunity she'd found to tell him about Zuppin, she'd been interrupted. Interested coffee clients had dragged her back to the roasting room. She decided that telling the Inspector about Zuppin could wait a minute, but only a minute. With hindsight, that would be a grave mistake. It was the same minute in which the Inspector had decided to make every effort to avoid her for the time being. He had a full team in this place and they would have their protective eyes on her.

Unhappy that her friend hadn't arrived to celebrate, Edith was distressed when Michel mentioned that Camille was going to attend a therapy session first.

"When?"

"About three or four champagne bottles ago," he laughed

"I'll go and meet her," she said, "I'll go through the kitchen to avoid the crowd."

"Where will you meet her?"

Edith was already gone.

It was almost dark when Camille arrived at the analyst's clinic. She hesitated a moment; all did not seem normal. She'd half expected to break a pane to gain access. Although the lights were out, and the outside door was shut, to her surprise it was unlocked. She went inside and could hear a cat mewing from the consulting room. As she opened the door the cat fled through, its wet fur brushing her leg. She stood and stared at the scene in front of her, transfixed as though she'd stepped into hell.

Urged on, Edith's taxi drove with haste back to the apartment and, despite the police guard insisting Camille hadn't signed out, all the apartment lights were off. The guard said the only place she ever seemed to go to was a bistro in the Rue des Lavandières. That's all she ever wrote in his register.

Edith phoned Kelile.

"Sorry, I should have told you," he said, "there's a back way out from her sixth floor, she often uses that."

Edith got back into the taxi and in minutes reached the Rue des Lavandières where there were a number of bistros to choose from.

"I'm looking for Camille Laroche," she asked again.

"At last," said the man, "you must be Lacey."

"No, is Camille here?"

"No, she left here alone about fifty minutes ago."

She was gone in the taxi before he'd said goodbye, her eyes searching both sides of the street.

It took a while for Camille to register what she was seeing: the analyst, naked, slumped over the Receptionist who lay face down on the desk, pooled in water. A whisky bottle stood next to them, upright, and both had the stillness of death imprinted on every feature. The analyst looked the more revolting of the two, she thought, a thought that would linger a while. Camille had to steel herself to go any closer. Were it not for the photo she would have turned and fled; however, the thought of their photo getting caught up in this enquiry was too much. The films kept flickering away next to her, but she hardly noticed under the spell of the moment. She didn't stop to watch; she rolled the photo up as best she could, snapping a rubber band from the desk around it, her eyes returning to the scene. She put the photo in her bag, wiped the door handles down and left, putting distance between herself and this horror.

An anonymous call to the police from a public phone was received less than five minutes later. The caller, a female, not only disguised her voice, but said fewer than ten words, the address included.

Some time after the Stalker regained consciousness, on the afternoon of the opening, the hospital staff allowed a brief discussion. The officer No.4 had long since excused himself from duty. She co-operated, but the initial discussions with the police were fruitless. She had seen nothing untoward, and was concerned only for the safety of Edith. The Paymaster was another patient of the analyst, "a crazy one", she said. The Inspector and team remained oblivious to the central role of analyst Zuppin. They scheduled an urgent visit in the next 24 hours to this man – they knew he'd plead patient confidentiality; they all did. The team had the imminent opening to attend, and knew the Paymaster might also attend, uninvited.

Feeling the buzz in his pocket, Inspector Vasseur took the call and spoke to the caller. He then summoned officer No.3 away from the team in the area, and told him to mingle inside the venue, keep a watch for the Paymaster, and phone officer No.1 with developments. He had to attend an incident; he would be back.

"Stay alert, watch everyone. If concerned, call for help."

Officer No.3 recalled the rumour that had been circling – that the Inspector thought there was a team at play in this case – and he moved his elbow to feel the pistol that rested at his side. Its presence gave him a surge of confidence. He could shoot with the best of them. He stared at Michel unblinking, promotion beckoning.

The Inspector, unable to locate Edith, requested Kelile to tell her that he had no choice but to leave, and expected to return later.

"Of course," said Kelile, "she went to fetch Camille. We look forward to seeing you back."

From his vantage point the Paymaster saw the Inspector drive away. He waited for his moment to get into the venue again, wondering if they were still serving free vodka and beer. He could be patient. Edith would arrive; it was her destiny.

Edith's police guard called the Inspector.

"I'm inside the venue now. She doesn't seem to be here."

"Stay at the opening, she may well have gone to fetch a friend. Keep looking and next time think ahead – 'no invite' is a dead man's excuse."

With lights flashing, officer No.1 arrived at the clinic minutes after being summoned by the response team. He had a quick glance at the videos and called his boss. On arrival, the Inspector took less than fifteen seconds to know this was the break he'd been looking for. On the desk in the consulting room, placed on one corner, and untouched by the water, was a leather bound folio titled 'The Psychotropic Blends: Series Seven'. The logo was identical to the symbol on the murdered girls' hands and the advisor's door in Berlin.

"The magic seven," said the Inspector, as much to himself as anyone in earshot. "The planets are lining up. This was the mastermind." He looked at the bodies, taking particular interest in the analyst's ankles under the table. The electro-pulsar had switched itself off, but only after the water spilt by the cat had poured into it. Fate electrocuted the lovers, dishing out the ultimate death sentence. The Inspector surveyed the desk: two empty whisky glasses, unused, the folio to be analysed, the jug lying on its side, and a few lumps of chewed leaves.

"Looks like *Salvia divinorum*, the divine leaf," said the Inspector, "and that's quality whisky. Seems the water killed them."

While the Inspector watched the bridge murder films, sequencing them into murder 1 and murder 2, the team continued with the assignment they knew too well. The photographer was already well into his work. This would take some hours. The Inspector's eyes switched between films. With the camera avoiding the killer's face, he struggled to recognise a distinguishing feature. Had he not been familiar with the two girls' faces, it would have been difficult to tell they were being murdered. No wonder there was a lack of witnesses – it all seemed too damn natural, just a couple interacting. When victim 2 reached for her attacker's gloved hands high up near his neck, the camera followed the movement, and for a brief moment the Inspector had exactly what he needed. In reviewing his most recent photos from the opening, he stopped at one and zoomed in on the Paymaster. He then studied the killers in the two films; they were the same man.

"This is our man. He's very much alive, and we're being side-tracked here," said the Inspector. He took the card out of the camera and gave it to officer No.1.

"The films show his eyes, nose and mouth. That nose has since been broken, get a bigger team to the café opening," he said, "you can pull them all off the bridges, make it look like crowd-control for the event. Get this man's photo out to our people. He won't go home tonight, no more bridges. Don't let any male in or out of the café cordon to be on the safe side, no exceptions."

A few blocks from the analyst's death scene, in the same café on the Ile de la Cité where they'd earlier discussed Lacey, Edith found Camille. She had not been the only one trying to find her.

"I made a choice. I'm learning about loyalty. Trying to be loyal to you is not that simple. And now they're dead." said Camille.

"Who's dead?"

"Zuppin and his lady friend."

"You killed them?"

"No, I think the cat killed them. Cats have lots of lives."

Edith stared at Camille who seemed elsewhere for the moment. Camille picked up her phone and dialled out.

"… to let you know, a cat killed some sleazy people tonight, that's karma."

"Thanks," said Danna, "I'll tell Marko. I know he hasn't forgiven himself. He doesn't believe cats have more lives, this might help."

"Good, visit me soon."

"We will."

"Who was that?" said Edith

"A friend."

"Let me take you home."

"No, it's the opening, I'll manage. They're dead. That's final. I learnt about all that years ago."

This area was notoriously dark, which suited the Paymaster, and the light of street lamps broke the darkness only on occasion. He could see the undercover police ringing the area and acted as if he was one of them. On the other side of the police cordon things were a lot calmer, and instincts told him the girls would walk to the party, but from which direction? As long as he stayed in the two-block circuit he could cut the time of circling down to a bare minimum. The rest was fate. Fate dictated he picked them up on the third attempt, coming in from the south. They were arm in arm, and while he knew this friendliness must be an act on Camille's side, she could not have known she was shielding Edith from death.

He got to within fifteen metres and pulled back when he noticed Edith scanning the streets repeatedly. He remembered her right hand and the oyster knife – he wouldn't make that mistake twice, she might be armed. She seemed more efficient with a knife than he was, and his injured leg slowed him down. Following them in would be the best option. He could mingle with the crowd. The public had been welcomed to the venue and the police were overstretched. With the free bar closed, it was time for business, and he presumed he was the only one not bothered about dying. The Paymaster began to feel the first doubts about Camille's loyalty to him. Was she acting, trying to lull Edith into a sense of false security? Perhaps, he'd give her more time to make her own move. He knew she wanted to – she wanted him with the same passion as he wanted her.

With Colombia once more an option, he decided that he would change his appearance once again, before going back inside. He disposed of the jacket he'd chosen for the night, squeezed a sachet of hair crème into his hands and combed what little hair had regrown these last few weeks back off his face. He moved the black bandana from his neck to forehead and put a bounce in his step, a painful bounce. The snake tattoo loomed large and he was looking forward to seeing the brooch pinned on his girl.

Michel decided to go and fetch his brother himself, and was turned back at the intersection.

"I'm the host," he said, "I'm going fetch my brother."

"Host or no host, tell him to take a taxi, and I suggest you go back and look after your guests."

"This is madness," said Michel.

"Life is mad sir, please return to your guests."

Realising the futility of his mission, Michel turned around. He did not want to spoil the night. He phoned his brother and insisted they come – they agreed, and he went back into the building. Kelile was standing near the kitchen outside the glass room.

"They're blocking the roads."

"Good," said Kelile "I think I saw Edith's attacker here. It worries me. Please go back to the terrace and be the host – give out more champagne. I can't ignore what's happening, it's ominous. I need a diversion, I'll find him."

Michel went back out. One look from Kelile convinced him. One look at Michel's face also told officer No.3 he had his man. He wondered if he should end this, and arrest him. He decided to wait; he'd practised shooting in confined spaces.

Michel said something aside to his mother who nodded back to him, and he went back inside. He was part of the team; he needed to be there at the death.

36

The arrival of Camille and Edith caused the expected stir. Most of the Parisian press and TV had featured positive reviews of her gala appearance. Michel greeted the girls with champagne, and couldn't resist showing Camille that her name was embossed on her glass, with the concert date beneath. She burst into tears, and he stood looking mystified before putting his arms around her.

"Thank you," she whispered, "and now it's our time, just like Addis."

The two girls disappeared deeper into the crowd, weaving their way in amongst the people.

Two pairs of eyes watched as the girls moved into the crowd; the two men were having very different thoughts. The Paymaster took a slower route around the throngs inside. Kelile, careful not to be seen by the Paymaster, inched sideways, smiling at everyone in general. Without causing alarm, he positioned himself a metre or two behind the man with the limp. The man remained too close to the girls for his liking.

The Paymaster was infuriated to see Edith and Camille hand in hand, talking, and joining the festivities. Camille seemed to be ignoring him. He felt the painful spasms once again inside his head, and it dawned on him that Camille had no intention whatsoever of acknowledging him.

Why did she come inside here without contacting me? She must have avoided me. She knows I'm following her, protecting her from the knife woman. In that moment he decided there would be no flights, she'd made the decision for him. Edith was the same bitch who'd stabbed him in the leg, and Camille was acting as her friend. Rage gripped his senses.

I'll take them both with me, he thought and he reached both hands into his pockets, coming out with a concealed Spyderco knife in each. The blades were shut. He palmed the knives and watched, keeping his thumbs above the thumbholes. Kelile saw the familiar tension cross the man's back. He knew he was too distant to react in time, should this man launch an attack. The man was psycho, and for once Kelile was uncertain how his quarry would act. He made slight adjustments himself as he continued to edge forward.

The crowd remained oblivious to the danger as the Inspector made his way through the people on the terrace, ignoring the journalists. He saw the Paymaster almost at once, standing behind the two girls, the tattoo now bold on his neck. Michel stood a few metres in front, and officer No.3 fewer than six feet away from him. Vasseur could see the officer's hand flexing an inch or two from his gun.

In our sights, he thought, and felt his own pistol tucked against his back. He couldn't pull it out in here in complete safety, no one could. The officer was closer, and he wished the officer had been unarmed. This was no place for guns.

The Inspector read the Paymaster's body language. He knew Kelile had taken the better position, which was another concern. He wished he'd experienced the Ethiopian's capabilities. He was making life and death decisions here based on perceptions of the man from Addis. Their eyes met for an imperceptible moment and Kelile acknowledged the flicker – they were comrades. Kelile balanced himself, visualising in ultra-slow motion every move he'd need to make to neutralise this 'Paymaster'. He had a fleeting instant to prepare for whatever action the man intended.

Vasseur picked up a glass with his left hand, his right hand hovering millimetres from his SP 2022. If he pulled it out, he'd be pulling the trigger. He took a sip of whatever was in the glass and forced his body to relax. The Inspector felt sick, knowing he had no clear shot and no time. He felt he'd misread his officer, who was too intent on watching Michel, and kept touching his own gun, an act that concerned the Inspector. *Don't do it*, he willed.

Frozen, waiting for his internal switch, the Paymaster fixated on the girls. He made two decisions on how he'd use the knives. For Edith, revenge: he'd hit a kidney and rip upwards. For Camille, he'd mingle his blood with hers in one glorious union; the same violent stroke of the blade ripping the life from their bodies. His chest expanded, taking a long slow breath as his thumbs curled open the blades. He launched, throwing his full weight into the attack, the time for death.

As the blades snap-locked Kelile reacted and the world stood still. The Paymaster closed on the targets, his mind focused into the killing rhythm, blades upright. Mid lunge, immovable steel hands locked onto his wrists. He shuddered to a halt. It was so sudden that he uttered no sound.

Man of iron, thought Vasseur, as he reacted himself. Officers surrounded them. Inch by inch he watched the attacker dragged backwards by Kelile, gripped by a force he was powerless to prevent.

In the fracas, the Inspector smashed Michel to the ground. Being a big man, Michel went down hard. Officer No.3 stood frozen. He watched his moment of glory turn to vapour; the Inspector had beaten him to it. The girls looked bewildered. Michel was stunned.

"Apologies," the Inspector said to Michel, "you were in the line of fire."

"My lucky day," said Michel, still gripping his bottle of Pol Roger.

From both intersections, left and right of the event, the police closed in, alarmed by the surge of people surrounding the terrace. There'd been a roar from the crowd outside as Michel's mother began the table-dancing. She moved with a finesse of the French. People from the inside were anxious to join in the celebrations.

"Did you see the ruckus?" Edith asked Michel's mother.

"It was dancing," interjected Michel, "dancing on tables at our openings is traditional. Father would have been up on the tables in the old days."

Few outsiders noticed the scuffle inside, and the bar trade increased as the night progressed. In the morning crime reporters had a long-sought closure, and spent the day piecing the stories together.

Realising he wasn't dead, the Paymaster felt a disconnect from life. He was sick and tired of questions, and withdrawal pains were a nightmare. He'd escape; he always did, and sat in his corner thinking about the cash behind the fridge. They wouldn't find it. The analysis of his pills alarmed his custodians; there was no doubt he should be institutionalised pending assessment. Psychologists insisted that monitoring and medical interventions were crucial. In turn, the prosecutor had more time to build the cases against him.

The IT department worked on the Receptionist's computer. Despite her encryption measures they were winning a battle. It would take time to reconstruct client lists, and they knew other invisible hands were manipulating data. The war was on. The endgame was around the corner. There had been no mention of the analyst in any news report; that was kept deep in the dark. The Inspector was conscious that they'd foul-hooked an evil syndicate, one that would take an international effort to smash.

The Founders rode in the chauffeur-driven car to the airport, and saw Kelile through the barriers. This time there were no watchers, but Kelile would feel the madness of airports well before boarding was called. He knew he'd been safer in the mountains, and longed for the tranquillity of coffee plantations.

⸻ ∞⦿∞ ⸻

The call from the Inspector was no surprise to Edith. He begged forgiveness for being presumptuous; he'd pre-ordered food at the Proprietor's café for service in three hours.

"Forgiveness is a tall order. Sundowners first?"

"Chilled as appropriate."

"I accept. Walk me home afterwards. This is Paris, you'll be off duty."

The Proprietor was ecstatic; his friend had heeded advice and invited Edith. He gave special instructions to the kitchen.

"Welcome Edith," he said, "I'm glad to be of service."

"Thanks, you know I wouldn't have accepted were it anywhere else."

Edith ordered a beer, and Vasseur followed suit.

"I'm relieved to hear the Peress girl is recovering, and visiting a genuine therapist."

"Yes, I'm told she has great taste in women."

"That's not amusing."

"And Camille is going to be dependent on you in future, how does that feel?"

"Not dependent, a friend. Agents are lining up to sign her. Her lawyers are handling negotiations and she's driving a hard bargain. My only advice was to make sure she knows what she's fishing for."

"Sounds like your father's advice."

"It was, and I need another beer. How are your days hunting villains?"

"Meyer will pay for his crimes. He's crossed the wrong lines. His body is a chemical mess. He has no idea that he killed those girls, we'll see. He's convinced he killed the old people. He keeps reciting the same line over and over, like he's searching for the message:

only the universe knows why the bullet flies through the eagle's nest, and out into space untouched

"My concern is with the families of the dead girls – that's where the hurt lies. Justice is hard for the families…"
"… and the analyst left a can of worms, evil worms we'll need to unearth."
"But not before you walk me home."
"And my Society application?"
"Accepted, we'll surprise the others."
"Don't you need ask them?"
"No, it's become a dictatorship, I've decided for them."

The Society meeting a week later was a regrouping in the wake of Kelile's departure. Soon after commencement, on time, at 20:00, Michel realised that he'd need more than his charms to connect with these girls. He'd have to pull out all the stops, show his better self. It was time for another new start, and he was confident one of them would be his bride.

At 20:10, moments after the meeting began, a solid knock on the apartment door interrupted the Founders. *A man's knock, a challenging man*, thought Edith, and with foresight she rushed to the door to open it.

"Our new member," she said. "Let me introduce Jean-Luc Vasseur."

Camille felt elated, and was intrigued to hear the Society waiting list was growing. She had no idea the surge of interest was connected to her own fame, preferring to believe Michel and Edith's were the cause, which may have been true. Michel realised why Edith had set out four cups. He knew the going just got a whole lot tougher, he needed to lift his game, and he still had eyes on the girls. Decisions were hard, yet the choice was his for the making.

During the meeting, Edith kept to the same Yirgacheffe beans that had been loved on the opening night. She felt full of life being with the Inspector, and watched as he leaned forward to taste the first sip. Her hand on the back of his neck felt natural, as if it had always been there, stroking him. Their last two days together had been surreal. Michel watched, perturbed.

As the night settled in, the Inspector opened the wine he'd brought as a new member offering. It was from the Pécharmant area, a wine he'd noticed was absent from her late father's collection.

"Strange choice," said Michel "thanks for the almonds?"

"A habit I hope you catch," he said, "a speciality, and something to take home with you. These are Marconas from Spain, sautéed in virgin olive oil and rolled in sea-salt, magnificent – like Edith's brew."

Edith proposed they make a private wish, a variation on the Ethiopian rite. Michel wished Vasseur would leave, and Camille told them she'd wish for wine.

"That's not private," said Edith.

"Come upstairs, I'll show you private," said Camille, taking Edith's hand.

"As long as you lock the Inspector and me in for the night."

"Of course I will. Michel wants me to play *The Saturn River* for him. Says he's a romantic."

"He's talking romance? Will you?"

"No, for you all, yes. He's not my type. I like a Spanish artist, Marko; he's rough but great. He and his sister Danna are full of life. I love listening to their stories of life on the streets of Paris. I've missed Paris life, now it's my time. He draws the most incredible works, using graphite pencils, works of Paris streetlights and statues. He sells them by the Seine. I'd love to play my music for him, while he sketches. We're setting up a small studio for him here."

"Tell me more."

"Why?"

Camille removed the rubber band and unrolled the signed photo she'd retrieved from the analyst's rooms.

"Here it is, inside," she said, "your oyster knife."

"Where the hell did you get that?" asked Edith.

"At the analysts, when I went to get our photo back. I'd seen the knife and photo on the desk, when I was there as Lacey." said Camille laughing.

Edith picked up the knife and flipped it in the air, catching it cleanly on the fifth spin, before kissing Camille and saying,

"That's true loyalty."

"It's family, your mother had given it to you."

Camille held Edith's hand to take her downstairs to the party.

"Will you tell the Inspector about the knife?"

"Not if you tell me about the Spaniard."

"Another day," said Camille, "another day."

Towards the end of the summer, on a rather early morning for the majority of Parisians, officer No.1 saw a drifting haze riding on the river water. In the distance above the haze, Inspector Jean-Luc Vasseur was sitting next to Danna, the Spanish girl, on his favourite bench by the Seine. They were discussing intuition. The Inspector held what looked like a pencil in his left hand and, in his right hand, a Department dossier. This was not the normal dossier they were all accustomed to holding. Instead it was the type of dossier that demanded respect, its cover displaying the distinctive 'for your eyes only' stamp. This dossier had not been copied to No.1, leading him to the simple conclusion this latest felony was of an international nature. The officer felt a familiar ominous tightening to his spirit, and turned and walked away. This was not the time to approach the Inspector, that much was obvious; he'd seen the Inspector kick out at his coffee flask, placed near at hand on the stone paving. The Inspector had missed the flask of course; he was no fool, the coffee was grand, and winter was about to set in.

Edith was still in the depths of sleep. Her life had been dominated by this new relationship with Jean-Luc Vasseur, and she'd learnt that sharing him with the Department was par for the course. That was fine, she had her own tourist and coffee businesses to run, and both were making money. She'd watched her mother and father give each other space back in her hometown on the southern French coast. Their love had never diminished; it had only grown deeper and wiser. They had welcomed Jean-Luc when she'd taken him to meet them, and had never thought to query the age gap, as nor had she.

In her own apartment on the other side of the River Seine, Camille was also sound asleep. Not the same soundness Edith knew, that being a deep contentment. In contrast, Camille's soundness came from the overwhelming joy of having had the first man in her life make love to her. Marko was barely twenty-one, not much younger than Camille, yet to her he smelt and felt all man, and making love was akin to the excitement of composing. It was perhaps more physically intimate, and more exhausting. Marko was still lying in her arms, and she was not aware of his body.

Camille woke to the warmth of her own nakedness. Sitting up, she looked at the shape of Marko's back and marvelled at the sculpture of his body. She could hear a silence, and only the soft breath of the artist moved that silence. She watched as her hand stroked his skin. Her new composition was crammed with the essence of their nights, matching the rhythms of his chest. Camille considered her own naked body and it looked serene, like Edith's, when she'd first seen her sleeping. She thought of Edith back then, peaceful, unperturbed by tribulations, and alive in her existence.

This was Camille's morning, and as her fingers lazed across his muscles, it was her body that stirred.